I0549162

TAKE
2 TABS
THEN
DIE!

TAKE 2 TABS THEN DIE!

A. J. HARRIS, M.D.

Murder Mystery Press
Palm Desert • California

Copyright © 2011 Murder Mystery Press
ISBN   978-0-9829361-6-0 (paperback)
       978-0-9829361-7-7 (hardcover)
       978-0-9829361-8-4 (ebook)
Published by Murder Mystery Press, www.murdermysterypress.com

Publishing Consulting and Product Development:
BookStudio, LLC, www.bookstudiobooks.com
Jacket and Interior Design:
Bill Greaves, Concept West Design, www.conceptwest.com

Library of Congress Control Number: 2010934436

Publishers Cataloging in Publication Data:
Available from the publisher

Printed in the United States of America

*To my ever-loving wife, Yetta,
who is a constant source of patience,
inspiration, and encouragement.*

Acknowledgments

The following people were exceedingly helpful in providing information and technical data. I am most grateful to them. If mistakes have appeared, they are mine and not those of the persons listed:

Dr. Joyce Wade Maltaise, my mentor, Allen Killfoile, and Nina Markos.

ONE

Dr. Andersen, the anesthesiologist, gave the okay to begin surgery. After the incision, my assistant retracted the tissues as I named the anatomical structures to the second-year nursing students seated in the surgical amphitheater. Using a rubber mallet, I began to pound the hip prosthesis into place when the anesthesiologist suddenly called out, "Hold it! Stop pounding! I can't get a blood pressure!"

A numbing paralysis gripped the OR except for the anesthesiologist who, agitated, tilted the patient's head back, made rapid adjustments in the breathing apparatus, injected IV drugs, and then started forcing a unit of blood into the IV tubing. I moved to the patient's head to confront the anesthesiologist. With hushed, controlled anger I demanded, "What the hell's going on, Andy?"

Without looking at me he commanded, "Pump in the blood!"

The students watched the beleaguered anesthesiologist whose concerned eyes shown above his mask. The scrub nurse covered the exposed operative site with warm saline solution packs, and we waited—and waited a seemingly interminable two to three minutes until the anesthesiologist said, "She's controlled, you can continue now. Your pounding put her in shock."

I had my own notion why the patient went into shock. She simply wasn't properly anesthetized, but I was not about to argue in front of the students. Besides, I was simply grateful her vital signs had returned to normal. I changed my gown, regloved, and continued the surgery.

Two hours later, the patient was wheeled into the recovery room, and I remained with her for an additional half hour. Although groggy, she reached for my hand and mumbled incoherently. I bent towards her ear. "Sarah, you've got a new hip, and you're going to be fine."

I was an hour late for my office patients. On my cell phone, I called and spoke to the new employee, Elise, telling her I was on my way. Before she could engage me in conversation, I closed the phone lid, ran out of the doctors' dressing room, and headed for my car.

A waiting room of irritated patients was always unsettling. No matter how I tried, I knew I would remain behind schedule the rest of the day. Catch-up was difficult, if not impossible. Maggie approached me as soon as I entered the back door and spoke in subdued tones. Ordinarily, I would have kissed my dear wife and perhaps patted her derriere, but she was preoccupied if not tense and not about to permit any intimacies.

"Josh, the person in room three came in ten minutes ago, and he looks bad."

"What do you mean?"

"He's dyspneic, clutching his chest and having breathing trouble. There's panic written all over his *face.*"

"Why didn't you send him to the emergency room? Was he alone?"

"He insisted on seeing you and refused to let me call the EMTs. Yes, he was alone. He wouldn't let me take a history, and he wouldn't put on an examining gown. I've looked in on him twice, no change in his condition. He's lying on the examining table with his head elevated. His color is awful!"

Maggie helped me with my examining coat then hurried me to room three. I had an ominous feeling, an intuitive response, following twenty-five years of anticipating and confronting medical emergencies. I opened the door to see a middle-aged, overweight man lying on his back, eyes glazed and fixed staring at the ceiling, mouth agape, lips blue, and body motionless. I rushed to his side, tore open his shirt, and placed my stethoscope on his barrel chest. Damn! No heart sounds! No breathing motion! I pounded his sternum and began CPR. "Have one of the girls call 911, right now! Get me the defibrillator and a vial of adrenaline!"

With the two defib paddles in place, I warned Maggie, "Stand clear!" I zapped his chest with two hundred joules, and the upper body went into a slight convulsive contraction. I increased the joules to three hundred then to three hundred sixty, once—twice—three—then four times. No cardiac response. I turned to the medicine cabinet on the wall behind me, grabbed the emergency kit, ripped the cover off a sterile syringe and plunged the needle into a vial of adrenaline. After putting a four-inch needle on the syringe, I injected the heart muscle. I withdrew the needle and watched then hoped . . . No reaction. No damn reaction at all. This guy was dead . . . dead . . . dead . . .

Maggie, wide-eyed, looked at the unresponsive body then at me. "Josh, is there anything I can do?" She grabbed a towel and wiped my forehead.

"No. There's nothing anyone can do, he's gone." I took a step backwards and surveyed the body. "Who was he, and why did he insist on coming here to see me?" I reached in his inner jacket pocket and found a worn leather wallet, a California driver's license indicating his name: Oferi Soldato, 42778 Corona Street, Palm Springs, California. Height 5'10", Weight 197, Eyes brown, DOB. 06-18-48. In the money compartment there was a total of $610.00, no credit cards or other identification and no phone numbers. Two of our office girls came in with two uniformed officers who made a quick assessment and asked questions. Almost immediately, they requested the EMTs, who responded within minutes.

"Shall we try resuscitation, Doc?"

"That'll be like whipping a dead horse. The coroner can work on him now." The corpse was bagged, put on a collapsible gurney, and wheeled out the back door to the boxy red and white conveyance, which headed to the coroner's in Indio.

In twenty-five years of practice, I had experienced death in the office only once before. It was unforgettable, an event that haunts and scars the psyche of every practitioner who experiences it. I returned to my office patients and tried to maintain an attentive and calm attitude, but the death of the stranger coupled with the morning's operative misadventure left me physically and emotionally exhausted. By late afternoon, I had seen all of my sixteen patients and moved like a zombie. Maggie had sensed my weariness and anticipated my need for a breather.

"Josh, you look bushed. Why don't you go to your consultation room, loosen your tie, and put your feet up on the desk. I'll bring you a cup of coffee." Maggie returned with the coffee, closed the door, studied me with her big, blue, compassionate eyes and kissed my forehead. While she stood beside me, I placed my arm around her waist, drew her towards me and buried my face in her abdomen.

I looked up and smiled, "Maggie, you're my salvation and my reward after a terribly long and miserable day." She bent towards me, held my face in her hands and gave me a long moist kiss.

"That's just for starters, love, take me to dinner, and I'll let you have your way with me tonight, not that I've ever denied you." She removed her nurse's uniform slowly and deliberately to tease and then slipped into her dress.

"Maggie, for a married woman, you sure know how to keep this old pot boiling."

We drove to one of our favorite restaurants in Rancho Mirage, Shame on the Moon, where the valet took our car and the doorman opened the heavily carved wooden door. Ginger, the hostess greeted us, "Good evening, Doctor and Mrs. Harrington. So good to see you both again." She checked the reservations list, "Here we are, seven o'clock in the Garden Room." We were escorted to our favorite table in a relatively secluded area away from the main dining room where the noise level interfered with conversation. The waiter helped Maggie into her chair and placed a napkin on her lap.

The table to my right across a narrow aisle was about to be occupied by a single man. With the restaurant only partially filled, I wondered why the hostess directed him to a table next to ours. I leaned over and whispered, "Notice how this guy's dressed for this time of year—dark conservative business suit, white starched collar and dark tie, hair cut military style. I'll bet he's Northern European."

Maggie gave him a cursory glance, "Josh, I'm not interested in him; I want to know about the man who died in our office this afternoon. Why did he insist on seeing you, and why wouldn't he let me take a medical history or at least tell me what was wrong with him? I never should have permitted him to stay."

"No, it's better that you put him in an examining room. He might have died in the reception area and that would have created bigger problems."

"I suppose you're right."

The man seated at the table to our right turned unobtrusively to look at us occasionally.

"In the short time you had talked with him, what impressed you, what did he sound like? Did he have an accent? Was there anything unusual in his mannerisms?"

"Everything about him was unusual. He had this pleading, frightened look as though he were being pursued. He didn't ask, he demanded to see you and refused to sit in the waiting room. He was sweating and had a sort of sour, unclean perspiration odor about him."

"Well, what about his speech, anything different or peculiar about it?"

Maggie knitted her brows, "Now that I recall, his speech was different, maybe German, Austrian or Swiss, sort of guttural." Looking at me, she asked, "What did *you* notice about him while you were trying to revive him?"

"He was well-groomed. His hair was recently cut and his brows were trimmed. He was clean shaven and used an expensive after-shave lotion. His teeth showed extensive and costly repairs, implants and porcelain caps. His fingernails were manicured, his hands were soft, no evidence of hard or dirty work, probably a white-collar worker, wore a Rolex watch, a simple wedding band, and his suit was costly. I'd say he was fairly affluent."

"Josh, you amaze me! You saw all that while trying to revive him?"

"Yes. It's what I've been trained to do." I was pleased Maggie was impressed. "Would you like a cup of decaf'?"

Maggie dabbed her mouth with her napkin. "No thank you. I've had quite enough. If you'll excuse me, I'll use the powder room."

I stood as Maggie rose and I looked after her. Her delightful femininity, the rhythmic movement of her hips and those well-turned legs still gave me a charge. Almost simultaneously, the man at the table to my right stood. He removed what appeared to be a hearing aid to which was attached a long fine filament and placed it in his

5

jacket pocket. He moved out smartly towards the exit. When Maggie returned, I told her what had happened.

"Well, if he has a listening or recording device, I don't know what he gleaned from our conversation. You didn't even make an indecent proposal to me."

On our way out, I stopped to ask the hostess, "Ginger, the man seated at the table next to us in the Garden Room, who was he?"

"I've never seen him before. He came in just after both of you arrived and requested a table near you. I thought you might have known him."

"Did he give you his name?"

"Oh, certainly." Ginger looked at the seating chart. "Here it is, his name was John Smith."

"Sure, and I'm Peter Pan. Do you recall anything unusual about him?"

"He seemed to be quite polite, maybe a little stiff or formal. I thought he had a foreign accent."

"Did he pay with a credit card or check?" Maggie asked.

"Neither, he paid the waiter in cash, the exact amount plus a gratuity."

In the parking lot, the valet approached me. I gave him my stub with a tip and asked about the man who had left just before us. "What kind of car was he driving? Did you get his license number?"

"Nah, I don't take license numbers. I remember every car, and I can match 'em with the owner. His car was a blue Hertz Ford Focus, strictly low budget stuff."

In the car, Maggie turned towards me, "Josh, perhaps we're making more of this than is warranted."

"Yeah, right. Why would a guy want to sit next to us with an electronic device? Furthermore, he had to be tailing us from the time we left the office." I looked in the rearview mirror and did a double-take. "That guy is following us."

On Fred Waring Avenue, I made a quick left turn into the Palm Desert Sheriffs parking lot. I stopped, waited and looked around anxiously. Maggie held my hand tightly, her eyes glancing around expectantly. No one followed after 10 minutes.

TWO

Our home is one of those recently constructed desert adobe-like structures that have mushroomed on every vacant plot of sand in the Coachella Valley. It has the heralding reddish-brown ersatz tile roof and a minimal care lawn of cacti and crushed rock. In our courtyard a three-tiered fountain with an Indian maiden kneeling, holds an urn through which water flows into two bowls below. It may be the only ornamentation that identifies our place from our neighbors'. The interior of our home is sunshiny bright during the day with splashes of vividly colored accessories added by Maggie. Through tall kitchen and living room windows we enjoyed the verdant expanse of a manicured golf course where we play occasionally on weekends.

Coming from the Midwest with its harsh winters this was as close to idyllic living as I could have imagined twenty-five years ago. Maggie, recently from Chicago, was still in awe of the desert and its beauty. More importantly, her love for me seemed as fresh and eager as it was the day we met. She continued to flirt much to my enjoyment. That and our busy practice propelled us rocket-like from one day to the next. The bedchamber allowed the conjugal bliss that had not waned since our first glorious affair six months ago. Maggie would ask, "Darling, do you have any idea of the number of children we could have . . . ?"

I interrupted, "If we were about twenty years younger? Better this way, my Sweet, I can enjoy all of you without sharing—not that I don't love my children, but . . ."

Maggie in her short silk nightie on that warm May evening led me in my cut-off pajamas to our king-sized bed. She turned off the bedside lamps. "No reading tonight, my love. This is playtime." With that, she lifted her nightie over her head and pulled my bottoms down. "Now show me how much you love me."

The following morning we shared a leisurely breakfast. Maggie had that sweet post-coital glow. She hummed and smiled and moved coquettishly. I embraced her from behind and nuzzled her neck. "Didn't you have enough last night?" She asked.
"That was a long time ago."

We left for the office together, since I had no surgery scheduled. Our suite of offices was shared with another doctor, Basil André Stuckley, a rheumatologist and graduate of Harvard Medical School, class of '84. Basil at age forty-nine about five feet nine inches, handsome and polished had a large practice consisting mainly of middle-aged and elderly women suffering various stages of osteo and rheumatoid arthritis. He was a divorced father of two teenage boys, ages fifteen and seventeen who lived with their mother in a Beverly Hills home.

He lived in a home on tony Clancy Lane in Rancho Mirage. He remodeled his house as a bachelor's pad complete with an s-shaped indoor spa, a fitness center and an exotic master bedroom fit for a Saudi prince. I had seen it last year when I was invited with several others to watch a movie preview in his home theatre. That evening he entertained a strikingly beautiful young woman as comely as a Hollywood starlet. For all I knew she might have been one.

I knew little about Stuckley's family. I figured his folks were wealthy enough to support his lifestyle. Or more facetiously, I fancied he might have been engaged in trafficking drugs, promoting illicit sex, or fencing stolen jewels. He took me by the arm and escorted me to his four-car garage. In the first stall was a new Bentley sport coupe. "How do you like this little baby?" He patted the hood lovingly, "Five hundred horsepower, twelve cylinders, all wheel drive." Then he opened the door to point out the magnificent exotic wood trim on the steering wheel and dash and the buttery smooth leather upholstery.

With a price tag of a quarter mill, I asked, "Basil, how in the hell can you afford this sort of thing?"

With a complacent smile, he said, "You just go down to the foreign car dealer, put on a bit of the Ritz, plunk down a few grand, promise to make monthly payments and take possession."

His glibness could hardly obscure the fact that a sizable down payment had to be made, and his financial statement had to satisfy the lending agency.

The following morning Maggie asked me "What did you hear from the coroner about the man who died in our office?"

"An autopsy revealed patches of atherosclerotic plaque in his coronary arteries and a large ischemic area in the heart wall."

"Meaning?"

"He most probably died of a severe heart attack. He also had to have a history of prior cardiac illness."

"If he had symptoms to indicate heart trouble, and he knew what they were, why wouldn't he go directly to the emergency room or call 911? And why did he insist on seeing you? You're an orthopedic surgeon. Surely, he knew that."

"Maggie, my love, I haven't the foggiest notion."

Maggie shook her head, "Did the police identify him or locate his family?"

"Not to my knowledge. Besides, I think his name sounds phony."

"What do you mean?"

"Oferi Soldato, sounds like Esperanto, roughly translated *sacrificial soldier*. It could be legit, but I doubt it."

"Do you know Esperanto?" Maggie turned and studied my face.

"The army provided me with a brief course which I never used."

"If he's a soldier, does that mean he's part of an army?"

"I don't know, maybe."

Maggie placed the charts for the day on my desk. "Josh, we're running out of file cabinet space for our charts. Can we remove those charts concerning your experimental drugs? They take up an awful lot of space in that cabinet, and you won't allow us to use that cabinet for anything else. Since you're no longer engaged in clinical experiments, why can't we empty that cabinet and put our other patients' records in there?"

Peering over the top of my glasses, I said, "We have to keep the data under lock and key as per Magna Pharmex protocol. At a specified time they'll request all that data, and we'll ship it back to Switzerland."

"What impressions did you get from using those experimental drugs? Are they of any value?"

"We gave those drugs as part of a double blind study. Some were placebos which shouldn't have altered pain symptoms, and the new medications which should have improved our patients' symptoms."

"Did you know which was which?"

"No. The patients were given numbered medications, and I recorded the clinical responses. Some patients improved, some felt surprisingly better, some had no relief at all, and four . . ."

"Why did you stop the study?"

"I was concerned about some of the results. In my series of a hundred and twenty-five patients, four died . . ."

"Is that a significant figure?"

"Yes, if the drug was responsible for some or all of those deaths."

"Wouldn't you be able to detect that?"

"I can only suspect, but without an autopsy I can't know precisely."

"Did you request any autopsies?"

"I did and got two families to consent."

"What were the results?"

"Both patients died of heart, liver and kidney failure, with no clear-cut history of prior illness. One was eighty-seven and the other sixty years of age."

"You reported all that to the drug manufacturer, didn't you?"

"Yes, of course."

"What was their response?"

"After ignoring my letters for several months, they finally thanked me for my participation in their clinical trials and sent me a generous check. I was told that the program was terminated and that the clinical trials were most gratifying."

"And that was the end of that?"

"Well, not exactly. The families of those patients who died were very unhappy and threatened to . . ."

Basil Stuckley appeared at our consultation room door. "Sorry to interrupt Josh, Maggie, but I wonder if I can ask a big favor?" "Go ahead," I said. "The worst that can happen is that I'll refuse you. What would you like?"

"I just had a request to appear on a TV talk show to discuss certain anti-arthritic drugs. One of the scheduled participants fell ill, and I'm a last minute replacement. I had the girls cancel my patient appointments, but in the event of an emergency, I'd like to be covered. I'll be gone for several hours this afternoon. Is that okay?"

"Go with my blessings." As soon as he left the office, Maggie asked, "Does he get paid well for that?"

"He told me if he continued this subtle kind of advertising for Magna Pharmex he'll be able to retire in five years. His annual investment dividends will exceed the salary of the President of the United States. He's become sort of an icon among many arthritis sufferers. His weekly columns in the local newspapers, his personal appearances and television programs make him quite bankable."

"Isn't he conducting a research program with new drugs?"

"Oh, yes! Big time. My protocols were like small potatoes compared to his. His roster, he tells me, consists of over five hundred patients on new medications and placebos.

"Have any of his patients died suddenly?"

"I don't know. He certainly hasn't volunteered that information, but when I asked him about his death rate he told me he treats many elderly patients who have age-related problems and death is a relatively frequent occurrence."

"He certainly finessed that." Maggie arose, "Well doctor, I believe our patients are arriving."

"Elise, hired by Basil a month ago, approached me apologetically with a patient's chart, "Dr. Harrington, one of Dr. Stuckley's patients, Mrs. Van Offing, has just arrived in a wheel chair and is complaining of knee pain and abdominal cramps for several hours."

"Give me her chart, please."

The patient was seen initially for pain resulting from osteoarthritis affecting both knees and the left hip joint. "Put the patient in an examining room and we'll take a look."

The patient, a frail sixty-seven year old, had the haggard, lifeless but worried expression of one experiencing crippling joint pain. She was being tended by her husband pushing her in a wheel chair. The patient explained that her symptoms seemed to be worse since Dr. Stuckley had given her the last sample of medication a week ago.

"Did he prescribe any other medicine for pain such as Tylenol, codeine, Demerol or morphine?"

"He asked me not to take anything else since he was trying to determine the effect of the tablets he had given me. Frankly, doctor, I think I'm worse now than before. Can you give me something to take away this awful hurt? I don't know what bothers me more, my belly or my knees."

I took Maggie aside, "Ask Elise to contact Dr. Stuckley on his cell phone. This patient is suffering needlessly."

Basil, this gal needs help—you don't want her to have other medication? You'll get in touch with her later today—fine. I think you had better.

I felt absolutely useless, but I advised the patient just as Stuckley ordered. I made an entry visit in her chart and reviewed the initial visit and subsequent progress notes. On her first visit, she had mild knee discomfort on arising from a bed or a chair, but no complaints referable to the abdomen. Initially she limped into the office two weeks ago without assistive devices. Now she required a walker or a wheelchair.

Outside the examining room Maggie asked, "Why does she tolerate Stuckley's treatment, or rather the lack of it?"

"I don't have a good answer unless it's because she's enamored of the guy. I'm sure he'll alter her treatment or give her some other medication." I looked at the recent blood studies and was concerned by the decrease in the total cell count. "This is a type of anemia I don't like. This patient needs more workup and should have hematological consultation." I gave the chart to Elise and reminded her to place it where Stuckley would see it when he returned.

THREE

Maggie, good nurse that she is, reviewed each patient's chart before I saw it and gave me a brief synopsis. "Mr. Effingwell is a new patient, seventy-eight years of age, a former merchant seaman with a large unstable knee. Dr. Stuckley has seen him three times. X-rays were taken and the patient received some of the doctor's magic medicine." Maggie was openly sarcastic.

I put the x-rays on the view box. "This is really interesting. Here's a condition we rarely see anymore."

"What is it?"

"A Charcot knee. With my pen, I pointed to the pathological characteristics. "Look at the disorganization of the joint surfaces, the disappearance of the cartilage, the fragments of bone floating in the joint—it's a mess."

"Is it painful?"

"Usually not."

"What's the cause?"

"In an old sailor? Most probably long-standing syphilis."

"What's the treatment?"

"Certainly not the medicine Basil was giving him. Basil knows better than that. The only treatment, unfortunately, is a fusion of the joint, making the leg stiff, or an amputation above the knee. Of course, a guy could wear a cumbersome brace but that's not altogether satisfactory."

"If, as you say, Basil knows better, why would he give this patient medicine?"

"Maybe the drug manufacturer pays him every time he doles it out."

"Josh, that's unconscionable."

"I agree, but not every doctor is a paragon of virtue. Some worship at the feet of Mammon."

"What are you going to tell the patient?"

"The truth. Most of these old guys can accept a diagnosis resulting from youthful indiscretions. He's a lot luckier than many old syphilitics who suffer brain and spinal cord involvement."

The patient, hunched over crutches and bearing little weight on the involved leg, entered the room. He was a grizzly bear of a man. Toothless, with facial stubble and dried tobacco juice in grooves angling from the corners of his mouth. A wad of tobacco formed a pouch in his left cheek. I directed him to the examining table where he sat with his legs hanging over the side. Despite his unkempt appearance, he looked at us with clear and understanding eyes. I examined the boggy knee and discussed his options for treatment. He rubbed his chin slowly then reached for his crutches. In his gruff voice he said, "Thanks, Doc, I gotta think on it."

Maggie pulled me aside, "Josh, you've reviewed just two of Stuckley's patients and already you've found mistreatment in both. What do you think you'd find if you were to review more of his cases?"

"Don't wish that on me." In Basil's defense I said, "He comes with good academic credentials. Frankly, I don't know what he's thinking. I hope he isn't collecting data to put into a chart just to impress some drug company officials."

"That's a horrible possibility." Maggie, like me, was cynical about clinical trials of proprietary drugs.

Elise walked by the open examining room just as Mr. Effingwell was leaving. She stopped. "Why Mr. Effingwell, what are you doing here? Aren't you Dr. Stuckley's patient?"

Effingwell croaked, "I was, missy, 'til I got one of the gals in the office to gimme my x-rays and copies of my chart. Your Dr. Stuckley wasn't helping me one goddamned bit and you c'n tell 'im that fer me."

Elise responded with a twisted smile, "I see," and walked off stiffly.

Maggie looked at me, "What's that supposed to mean?"

"She probably has a strong sense of loyalty to Basil and losing a patient to another doctor is something she takes personally."

"She better not forget that half her salary is paid by you, that little snip." Maggie gathered my charts for re-filing. The office was quiet. Elise, as well as the other office girls and the x-ray tech had gone for the day. Maggie, with a plastic container gathered used syringes, needles and empty vials from our treatment rooms. As she passed Stuckley's office, she noticed the open closet door and stepped into the office to close it. "Josh," she called, "here's something I think you'll find interesting." She pulled me by my arm to show me a woman's blonde wig setting on a self. "What do you make of that?"

"Maggie, don't go poking your pretty little Irish nose where it doesn't belong."

"You have no appreciation for gossip and intrigue. Who would wear that?" Maggie had an impish grin. "Do you think Stuckley's a cross-dresser?"

"I doubt that."

Maggie seemed delighted with the possibility.

"Come princess. I'll take you home, and think about making love to you."

"Oh, I'd like that," Maggie pushed against me giving me a moist kiss. "That's just for starters."

In the car, Maggie turned towards me, "Josh, I've wondered for the longest time, why did you and Stuckley decide to share an office? You two are so different."

"How so?"

"Now don't go looking for flattery, but since you're so much nicer, you're honest and forthright, no pretense or showmanship. He's really such a con artist."

"Our association in the desert goes back several years when office space in the mid-valley was scarce. Both of us shared an office with four others until our practices started to grow, and we simply needed more space. Because we were the last to join the group, we were given the least amount of space. The two of us formed a kind of understanding; we would leave as soon as we could find more space. About a year ago, Basil told me he had seen an elegant new building on north Monterey Avenue, one we could lease at an attractive rental. On that same day, problems occurred causing me more frustration and an overwhelming urge to break out of my cramped quarters. I was ready to go anywhere."

"Did you have any doubts about sharing space with Basil?"

"Not really, although, I knew there had been rumors that he had problems years ago in L.A., long before I knew him. When he came to the desert, I was told, he convinced members of the local medical society that he'd reformed and had been born again—whatever that meant. He created the impression that he had adopted an ascetic lifestyle. Can you believe that? Anyway, he did settle down, and in a short time became quite busy."

"Sounds as though he had woman trouble before."

"I guess that was a large part of it. However, during the time I had worked with him, there were no problems. As I said, I was desperate for more space and this new building, close to Eisenhower Hospital, seemed ideal. I'd have shared space with the devil if I had to.

"We signed a long-term lease with an option to buy. I had no reason to believe our business relationship wouldn't work. As a rheumatologist, Stuckley saw patients who needed surgery and referred them to me. That meant hip and knee replacements as well as hand and wrist surgeries. On the other hand, I referred patients with medical problems to him. We enjoyed a type of symbiotic relationship."

"Are you satisfied with your business relationship?"

"I'm not unhappy, and yet, even though I'm not an envious person, I can't help wondering at times: how is it that he's so much more successful, financially, that is?"

"Does he see more patients than you do?"

"Oh, yes, but remember I do surgery and that brings in large fees, you know."

"Maybe he's made good investments, or maybe someone's invested in him."

I looked at Maggie, "What do you mean by invested in him?"

"Oh, nothing, just sort of thinking out loud."

After we cleared the table and filled the dishwasher, I reached for *The Desert Sun* and *USA Today* and then headed for the couch. Maggie sat beside me. With mischievous eyes, she searched mine, then put her arm around my waist.

I had seen that flirtatious look many times before. I put the newspapers on the floor. The pulsating rhythm of romance was interrupted only slightly when I got up to turn the lights low and to place a CD of Sinatra's greatest hits on. I made a quick stop to the bedroom to remove my outer clothes and shoes before returning to the living room. Maggie was sitting in her slip with legs folded under. She placed her bra and panties neatly beside her as she patted the sofa cushion. "Come, my handsome prince, make love to me."

"What makes you think I want to, fair maiden?"

Maggie glanced at my briefs. "You may not be ready, but your friend there certainly is." She touched me, and slid the straps of her slip off her smooth shoulders. She wiggled free of the straps. I looked at her voluptuous breasts and remained in awe of their youthful, globular symmetry and the deep cleavage that enhanced their form. Her nipples protruded from broad areolar bases, which begged to be suckled. I caressed and kissed them lovingly. Maggie held me closely then pulled down my briefs and directed my eager member. "Oh Josh, I love you so."

We lay exhausted on the couch, our skin moist with perspiration. As I prepared to get up, Maggie held me tightly and pleaded with me to stay. "Don't leave yet. I love the feel of you."

I continued to hold her closely, then ran my hands through her hair and kissed her sweet, loving face.

The following morning after performing a knee arthrogram, which showed considerable arthritic deterioration on a fifty-eight year old housewife, I left the OR to talk with the patient's family in the waiting room, an obligation to allay fears and to reassure. The arthrogram is a method for looking inside the joint without making the customary two-inch incisions. I approached the husband to tell him that his wife would have only temporary relief from a local anesthetic and a steroid compound injection, but I believed she would have need of a total knee prosthesis within a year. He thanked me then mentioned he had heard of a wonderful new experimental arthritis drug a *Dr. Sickley* was using.

"Dr. Stuckley," I corrected him. "I don't think any medication is going to have a lasting effect on your wife's knee."

"Dr. Harrington, for the cost of a visit to *Dr. Sickley's* office, we surely ought to have good results."

"What, may I ask, are you paying for . . . ?" At that moment my cell phone rang. "Excuse me please." I walked several feet away to answer.

Josh, are you ready to leave?—Good.—Bad news! I'll pick you up in ten minutes.

"Hello? Hello?" Nothing, I rushed to the doctors' dressing room, changed clothes and hurried to the parking lot.

Maggie, agitated, waited in the car and waved frantically. "Josh, you won't believe this!"

"Calm down, what is it?"

"Someone broke into our office and made a mess of our records!"

"What?"

"Our locked file cabinet—they must have used a crow bar on the drawer and took our files. I feel so bad, all your months, years of work stolen! What were they looking for?"

"Easy, Maggie. Start from the beginning." As we drove to the office Maggie filled in the details.

Two plainclothes men were sitting in my consultation room. They stood as Maggie and I entered. "I'm Sergeant Tim Mannheim and this is my partner, Officer Bob Hernandez." Mannheim, at about six feet one or two, gaunt with deep-set eyes and bushy brows was unsmiling with a sallow complexion. His dark jacket hung loosely on a narrow frame. Hernandez at about five feet seven, swarthy, muscular and compact, stood with massive upper arms. A holstered pistol at his side completed an almost menacing appearance.

"Dr. Harrington," Mannheim said in a deep monotone, "we'd appreciate it if you didn't touch the file cabinet until the crime scene unit gets here." He looked around, "Do you have accessible narcotics?" "Not any significant amount. Let me check the supply room where we keep most of them." The officers followed Maggie and me closely. I opened the locked door, and zeroed in on the shelf, which housed the pain medication. I froze. "Well, I'll be damned! The samples of scheduled narcotics are gone, and the locked steel box with Demerol is missing." My anxiety mounted.

"What do you make of this, Doc?" Sergeant Mannheim asked.

"Stealing drugs I understand, but why the medical records?"

"That's what we'd like to know," Officer Hernandez said.

Maggie asked, "How did the thieves get in here?"

"Good question." The front office door locks are intact and the windows which don't open aren't broken," said Mannheim.

"Are you suggesting this might be an inside job?" I asked.

"Yeah, unless you have a better explanation," Mannheim said.

"The cleanup crew?" Maggie asked.

"They're number one on our suspect list," Hernandez said as he looked about the boxes of medical samples and ortho supplies.

"Would you have any reason to suspect Dr. Stuckley's?"

"Certainly not."

Elise approached, "Dr. Harrington I'm terribly sorry all this has happened. I just don't understand it."

"Thanks for your concern, dear. Did Dr. Stuckley have any damage to his part of the office? Were any of his file cabinets broken into?"

"No, not at all."

Maggie, arms folded, studied the youthful Elise whose high-pitched voice, short-bobbed black hair, over-sized glasses and braced teeth gave her a teen-aged appearance, all of which seemed to irritate Maggie.

"Were any drugs stolen?" Officer Hernandez asked Elise.

"Just a few samples," I think.

The officers walked with Maggie and me back to my consultation room. "What was in that locked file cabinet?" Mannheim asked. "Any drugs, narcotics, needles, syringes . . . ?"

"Nothing like that, just medical records." I did not feel the necessity of going into details over the experimental drug program. Mannheim gave me his card and asked me to call him if anything helpful came to mind.

"Don't touch the file cabinet! We'll have forensics dust it for prints."

Hernandez followed Elise after he requested to see Dr. Stuckley's suite.

FOUR

The mess in the office had been cleared after CSU had taken photographs and dusted for fingerprints. The day proceeded with all of our patients having been seen on schedule. The time was six o'clock and we were ready to close.

"Josh, I've been thinking: the break-in had to occur sometime between the cleanup crew's work and opening time. If there were an illegal entry to the building, the alarm would have gone off, wouldn't it?"

"I would think so. You're thinking that it may be someone among the cleanup crew—wait a minute, what about the security service?"

"And what about the maintenance crew?" Maggie asked. "All of them carry keys to the building. Josh, how valuable are those stolen charts?"

"Obviously, they're valuable to someone."

"But there's the matter of the stolen narcotics."

"Probably just a red herring. The real target was those charts."

"All your time and effort gathering data—gone. That's terrible!"

I looked around cautiously even though I knew we were the only ones in the office. I whispered to Maggie, "I have a summary sheet of all my important findings tucked away in our den file cabinet."

Maggie gave a sigh of relief. "Thank goodness. Does anyone else know this?"

"Just you and me, baby."

At that moment, I heard the front door closing. I dashed out of the room and ran towards the door, there was no one there. I looked down the hallway, no one. I ran back to the consultation room overlooking the parking lot. A small, dark sport coupe was turning around the corner of the building, but I could not see the driver, nor did I recognize the car.

"Do you think whoever that was heard us, Josh?"

"I don't know, but we can't assume that they didn't. Let's go directly home right now!"

As we approached our house, we looked for any strange automobile parked nearby. There were none. With the remote, I opened the garage door and looked behind me before entering. Maggie's Mercury SUV and the golf cart were as we left them. We entered the house cautiously. Maggie peered into each room, but there was no sign of disturbance. We went to the den, opened the closet and looked at the metal cabinet where summary sheets on the clinical trials were kept in a folder marked Magna Pharmex. All one hundred twenty-five pages of data remained intact. Looking around the room for a safe repository, I placed the folder on my desk.

Maggie sensed my dilemma.

"Josh, why not put that in the bank safe deposit box?"

"Good suggestion." I looked at the folder and opened it. "But who would want this material and why?"

Maggie shook her head but made no comment.

The telephone-answering device indicated two recorded messages.

Josh, Basil here. What the hell was that office break-in all about? Let me know what you're thinking—let's get together to discuss it. I've already talked with Mannheim and Hernandez. How's Maggie holding up? Talk with you later.

"He almost sounds sincere," Maggie said. "Who's the second caller?"

"Shush, listen."

Dr. Harrington, this is Sergeant Mannheim. Just wanted to tell you that our detective bureau has made a provisional ID on the dead man in your office. Give me a call.

Maggie looked at our fax machine. "Josh, here's a message from Magna Pharmex, dated May 16. That's today."

"What does it say?"

No response from message sent to your office fax on May 14. Hope this is received on your home fax. Will collect office filing cabinet with test data on May 18 via Worldwide Transport Carriers. Be sure all items are ready for shipment If any problems, please notify . . .

"They're going to pick up one battered file cabinet from the office?" Maggie asked.

"That file cabinet is their property, they installed it and according to the terms of the contract, it belongs to them."

"You'd better notify them that the file contents are gone."

Just as I shut the light in the den, I heard the sound of a car door closing. "Shush," I whispered. "Don't turn on the lights and don't make a sound." Footsteps coming up the path became louder. I stopped and held Maggie's wrist firmly. I could feel her pulse quicken while her breathing all but stopped. Shattering the silence, the doorbell chimes rang which seemed exaggerated in the still darkness.

"Fed Ex!" came the call from outside. Maggie relaxed and was about to step forward when I tightened my grip on her wrist and whispered for her to remain still. I tiptoed to the dining room window that faced the front of the house. A man dressed in Levis with tennis shoes and a baseball cap waited at the front door without an apparent package or letter. He peered through the side windows of the front door, rang the bell a second time, tried the doorknob and looked to either side of the house. Finally he turned and walked to a dark coupe at the curb and drove off, it appeared to be the same car I saw in our medical building parking lot earlier in the evening.

Maggie was tremulous. "Josh, should we call the police?"

"No. Just make a note of the time this occurred."

On the highest shelf in our clothes closet, I reached for a dusty brown leather holster. I ran my hand over the top side and unhooked the strap to remove a shiny Colt Python 357 magnum. I checked the empty cylinder, and then reached for a box of ammo also on the top shelf.

Maggie walked in. "Josh, what are you doing?" There was disapproval in every syllable.

"I think it may be wise to protect ourselves in the event . . ."

"Put that away, please! I don't want to see you with that thing ever!" Maggie walked out of the room, and I placed the holstered piece in the bottom drawer of my nightstand.

Maggie closed all the window blinds in each room, so that we were shut out or shut in from intruders. "*Let's* watch a little news on TV before turning in," I said. On the sofa, Maggie cuddled next to me and held my hand. Although appearing to watch TV, she seemed preoccupied and restless. "Josh, there are a lot of people who have keys to our office, four office girls, the cleanup crew . . ."

"I know, I know, Maggie. Getting back to the real problem, who wants the information on those drug tests?"

"The other question is, why weren't Basil's files violated? Wasn't he doing clinical research for Magna Pharmex, too?" She asked.

"Yes, he is, but I believe his protocols are different, and I don't know if we're even using the same drug."

Maggie persisted. "Let's think about who's trying to get to your files? Who would benefit from having them?"

"I don't know, but they're going through an awful lot of trouble and scaring the hell out of us. Let's consider the principal players: number one, the pharmaceutical company and its lawyers, and number two, the patients and their lawyers . . ."

"Any information you have could be subpoenaed. Why would it be necessary for anyone to break-in?"

"I've thought of that. Let's take a hypothetical case: supposing some law firm demands to see the clinical records of those who died while taking the experimental drug."

"Again, they could subpoena the records, right?" she asked.

"Yes, if those records were available. Now, if those records were sent to a foreign country a whole different set of legal rules might apply. A foreign manufacturer might not be obligated to reveal its records."

"Aren't you responsible for your patients' records?"

"Ordinarily, yes. However, when the patient submits to an experimental drug program, he or she signs a waiver giving the manufacturer sole ownership of those records. The drug manufacturer may be able to bury data or alter them so that a case of liability would be difficult to establish."

Maggie became pensive. "Okay, I think I understand all that. Now who wants to break into your files and why?"

"Someone who wants the data on the drugs before they're shipped out."

"You mean like a lawyer representing a drug victim's family?"

"Maggie you're beginning to see the picture more clearly."

"Haven't you sent monthly reports to the pharmaceutical firm?"

"I did, in fact, I sent more information than was requested."

"For example?"

"They didn't anticipate autopsies on two of those deaths, and they didn't request the results of some of the tests I ordered."

"Weren't you obligated to give the drug house all that information?"

"Yes, but my primary obligation was to the patient's well-being. Furthermore, I informed the drug manufacturer of my findings."

"What were their responses?"

"They made no reference to unfavorable data. It was as though that information was unimportant, ignored or lost."

"Go on."

"More recently I received letters from lawyers representing the families of the two deceased patients who had been on the drug."

"What did you do?"

"I got in touch with Magna Pharmex's Pharmaceuticals legal department and advised them. They demanded I do nothing and told me that they would conduct all future correspondence.

"I had serious concerns about the toxicity of the medication, so I refused to participate in further clinical trials. I wanted nothing further to do with that drug. Since MP did not respond, two months after I stopped, I sent a letter to the Food and Drug Administration. They advised me that my concerns would be addressed in a timely manner. That was months ago."

"Seems as though teh FDA dropped the ball, too."

"Six months after I forwarded my last monthly report, I received a letter from MP telling me that the trial studies had been concluded. They paid me generously, and you know the rest. They conveyed the impression that the medicine was highly effective and would probably be promoted to the medical profession and sold only by prescription in the near future with the blessings of the FDA."

"Do you still have some of their trial medication?"

"Enough for about twenty patients."

"Where is it?"

"In the storage room at the medical building."

"Josh, are the keys to the storage room available to the same people who service the rest of the building?"

"No, they're not. Remember this is the storage room, not the supply room. Only Basil and I have keys to this room. He has records and medications that are stored there."

"Are you sure no one else has access to that room?"

Before I could answer, Maggie bounded off her chair and pulled me off mine. "Let's examine that room now."

I looked at my watch. "It's late. It's nine thirty. We can examine that room tomorrow. Why the urgency?"

Maggie was not deterred. "Josh, it'll take us only fifteen minutes to get there, and I'll feel a lot better. Besides, you might need that medicine to prove its toxicity."

"Remember some of it is an inert or benign placebo," I said, hoping to discourage her insistence.

Maggie handed me my jacket. "Any lab can determine which samples are placebos and which have the drug in no time at all."

"How can a gal who is so sexy be so clever and analytical?"

"If that intrigues you, deary, never let me go."

"I have no intention of ever doing so."

FIVE

Traffic at that hour, nine forty-five p.m., was light. We drove north on Monterey Avenue; the office buildings were dark. Approaching ours, we saw a light from the first floor; in fact, it was Basil's suite. "Maybe it's the cleaning crew," I suggested.

"Isn't that Basil's Bentley parked there?" Maggie asked.

I turned off the headlights and pulled into a parking space next to the Bentley. "Basil must be working late."

"Maybe he's cooking the books."

"Maggie, don't be so cynical."

It was one of Basil's examining rooms. The venetian blinds were partially opened. Maggie sidled up to the edge of the window and peered inside. She made excited gestures and pointed. I figured she was watching something illicit, indecent, or both. Standing behind her and looking over her shoulder, I saw something that caused instant embarrassment, and I don't embarrass easily.

Basil seated in a chair, head tilted back, eyes closed, was smiling blissfully. An examining table obscured his lower body. The back of a petite blonde, a curvaceous nude rose from below, picked up a dress and ambled out of the room. Basil stood, pulled up his pants and zipped up his fly. He turned out the lights and left the room.

"Maggie, let's get out of here. I knew we shouldn't have come."

"Well, I'll bet Basil did." Maggie covered her mouth to prevent audible giggles. "Josh, don't be so mid-Victorian. Everyone knew

27

about Clinton, and the world is still spinning on its axis. Besides, we're not leaving without knowing whether the trial medication is in the storage room or not."

"Well, I'm not staying here to confront Basil and whoever he's with. We'll pull around to the side of the building and wait until they're gone. If they're not gone in ten minutes, we're leaving."

In less then five minutes, two shadowy forms got into the Bentley and drove away. We walked towards the entrance. I still felt uneasy and wished that we had not come. Maggie seemed to enjoy the salacious, covert activity. She preceded me and took my hand to pull me forward. With my keys and the attached mini-flashlight, I turned off the alarm system. The scent of perfume lingered in the hall. I turned on the lights, and we headed for the storage room. I selected a key from my key ring and opened the door. A musty smell permeated the dimly lit room filled with old charts, obsolete equipment, and outdated journals.

In the far left corner of this pantry-sized room with its shelves and partitions, a square cardboard box measuring about twelve by twelve inches, marked TRO-129 Dolorean β, was slightly askew on the top shelf. I reached up and removed it to find the seal had been broken. "I'll be damned, it's been emptied." I looked around the shelves kind of absently, hoping for an explanation.

"Seems as though someone's trying to collect all the existing evidence. Josh, surely there are others who conducted trials with that drug. Do you think their drugs have been stolen also?"

"Stolen? I can't believe that. Maybe Basil used it . . . Yet . . ."

Maggie pondered. "What troubles me, Magna Pharmex had enough data from you alone to make them suspect that the drug could be lethal . . ."

"MP may have known full well about the drug's toxicity, but they tried to satisfy investors to get to the market place before the competition, safety standards be damned!"

"So drugs not thoroughly tested are still being released to the unsuspecting public?"

"Not only the public, but doctors as well. Since information may come solely from the detail person, that is, the drug representative who touts the new product to the doctor in his office. Glowing reports, masquerading as scientific facts, are given for new antibiotics, pain relievers, youth restorers, and sustainers of penile erections . . ." I glanced at Maggie, tongue in cheek, "Should I invest in that type of preparation?"

"I've no complaints in that department, thank you."

We walked to my consultation room. Maggie thumbed through a surgery journal on my desk and looked at costly and colorful ads promoting new drugs.

She shook her head, "I'm becoming cynical about the whole pharmaceutical industry."

"Don't condemn the entire industry for the greed of a few ruthless CEOs. There are more wonderful life-saving drugs like biologicals and anti-cancer preparations than ever and many more are in the pipeline. Researchers are sincere, dedicated, hardworking people . . ."

"Okay, Doctor, you've made your point. What do you suggest we do next? Should we notify the police about the theft of the drugs?"

"Not until I ask Basil if he took them."

"Now, aren't you glad I insisted on coming here tonight?"

"Not entirely."

The following morning, from my bedside, I called Basil and asked him if he had broken into my supply of Dolorean β in the supply room. He vehemently denied any knowledge of the matter and registered a deep concern.

Mannheim and Hernandez were waiting in my consultation room when I returned from morning surgery. Without preliminary conversation, they made inquiries about the medications taken from the storage room. "How long has it been since you've looked at that box?"

"Maybe two weeks, I don't remember exactly. I haven't much reason to go into that room."

"What value are those drugs to anyone?" Mannheim asked.

"They might be of value to the drug manufacturer, possibly to attorneys representing families of those who died . . ."

As Mannheim made notes in his small spiral book, I asked, "Sergeant, you left a message on my phone that you had an ID on the man who died in our office."

"That's right. His name was Karl Hoffman, a Swiss national who left Geneva airport on May 12 for New York. He arrived at Palm Springs International on May 13, checked in at the Hilton, then rented a car to go to your office."

"How was he identified?"

"At the coroner's office, his finger prints were taken on a gadget called a *Live Scan* and forwarded electronically."

"Forwarded where?"

"You remember the guy had no ID except for his California driver's license which was as phony as the name he gave himself. The guy's clothes were examined including his shoes that had a label on the insole from a department store in Geneva. The Geneva police were contacted. The dead guy's fingerprints were in their files and a positive ID was made. Some member of his family verified his absence."

"So who was he and why was he here?"

Mannheim referred to his notebook. "The guy was a fifty-eight-year-old vice president of Swiss Union Bank. He was recently widowed and was on health leave."

"Sergeant, what was he doing here and what did he want with us—I mean with me?"

"Doc, I'm happy we were able to make an ID and ship the remains back to Switzerland. I can't answer your other questions, at least not now."

Maggie walked into the room, excused herself and reminded me there were patients to be seen. When the officers left, Maggie pressed me to learn what was said. "Josh, don't wait to hear from the police, get the dead man's home phone number and make your own calls to Geneva."

"Do we really want to get more involved with this? Who knows where this will lead?"

"Maggie stopped in front of me, hands on hips, ready for verbal battle. "I can't figure you out."

"Okay, tell me where I've failed."

"This dead man made a trip of about five thousand miles presumably to see you. We don't know why, and you aren't curious enough to . . ."

"For heaven sake, the next thing you'll propose is a trip to Switzerland . . ."

"That may be necessary." Maggie paused, cocked her head and asked, "Where are the main offices of Magna Pharmex?"

"Geneva, Switzerland."

"Bingo!"

"Maggie, if you're thinking there is a connection between Magna Pharmex and this guy Hoffman's death in our office, you're making a mighty big assumption."

"I'll let you digest the turn of events in the past three days and then tell me I'm wrong." Maggie didn't wait for my response but started by counting on her fingers.

"Number one, a man from Switzerland, where the drugs are manufactured, seeks you out and dies in your office. Number two, a Teutonic-looking guy who may be Swiss, sits next to us in a restaurant with an electronic device trying to hear our conversation. Number three, your office files are stolen and somebody tries to gain access to our house posing as a Fed Ex delivery guy. Oh, yes, and what about the car that followed us? To me, all that is more than just coincidental. What's more, I believe your reports on the deaths of some of your patients taking the trial drug are linked to all of this." Replacing her hands on her hips, she paused. "Well?"

"Maggie, your deductive reasoning is almost flawless—or is that inductive reasoning?"

With Elise following him closely in the hallway, Basil stopped me before I was about to enter an examining room.

"Josh, are you going to the dinner and lecture sponsored by Magna Pharmex at the Los Angeles Tower, tomorrow?"

"Yes, I've already signed out to one of the orthopods. Maggie and I plan to attend. We'll be staying overnight, I don't care to drive back to the desert in the late evening."

"Good, I'll see you there."

Maggie approached just as Basil left. "What did lover boy want?"

After I told her she gasped and put her hand to her mouth, "Oh, Josh, please forgive me. I've been meaning to tell you all day: just this morning I heard from my niece, Judy, the nurse at Northwestern Hospital. She's decided at the last minute to come to the desert for a nurses' meeting at the Eisenhower Medical Center, the very two days we planned to spend in L.A. I think I'd like to be with her, she's my only living relative. I'm terribly sorry, I hope you don't mind."

"That's all right. I'll just cancel the L.A. trip."

"No, no! I insist you go and get whatever information you can from someone who knows what's going on at Magna Pharmex. I'll entertain Judy, we'll enjoy some nurse-talk, and I'll learn some gossip about my Chicago friends." I started to object, but Maggie anticipating my reluctance, put her hand to my mouth and insisted that I go. "Just don't let a hussy set a trap for you."

"What makes you think I'll be that lucky?"

With my overnight bag, I stopped at the hotel's daily activities board to locate the Magna Pharmex dinner meeting held in one of the larger banquet halls. At the registration desk a young woman took my charge card and verified that my mini-suite was non-smoking with a king-sized bed. She looked to either side and over my shoulder. "Would Mrs. Harrington prefer her own room key?"

I explained that I was alone and would have been happy with smaller accommodations. The young woman apologized explaining the hotel was completely booked and since my accommodations were prepaid by Magna Pharmex, I should find the larger suite more comfortable. I thought it best not to argue.

When I opened the door to the commodious suite, I found a bottle of champagne in an ice bucket and a basket of fruit on the cocktail table, a card read: "Compliments of Magna Pharmex and Mei Ling Bolton."

I picked up the card and examined both sides. Who was Mei Ling Bolton?

SIX

At the host's bar, I ordered a gin and tonic and scouted the room for a familiar face. A long draped table set for eight at the front of the room was divided by a speaker's stand. On the wall behind, a long banner proclaimed, Magna Pharmex, Provider of Ethical Drugs to the Medical Profession since 1923. Vertical columns at each end of the banner listed the current products of the giant firm. Looking across the room, I saw the profile of Basil seated next to a blonde whose back faced me. I was about to cross the room when an attractive, petite brunette sidled up to me and smiled with an intimacy suggesting an old friendship. I tried desperately to recall her face, name, place or situation where we might have met, but I came up empty.

"Dr. Harrington, I'm so happy to see you again." She extended her soft, delicate hand and held mine. "I'm Mei Ling Bolton. I called on you at your office about eight months ago to detail our newest generation of antibiotics. At that time, you were working on the clinical trials of batch number, TRO-129, code name, Dolorean β."

"Yes, yes, of course. Forgive me for not recalling such a beautiful young woman, I should have remembered. And I want to thank you for that basket of fruit and champagne sent to my room."

"*Il n'y a pas de quoi.* You were, as I recall, preoccupied with making arrangements for a trip to Chicago. Besides, I remember you very well, a handsome widower who was both kind and gracious to a novice drug saleswoman. I've thought about you often."

"Ms Bolton, you embarrass me. I'm happily married now, and besides, I'm old enough to be your father."

"My father is handsome, too, and I love him dearly."

She was as brazen as she was alluring. I thought I had better put some distance between us. As I stood to leave, she held my arm. "Is Mrs. Harrington here?" I explained why Maggie was not.

"I hope you don't mind if I sit at your table tonight. I'm also unescorted."

"Not at all." Actually, I was hoping she would sit elsewhere. An extra-marital affair or even the appearance of one was not something I needed to complicate my life. I excused myself and walked to the men's room to distance myself from this little vixen, she with her neatly styled black hair, pearly skin, delicate bow-shaped mouth, tiny nose, and eyes of mystic almond-shape with long fluttering lashes. Her figure, like an ingenue's approaching maturity, had all the feminine softness of a beckoning siren. I warned myself to ignore her advances.

Returning to the dining room, I looked for an MP company rep. They wore permanent badges with names embossed over the MP logo. Guests were given plastic badges with their names written with a felt pen.

A group of four men in business suits wearing company badges were chatting. A short, portly man who spoke English with a decided German accent seemed to be holding court. He rolled a long unlit cigar in his left hand. As I approached, he looked at my badge and extended his right hand.

"Dr. Harrington? How do you do? I'm Dr. Hans Becker from Geneva. Welcome to our meeting. I hope you prescribe our preparations often. Is there a particular product you are interested in?"

When I mentioned the experimental drug, TRO-129, he looked at me with greater interest, and then nodded almost imperceptibly to the others who drifted off. His beady eyes locked onto mine.

I explained that I ran clinical trials for the company; he listened and nodded but said nothing until I asked, "Did you know a Karl Hoffman from Geneva?"

He ran his tongue around the inside of his mouth, "Karl Hoffman is not an unusual name in Geneva. Can you give me more details?"

I told him about Hoffman's death in our office as well as the information we received from the Swiss police. Becker placed the long unlit cigar in his mouth and moved it slowly from side to side. "I'm sorry I cannot help you."

I thanked him and started to walk away when he reached for my arm and said, "Wait. Tell me about your drug trials. Were you pleased with the responses?"

I made an effort to be discreet and yet maintain my honesty. "Some patients seemed to be relieved of pain."

He smiled, his jowls expanded and his eyes became mere slits. I imagined he thought he had met a true devotee, a real promoter for Dolorean β. He reached up and put his arm on my shoulder.

Then I dropped the hammer. "But some patients died." His smile vanished; he cleared his throat and released his shoulder embrace.

His cigar was retrieved from a near fall, "Did-er-did you notify the company of this?"

"Yes, but when I got no response after more than a month, I notified the FDA."

Becker became agitated, beads of perspiration appeared on his brow. The glabrous folds on his neck reddened. "Do—do you still have those records?" He reaffirmed my thinking that MP was interested in obtaining all records relating to Dolorean β. He stared at me expectantly, but I hesitated before answering. I felt compelled to tell the truth but not to give more information than was requested. He didn't need to know that I had duplicate records at my home.

"I was ready to comply with the company's directives to forward my records, just before they were stolen."

"Humph," he muttered chomping down on his cigar. He turned to an approaching tall, bespectacled balding man, dressed immaculately in a pin-striped suit and a shirt with a high stiff collar, French cuffs and a Hermes tie with a diamond stickpin. My impression was that of a supreme egotist who was smooth if not unctuous. Although cigarette smoking was considered passé among successful American men, he of course was exempt. He reached into his suit jacket pocket and pulled out a classic, thin striped silver cigarette case with the

Dunhill logo and his scrolled initials. I put my hand up to decline his offer, which he seemed to expect.

He placed the filtered tip in his mouth then reached in his trouser pocket for a thin silver lighter that matched the cigarette case. Raising his head to exhale from a long drag, he looked beyond me even as I extended my hand.

"Dr. Mueller, this is Dr. Harrington, one of our test pilots for Dolorean β." Becker forced a chuckle. Mueller did not smile and appeared preoccupied. "Dr. Mueller is the scientist in charge of the development of Dolorean β," Becker continued.

As I extended my hand again, Mueller looked beyond me, then walked away with a curt, "Excuse me." Awkwardly, I withdrew my hand.

Becker embarrassed by Mueller's aloofness, said, "Ach, you know these scientists, their heads are in the clouds."

The numbered tables and place cards indicated our seating. Mei Ling had succeeded in placing her name card next to mine. She arrived as I approached the table. Standing behind her, I eased her chair into place as she sat. She turned, looked up at me with a beguiling smile to thank me and touched my arm gently. The other three couples at the table watched and probably wondered about our relationship. I was flattered but also embarrassed to think anyone might have linked us romantically. I felt compelled to engage her in conversation.

"Tell me about yourself, Mei Ling."

She sat up brightly and looked into my eyes. "I was born in Chinatown, San Francisco. My mother is a second generation American whose grandparents came from Peking. She attended U.C. Berkeley and fell madly in love with her handsome psychology T.A., Benson Ormand Bolton, a descendant of a Mayflower pilgrim. What a delightful couple they are, my mother at four feet eleven inches looking lovingly at my sky-high father at six foot three as they stand side by side. From his initials, B.O.B., he was known affectionately among students and faculty as Big Bob Bolton. They moved to Berkeley when I was quite young and raised two more children."

Mei Ling shifted her weight so that her arm touched my sleeve. Her brown eyes danced and surveyed my face. "Now tell me all about you."

I started a thumbnail sketch of my background before our Caesar salads arrived. Mei Ling pressed her thigh against mine. I tried to move my chair but was thwarted by an obese woman who sat to my left. I glanced upwards seeking divine guidance but received none. Across the room, I saw Basil as he held his companion's hand on the table and engaged in a tête-a-tête. I wondered if his blonde companion was the same one we had seen in his examining room the night before.

Mei Ling chatted throughout the main course as I nodded and smiled absently. When the desserts arrived, Dr. Becker approached the speaker's stand. The waiters and waitresses disappeared as the portly man tapped the microphone for an annoyingly loud click-click followed by an unnecessary, "Can you all hear me?"

He began a litany of the company's many products distributed globally under various names. He droned on about increasing profits, improved sales techniques and lastly about new and promising drugs. These new drugs were distributed to foreign markets before coming to the States, since product liability laws were less stringent outside of the United States.

Mei Ling moistened her bow-shaped lips provocatively with her tongue and smiled. I looked away in an effort to appear aloof. Dr. Mueller, the dandified head of the new drug development program, was introduced and began a monotonous description of new products. Using Power Point to illustrate his talk, he dwelled on molecular configurations, pie charts, algorithms, probability studies, grids and graphs to an audience that appeared to have lost interest or comprehension after two minutes of presentation. I looked around and saw some who were nodding and others who were obviously snoozing. His delivery was somewhat indistinct because of his accent, a curious combination of precise English and guttural German.

He reeled in the somnolent audience by speaking of the experimental drug, Dolorean β, the latest, best publicized, but as yet unavailable drug in the States. "Considering that nearly all persons over the age of sixty-five have some form of arthritis, ranging from mild to debilitating, I think you can see that the world-wide need is enormous . . ."

Mei Ling, elbows propped on the table, her chin resting on folded hands, turned her face towards me. I pretended not to notice. When

Dr. Mueller finally finished his presentation, he asked for questions. I wanted to confront the arrogant and pedantic S.O.B., so I stood and an usher handed me a cordless microphone.

"Doctor, how many deaths have occurred with Dolorean β?"

Mueller's eyes bored into mine and without emotion he declared, "Not vun!"

"Not one?"

"Dot's right! Not vun!" With that, he spun on his heels and walked off. I wanted to yell, "Yahwohl!" but thought better of it. The meeting had ended with Becker's closing remarks. I excused myself and walked towards Basil's table. His blonde companion's face was partially hidden by long tresses. When I looked at her, she turned away. Basil made excuses for both of them and escorted her off saying they were late for another engagement. Walking back towards my table, I could see that Mei Ling had gone, and I was relieved. What did she want of me? Let her get involved with someone her own age.

MP's pharmaceutical program boasted of preparations unrivaled for relieving pain and hastening healing. I had reached that stage in my professional life where cynicism became a handmaiden to acceptance. Out of six new products, one may have outstanding properties. As one of my friends would say, "There may be a gold nugget buried in that pile of horse shit, but you gotta do a lot of diggin' to get at it."

The distressing point for me was MP's complete denial of the toxicity, let alone the deadly effects of Dolorean β. How long could they keep that information under wraps? Then I wondered why I hadn't heard from the FDA.

I returned to my mini-suite and planned to call Maggie, who I knew was curious to know about everything. I undressed down to my shorts and punched in our home phone number.

Hello, Maggie—yes love—just a moment, there's someone at the door.

I set the phone down and asked who was there—no answer. Instinctively, I opened the door. Standing in an oversized terry cloth hotel robe, carrying a bottle of champagne in an ice bucket and two flutes was Mei Ling. She tilted her head and, with a seductive smile, asked, "May I?" Before I could respond, she stepped into the room. I turned my back to her and ran to the phone,

Uh—uh, Maggie, let me call you back—one of the company reps just came in.

Before Maggie could say another word, I placed the phone on its cradle. I was already riven with guilt and rushed to the bathroom for my hotel robe. Mel Ling with an impish smile started to titter as she walked towards the cocktail table. She was carrying the same kind of champagne sent to my room from MP Pharmaceuticals.

"Oh, what a wonderful supply of bubbly!" she said when she saw my unopened bottle. "We can drink and make love the whole night! Won't that be fun?"

"Oh, no it won't, my dear. Turn your pretty little tush around and get out of my life."

With a pleading smile, she turned then tripped and fell over her long robe. The ice and water in the bucket splashed across the room. The champagne bottle bounced but remained intact. One of the flutes broke. I carefully picked up the shards and with towels soaked up the ice water.

Sprawled on the floor, Mel Ling moaned softly. Her partially opened robe revealed delicate tea-cup-size breasts. She attempted to stand but was unable to bear weight on the left foot.

"Oh, my ankle is killing me. Let me rest for just a minute or two." Her complexion turned pasty, and she was about to lose consciousness.

I caught her and placed her on the sofa. Her robe fell open revealing an unblemished body magnificently proportioned, from her slender, sculpted neck to her pert breasts with upward-tilting nipples emerging from pink-beige areolar bases. A flat belly and an hourglass waist flared into a rounded pelvis with a triangle of scant pubic hair that did not completely conceal the vaginal cleft. Her eyes fluttered then opened slowly looking into mine as she murmured, "Do you like what you see?"

SEVEN

In my best detached, clinical assessment, Mei Ling's body represented the penultimate embodiment of the precious youthful female form on the brink of full maturity. I closed her robe, "Yes, I like what I see, now do me a favor . . ."

I was about to ask her to leave when she reached up, grabbed the lapels of my robe and pulled me on top of her. Before I could object, she kissed me and flicked her tongue rapidly in my mouth. I rolled off and ordered, "Okay, enough. Out you go, sprained ankle or not."

With a sound somewhere between a pitiable cry and a stifled laugh she said, "But I can't walk to my room on this ankle. Josh. You don't mind my calling you Josh, do you? Let me stay for a short while longer. I was hoping to seduce you, but that doesn't seem possible. You're such an honorable guy. Does your wife know how lucky she is?"

While she lay on her side on the sofa appearing doll-like, Mei Ling watched as I gathered ice cubes from my champagne bucket and placed them in a plastic bag. I wrapped a towel around the bag of ice, and placed it on her ankle.

Ooh, that feels so much better." She pulled her robe around closely to seal off any further exposure. The roaring tide of her passion seemed to have ebbed as swiftly as it had swelled, much to my relief. With her sensuous, almond-shaped eyes, she locked onto mine. "Josh, you're very sweet, and I wouldn't want any harm to come to you."

"What do you mean?"

"I was privy to the results of the drug trials you were conduct-ing on Dolorean β."

"How did you know about those drug results?"

"Would it surprise you to learn that I've had a close relationship with some of the big-wigs at MP?"

I did not respond.

"Let me tell you some of the things I learned, things that involved you."

Now she commanded my complete attention. For the next thirty minutes, I made mental notes underscoring names and events. There was a chilling objectivity to her story, an almost unbelievable account of corporate avarice and disregard for human life. Her talking was punctuated by occasional moans when she moved her foot.

"I think I can hobble to my room," she said. "I'm just four doors down."

I went to the dressing room, removed my robe and put on a shirt, trousers and shoes. "I'll carry you to your room. Keep the ice pack on your ankle and stay off your foot." I was more comfortable in a doctor-patient relationship rather than a ridiculous Lolita-adult affair.

"Before you carry me off, Sir Galahad, would you share a little champagne with me, pretty please?" She pouted and held on to a sofa pillow in defiance of my refusal. I reconsidered hoping to hasten her departure, "Okay, one small drink and you're out of here." I uncorked the bottle, a loud pop was followed by a jet stream of foam arching onto the coffee table and sofa.

"Oh, I wish you had done that to me." she quipped.

Ignoring the comment, I took a perfunctory sip then took both flutes and set them down. I handed her the ice bucket and bottle then reached down to pick her up. "That's it, my dear. Now, out you go!" At about a hundred pounds, she was an easy carry, especially with her arms wrapped around my neck. Before going into the hall, I looked in both directions, no one in sight. I carried her past three doors and was about to open her door when Dr. Mueller emerged from the room next to hers. He stopped momentarily and stared at us with steely eyes. His face, I thought, was a dead-ringer for Grant Wood's farmer in American Gothic—without the benignity.

"Oh, good evening, Kurt." Mei Ling cradled in my arms started to give Mueller an explanation, "I slipped and sprained my ankle . . ." Mueller, stiff-necked, ignored her comment and walked off. "Don't mind him, Josh. That poor man lacks the most basic social graces." Damn. This was all I needed, that jerk could start a rumor. I hoped to hell he was going to be as non-communicative with others as he was with us. I set Mei Ling down on her bed. Before I released her, she hugged me tightly.

"Won't you stay and tuck me in? My ankle won't interfere with what I have in mind for us, and I'll never tell."

Midnight, I can't call Maggie now, she's asleep. I'll call in the morning. I lay in bed and thought about Mei Ling as well as those things she had revealed about Magna Pharmex, then there appeared the creepy visage of Dr. Mueller.

Eight a.m. I was about to leave Los Angeles and called Maggie on her cell phone.

How are you, darling? I'm on my way—tell you all about it when I see you at the office at about 11:30.

How much do I dare tell Maggie about that visit with Mei Ling? Would she believe my innocence? Would I believe Maggie if the situation were reversed? Of course. That's what a faithful marriage is all about.

I left the hotel at eight-thirty to confront the downtown L.A. traffic, which had become fiercer with each passing year. On that mid-May morning, the freeway interchange showed the usual lock-step formation with barely perceptible progress. My strategy was not only to jockey into a moving lane, but to avoid getting too close to a truck or clunker where exhaust fumes would be sucked up by my air conditioner. If I allowed an extra car length or two, a third car raced in to fill the void, and my advantage would vanish. Meantime, the gray-green-brown layer of smog hovered like a pall. The infamous inversion layer and the crowding were the main reasons I had left the L.A. scene about twenty years ago.

Once I merged onto I-10, I had a sense of relief. The freeway widened, the air became cleaner, and I knew I was on *my* road, which was a straight shot home. The Cabazon Mall on the north side of the freeway was a mere forty minutes from home if I maintained a speed of seventy-five and no paralyzing accidents occurred.

About four miles east of the mall, there had risen out of the barren, scrubby sandy soil an incongruous structure, a tower, light-colored with an enormous green window on top like a giant periscope or an evil cyclops with a raised eyebrow beckoning gamblers to its casino and hotel. That, I thought, was the Morongo Tribe's altar for commemorating sacrifices at the gaming tables and electronic bandits.

Then the windmills came into view, some at a height of one hundred fifty feet with blades half the width of a football field. They covered the landscape in rows and formed undulating patterns over hills and valleys near the San Gorgonio Pass. If these windmills provided the source of energy for our valley, why were our electric bills so high? That was a question I asked whenever someone rode with me.

Just to the south of the freeway, around Banning, I could see the San Andreas Fault, a distinct rupture on the valley surface. Seismologists had been warning residents for years that a major earthquake was due anytime. Since the last quake in the Mojave region occurred one hundred forty-nine years ago, and the recorded intervals of time between major quakes were one hundred forty years, we have been living on borrowed time. That was a narrow concept and not worthy of constant concern.

My momentary concern was about last night's meeting with Mei Ling. In reconstructing the events of the evening, I learned that her flirtatious, no, her seductive enticements were designed to get me to stop revealing information I might have had on those patients who died while on the clinical trials of Dolorean β. Then she planned to make me promise not to divulge those deaths and autopsies to the FDA or any other agencies that might call for a moratorium on manufacturing and rescind an approval rating on the drug.

Getting back to Mei Ling, she was more than attractive and about as sexually desirable as a young woman could be. But my own code of ethics, my own inhibitions, my own sense of love and loyalty to Maggie wouldn't permit any philandering. I repeated the word "philandering" in my mind. It was such a pithy, old-fashioned word. Anyway, that episode had ended, and I really had no reason to recount those details to Maggie. I was sure she would have understood, but there was little point in tempting fate or arousing suspicions.

Maintaining a speed of seventy-five in the middle lane and driving defensively, I noticed a dark sport coupe coming up on my left side at an estimated speed of ninety to one hundred miles per hour. When he was parallel with my car, the driver waved me over to the right. The vehicle, a costly car, I knew was not official, and I decided to stay in my lane. Then the SOB started inching towards my left side in an obvious attempt to get me onto the right shoulder. What in the hell was the bastard trying to do? I had to make a decision, fast! At that moment the wailing siren of a highway patrolman with flashing roof lights roared up behind the sport coupe and forced it to the side of the freeway. Damn! That was a reprieve.

I took a couple of deep breaths and tried to relax. Maybe the guy had mistaken me for someone else, and I refused to let the episode bother me further. As I neared the Monterey exit, the Costco warehouse sign came into view. I decided on an antidote to defuse the excitement. I would buy Maggie a dozen roses and just maybe assuage any guilt I had about last night.

Springtime in the valley brought visual treats from the brilliant colors of flowers planted in the road medians and along the country clubs where Jacaranda trees with purple blossoms, bougainvilleas and oleanders with vivid hues decorated the streets. I could not identify many of the plants, and I always felt inadequate about my limited knowledge of horticulture.

Pulling into the office parking lot gave me a sense of security, it was my safe haven. Before emerging from the car with the bouquet, I looked around and saw a late model light blue Ford sedan with two spotlights and a light on the left side of the rear window shelf. This unmarked police vehicle announced itself to every law-breaker within sight.

Parked beside it was another unmarked sedan in black, a plain Jane with no buyer options. The tires, however, were heavy duty and it too had two spotlights mounted on the "A" posts. Peering into the driver's window, I saw the two-way radio system and the worn black vinyl upholstery as well as the lack of inner rear door hardware. Two police cars? What was going on?

When I entered the rear door, Elise motioned with her eyes and moved her head towards the consultation room. She mimed the word *police*, so I asked her to put the flowers in a vase and place them on Maggie's desk. I opened the door to find Detectives Mannheim and Hernandez sitting opposite my desk. Behind them stood two somber men wearing dark jackets. Both wore collared shirts and ties with weapons mounted on their sides. With five people, the room was crowded and the odor of body perspiration was not entirely masked by after-shave lotion.

"Looks like a small convention, fellas. What brings all of you here?" My cordiality was not reciprocated.

Mannheim said, "Doc, we've been asked by the L.A.P.D. here to verify a few things." He turned to face a balding man to his right. "This is Detective Bill Bisogno and his partner, Detective Bob Black. If you think your rights are being compromised, you can confer with your attorney. I'm sure you'll be able to straighten out any questions these L.A. men have."

I moved to my desk chair and sat.

"What's this all about, fellas?" There was a kind of bravado in my manner, something I needed for my own reassurance.

"Were you in L.A. last night at the Angeles Towers Hotel?" Detective Black asked.

"Yes."

"Were you in the company of a Ms. Mei Ling Bolton?" Detective Bisogno asked.

Heat rose from below my collar, and I had a sinking sensation in my gut. The bravado was gone. I measured my words and looked directly into the detective's eyes. "Yes, we talked for a while."

"Where?" Bisogno asked.

"In one of the banquet halls."

"Anywhere else?"

We entered the realm of cat and mouse. Obviously, they knew about our meeting in the hotel room and were toying with me. I wondered where this questioning was leading. Perhaps I should withhold information until I talked with my attorney, but I had no reason not to answer their questions. "Fellas, it's a little stuffy, in here. Mind if I open the door?"

"Dr. Harrington, we don't want to engage in any games," Mannheim continued. "The L.A.P.D. here already knows certain things." Detective Black referred to a spiral notebook. "At about eleven thirty last night you carried a Ms. Mei Ling Bolton to her room, is that right?"

My mouth went dry, and I knew I was starring. Were there surveillance cameras or was it that damned Dr. Strangelove-type character, Dr. Mueller? But wait, what did I do? I didn't rape her, I didn't harm her. Why all these questions? "That's right. Did I break any laws?"

Mannheim paused, looked at the ceiling then looked at the floor before locking onto my eyes, "Doc, Miss Bolton was found dead early this morning."

That hit me like a full body blow. I felt an immediate nausea. My throat was parched, and I tried clearing it. "What? What are you talking about?"

"We were hoping you could tell us." Mannheim said.

The picture was coming into focus. "Wait a goddamned minute. When I saw her last night, she was very much alive and healthy—except for a sprained ankle. We had an innocent conversation, and now I'm a *murder* suspect? Christ! Am I actually being charged with murder?"

"No, Doc, calm down," Bisogno said. "We don't even know if she was murdered. An external examination of the body didn't show any obvious trauma. We're going to get the coroner's report later today. Not that it makes any difference, but I thought you should know forensics has already identified her lipstick on a champagne flute in your hotel room. You wouldn't object if the lab tested your DNA, would you?"

"C'mon guys, what are you suggesting?"

No one volunteered an answer. "Doc, you're not planning to leave the area any time soon, are you?" Detective Black asked.

"Of course not. Look, I've done nothing wrong, and I've nothing to hide."

Mannheim set one half of his behind on the corner of my desk and leaned toward me as though preparing for a long interview. Hernandez stood with a broad base as though to secure his stability and prevent me from moving quickly. Was he thinking I would attack him? Fat chance.

"Doc, I'm curious: why was Ms. Bolton in your room?" Black asked.

That was none of his damned business, but I was not going to be confrontational. "I think she was lonesome and wanted to chat. Actually, we talked about the efficacy of some new drug products." As soon as I said that, I knew I sounded fatuous.

"Huh? Oh, yeah, sure. Efficacy?" He leaned forward. "C'mon, Doc, tell us what really happened."

Was this a serious interview or were these guys interested in gossip? "Fellas, you'll have to excuse me. I have patients to see."

Mannheim showed no concern for my time constraints. "Just a few more questions, of course, if you'd rather, all of us could go down to the station . . ." Mannheim lifted his behind off the desk, brought his shoulders back and looked down at me. The boys were starting to play hardball.

"No, I'd rather not," I was quick to add. "Ask me anything you want, the patients will wait awhile, but not too long, please."

"Doc, how well did you know the deceased?" Mannheim asked. He reached into his pocket for a toothpick and guided it around his mouth with his tongue, never taking his eyes off me. Hernandez with folded arms stared without expression, but at least he spared me questions.

"I hadn't seen her before last night . . ." Mannheim stared at me with his deep-set eyes partially concealed by bushy brows. ". . . except for a brief office visit she made about eight months ago when she was detailing for Magna Pharmex."

"You hadn't seen her since then?"

"That's right."

Detective Black asked, "Doc, an item in Ms Bolton's ledger, dated one month ago, indicated that she wanted to see you at this last meeting. Are you saying you knew nothing about that?"

"That's what I'm saying."

Detective Bisogno tossed a set of keys on my desk, "Do these look familiar, Doc?"

I quickly felt my pants pockets. The keys to the office were missing. "They must have fallen out of my pocket last night."

"Yeah, right into the deceased's purse. Fortunately, there's an ID tag on them."

The detectives finally left. I slumped into my chair emotionally drained and thought about the crazy turn of events that could only be a prelude to more grief.

EIGHT

Elise knocked, then without waiting came into the room. "Is everything all right, Dr. Harrington? Can I get you something, a cup of coffee?"

"Yes, please." The thought of Mei Ling's death was shocking and defied reason. I shook my head as though to dispel an unbelievable nightmare.

Elise placed the cup on my desk as Maggie walked in. She stopped and surveyed Elise with the protective eye of a tigress guarding her young. Elise made a hurried exit and closed the door behind her.

Maggie leaned over my desk and kissed me. "Darling, I just said goodbye to Judy. She was so sorry she missed you." Her eyes danced in that delightfully girlish way that captivated me. "We window-shopped in every store on El Paseo, tried on a zillion dresses and shoes. She was absolutely enchanted with everything, the metal art work and flowers in the median, the expensive showy cars, and the art galleries." She caught her breath and stopped abruptly. "Now, tell me about your evening: who you talked to, what you learned, and who attempted to steal you from me?"

My weak, forced smile must have set off a warning signal. I outlined every detail of the meeting until I got to the part about Mei Ling. In what proved to be flawed judgment, I made no reference to her, I wanted to spare both of us grief, at least for the moment.

"Josh, something's troubling you, what is it?" Maggie read me easily.

In spite of my initial reticence, I mentioned the meeting with Mei Ling, in the hotel suite, the police visit to the office just a few moments ago and their shocking report of Mei Ling's death. Maggie appeared devastated and dropped into a chair while I unraveled the details. A painful silence ensued. I could not be sure if she was terribly saddened by Mei Ling's death or whether her faith in me had been shaken or both.

"Maggie, I've never lied to you, I love and respect you too much. Please understand, I'm completely innocent in this unfortunate mess."

She stood slowly, took several steps and turned back. Her eyes were red and teary. Her voice quivery, "Josh, I believe you. I just wish I had been with you, all of this could have been avoided." She raised her chin and swallowed, walked over and put her arms around me and held me tightly, "Don't worry; we'll muddle through this somehow."

I brushed a tear from her cheek, placed my hand behind her head, and pressed it to my chest.

Elise's high-pitched voice on the intercom disturbed the serenity. "Dr. Harrington, a Dr. Thomas from the Indio coroner's office is on the phone."

> *Hello, Dr. Thomas—yes, on Mr. Hoffman who died in my office—what?—not the immediate cause of death?—not like alcoholic cirrhosis—that is weird—yes, please keep me informed.*

"What is it Josh?"

"Mr. Hoffman may not have died of a heart attack but rather a severe and acute destructive process of the liver. The coroner will let me know as soon as he gets information on tissue slides he sent to a hepatologist at Stanford."

For the next four hours, Maggie remained somber as we went through the routine of seeing our patients. There was a lack of the usual humor we injected to lighten the patients' concerns. After the last patient left, shortly after five thirty, Maggie went into each examining room to clean and check the supplies in the medicine cabinets. "Josh, did you use the Empirin Compound with codeine in room two today?"

"No, why?"

"A bottle has been emptied."

"Was the cabinet locked?"

"Yes. I thought there were only two keys. You and I have them, right?"

"Right."

At about five forty-five, the cleaning crew of three arrived with their paraphernalia. Charlie Ironsmith, the head of the crew, lowered his head slightly, excused his intrusion and entered with a mop and pail into the examining room. His bent posture suggested an attitude of perpetual submissiveness. At forty-five to fifty years of age and at about a height of five feet ten inches he was broad-shouldered with dark penetrating eyes. He said little but seemed to understand when we spoke to him. A bushy head of black curly hair and a full mustache I thought gave him a Mediterranean appearance. And yet, his skin was pale like those Irish who were supposed to have inherited the dark hair of the ill-fated Spanish Armada sailors who were imprisoned and later mated with Irish lasses.

"Charlie, do you know anything about this empty bottle?"

He studied it momentarily, raised his eyebrows, shook his head and shrugged. I would have been surprised had he given another response.

I must have appeared pensive while I drove home. Maggie turned to me. "Josh, I've already forgiven you for anything that might have happened last night in L.A. . . ."

"I was in no way involved in Mei Ling's death nor did I have sexual relations with her. Believe me."

"I believe you, but Mannheim may have his doubts. He called to say he'd like you to submit a specimen for DNA analysis."

"That's fine with me. I know I'm innocent, there's no way . . ."

Then I remembered Mei Ling's tongue darting in my mouth, but she had champagne after that and that should have washed away any of my DNA, or did it? Suddenly, my armor of righteous indignation developed chinks.

Maggie said matter-of-factly, "The L.A. coroner found semen in Mei Ling's vagina."

"Well, it sure as all hell wasn't mine!" Maggie assumed a subtle air of detachment in her questioning. "Are you convinced that this Mei Ling wanted to be with you because she was head-over-heels in love with you? It isn't as though she knew you well prior to that evening. You said you didn't even recognize her at the banquet until she reintroduced herself and jogged your memory."

"That's right."

Maggie was entitled to and expected more explanation. "Let me fill you in on a few more facts. After Mei Ling tried to seduce me, she confessed to having an ulterior motive but asked that under no circumstances was I to divulge the nature of our conversation to anyone, not even to my wife. Reluctantly, I agreed since I had to know what had driven her to throw herself at me. After all, she was beautiful, intelligent and probably could have had any man she wanted. She confided that she climbed the corporate ladder by granting favors to some of her superiors. In fact, she was on a mission when she approached me."

"What did she want?"

It was dusk when we neared our home. A dark sport coupe was parked across the street. I wondered if it was the same one that sped out of our parking lot as we were closing the office two nights ago. "Let's not open the garage door just yet. I want to check out that car."

I drove past it slowly and peered into its tinted windows. I could see only the indistinct outline of a driver, no facial features. At the end of the block, I made a u-turn. From a distance of about fifty feet the coupe suddenly screeched as its wheels spun, then it fishtailed leaving exhaust and skid marks. "Damn! Did you get a license number?"

"It sped away too fast. I couldn't!"

We entered the house and turned on the lights in each room, no sign of forced entry. The file cabinet in the den was intact.

"Josh, this frightens me. Who was in that car, what do they want of us?"

"I don't know, maybe our files."

"How would they know about our files, unless you mentioned that to someone?"

Maggie's question made me think. "I might have said something to Basil about having copies of the test trials at home, but I doubt that he would have any interest in them."

Maggie prepared a salad while I set the table. Maggie tried to sound nonchalant. "Let's get back to Mei Ling.

The phone rang.

Dr. Harrington? This is Sergeant Mannheim. The lab would like to test your saliva tomorrow. No, we'll send someone to the office—give me a time that's convenient—just routine—don't worry.

I told Maggie about the conversation, "Mannheim said, "Just routine. Don't worry." But my appetite was really compromised after he said that.

Sensing my disquietude, Maggie said, "Let's have a glass of Cabernet and talk a bit before dinner."

We sat on the sofa, and I continued, "Mei Ling said she came to my suite to get information and to have me cooperate in some scheme to endorse Dolorean β. Whatever it was she wanted, she didn't get."

"And?"

"Perhaps she realized I was too straight and wouldn't participate in promoting the drug because its toxicity concerned me."

"Why did MP keep pushing the drug if they suspected it could cause illness or deaths?"

"There were millions—probably billions riding on its potential sales world-wide. Mei Ling knew I had sent in my reports implicating the possible lethal effects of the drug. She said that someone at corporate headquarters wanted me to turn over all my remaining documents. They wanted me to deny the possibility of the drug's toxicity. For sure, they didn't want the reports of the autopsies I had authorized to be published. She hinted that if all my records were destroyed, and I wrote nothing else derogatory, I might receive a hefty grant for another research project. In other words, they were trying to buy me off with a handsome bribe."

"That's despicable." .

"I quite agree, but that's not the worst of it."

"What do you mean?"

"After Mei Ling had a couple glasses of champagne she spoke more freely. She said if I didn't cooperate, the alternatives could be a hell of a lot more drastic."

"More drastic?"

"Well, I don't know whether she was just being melodramatic, or . . ."

Maggie became impatient, "Josh, for heaven's sake, what did she say?"

"She said I could meet with an accidental death or just disappear forever."

Maggie paled and clutched her chest, "Oh, that really frightens me. Give them what they want and wash your hands of the whole thing."

NINE

Maggie called, "Darling, before you come to bed, please see that all the windows are closed and the doors are locked."

From the den I answered, "It's a warm, balmy evening, I'm going to leave some of the windows open for a bit of fresh air . . ." There was no response. After ten minutes of reading the sports section of the paper, I looked in on Maggie. She had fallen asleep with the reading lamp on and an open book resting on her chest. Gently, I removed the book, kissed her lightly on the forehead and shut the lamp. She stirred but did not awaken.

I slipped into bed behind her, placed my arm around her waist as she backed into me. I was about to sink into unconsciousness when I heard a faint rustle, a sound I had hoped would be transient. I heard it again and became concerned. My heart began to pound while my eyes accommodated to the diminished light. I concentrated on the sound, which came from the den. Rolling towards the night stand, and shifting toward the edge of the bed, I quietly opened the lower drawer to remove the Colt revolver from its holster. I walked slowly with both hands on the grip of the gun, my senses peaked to full alertness.

"Josh?" Maggie called.

I whispered, "Shush, go back to sleep." I moved towards the den and stopped at the doorway where I squinted to see the silhouette of someone with a mini flashlight in his mouth going through my cabinet file.

"Hey! What the hell are you doing?" I yelled. Suddenly I was blinded by the flashlight shining in my eyes. In a dizzy succession, my head smashed against the wall, a galaxy of bright stars and flashing comets whirled around me. A searing blow to the side of my head and face knocked me flat on my back. More painful blows rained down, but I held onto my gun and extended my arms forward and upward. I pulled the trigger. A deafening blast assaulted my ears as my hands and arms jerked back and up. Mercifully, the attack stopped.

A piercing cry came from the bedroom, "Josh! Are you all right? Where are you?" Maggie ran and screamed hysterically. She turned on the light and looked at me sprawled on the floor. "Oh, my God! What happened?" She bent over to examine my bloody, bruised lips and my right eye that had already swelled. "Oh, my God! My God! My God!" She invoked the Supreme Being three times, and still my head and face throbbed with an unbearable pain.

The den was in total disarray. The file cabinet drawers were open. Charts were strewn on the floor and the smell of gun powder lingered. Maggie rushed to the washroom and moistened a face cloth to apply to my lips and eye. She listened wide-eyed to what had happened then helped me to my feet. I staggered but still held the revolver as though in a catatonic state. Gingerly, she took the gun after prying my fingers off, and then helped me to the desk chair. I felt dizzy and nauseated. Like a good nurse, she had me lower my head on the desk, until the dizziness subsided. Then she made a quick examination of my head and neck as well as my arms and legs. She hurried to shut the window but called my attention to several drops of blood on the sill. On the floor, the intruder's flashlight was still lit.

Maggie looked around, "We'd better call the police."

While Maggie had me sitting and holding the moist compresses to my face, two Palm Desert police arrived and surveyed the mess in the den.

"What was he after?" One of them asked. "Do you keep valuables in this cabinet?"

The throbbing pain made me impatient, "I don't know what he was after and there were no valuables in there." I was in no mood for idle conversation.

"Do you think the guy meant to kill you?"

"Believe me that occurred to me every time he whacked me." One officer took notes while the other scanned the room and asked questions. When Maggie pointed to the drops of blood on the windowsill, the talking officer advised us not to wipe them off or touch anything near the window or file cabinet. Someone from forensics would be around in the morning to collect the blood and dust for fingerprints. He picked up the flashlight with a latex glove, clicked off the light and put it in a plastic bag.

"Do you mind if I take your revolver?" It was a rhetorical question since he intended to take it, anyway. "Not that I care," he said, "but I hope your gun is registered in Sacramento."

"It is."

Maggie drove us to the office the following morning. A butterfly Band Aid below my lip sealed the edges of a small laceration. Dark sunglasses concealed my black eye. Basil stared at my battered face and wanted to know what had happened. Elise stood between us, carrying Basil's charts. "Oh, Dr. Harrington, what happened to you? Are you all right?"

Maggie intervened, "Yes, Elise, Dr. Harrington will be fine, thank you."

Basil continued to study my face as I removed my dark glasses to expose my discolored and swollen eye. "Wow! That son-of-a-bitch really worked you over! Who did this? Did you get a look at him?"

Elise piped up, "Could you identify him?"

"No, but he left bleeding after I shot him."

"You shot him?" Basil's head jerked backward, and his eyes bulged. He wanted more details, but I had no intention of dwelling on the incident. Just recalling what happened seemed to intensify the pain and caused fine tremors. I changed the subject.

"Basil, whatever happened to Mrs. Van Offing, the one who complained of knee and abdominal pain the day you left for your TV appearance? I've wondered about her pains and severe anemia."

"She had to be hospitalized for a bleeding ulcer. I stopped the medication and transfused her. She improved considerably."

"So, you think the trial medication was responsible for her bleeding?"

"Maybe. Anyway, I'm happy I got to her in time. She could have bled out and died." Basil's comments were a kind of self-congratulatory paean to a mismanaged case that deserved the attention of the local medical board.

"Before you sent her to the hospital, why did you insist on keeping her on the trial medicine, and why didn't you permit her to take something else, even an over-the-counter pain reliever?"

"MP Pharmaceuticals requested the patients be kept only on the test drug until a distinct response occurred. Any outside drugs would have clouded the results." That was the lamest excuse, for an obvious case of malpractice.

"Basil, you ordered blood work on her a week before I saw her, you knew the blood count showed a severe generalized anemia."

"Josh, you're absolutely right. I should have done something about that much sooner. It's just that I'm so damned busy, I have lectures, newspaper and magazine deadlines, I just don't have enough time to review charts. I swear I'm on a perpetual merry-go-round."

"But you manage to find time to spend with women."

"When I can relax, I like to, you know, lower the old testosterone level." He winked and nudged me.

"By the way, who was the blonde with you at the MP conference in L.A.?"

"Just a friend."

Carmenita, a front office girl, interrupted our conversation. "Dr. Harrington, there's a Dr. Thomas from the Indio coroner's office asking to speak to you."

"Thank you. I'll take the call in my consultation room." Maggie followed me.

*Yes, Dr. Thomas—complete cellular destruction?—How?—
Would you repeat that please—World War One?—Sounds
bizarre. Do you know if any family members in Switzerland
have been contacted?—Good, thanks.*

"What did he say?"

"Some fantastic tale about Mr. Hoffman, alias Mr. Soldato, our deceased patient, had a liver that was almost completely destroyed."

"Why is that unusual?"

"A biochemical analysis from Stanford revealed a highly toxic substance within the liver. And here's the weird part, the toxicologists researched the poisonous stuff and discovered that it was formulated by German chemists during World War I. The formula was resurrected by the Nazis to exterminate camp prisoners but was discarded since it didn't kill large numbers fast enough. The Allied Forces supposedly destroyed all they found in a German concentration camp."

Maggie's jaw dropped. She slipped into a chair as though her legs were about to collapse. "Do you think Hoffman drank or ate something that was poisoned, or was he injected?"

"I don't know. The coroner's report didn't mention any needle marks."

"If it were in his food or drink wouldn't he have tasted or smelled it?"

"According to the toxicology report, the substance is odorless and has only the faintest taste of mint which could be masked. The strange part is this substance selectively destroys the liver within hours, and of course, death occurs soon after."

"How long after?"

"Two to four hours, the coroner wasn't sure."

"Who would have this poison and who would want him dead?"

"I don't know. I still don't know why he was in our office wanting to see me."

"Josh, if this substance destroys the liver in two to four hours and Hoffman spent a day in travel from Switzerland and another day in Palm Springs, he had to be poisoned here in the Valley sometime in the morning before he came to our office. Right?"

"I would think so."

"So, who was he with before he came to see us and what do we know about him, other than the fact that he was a vice-president in a Swiss bank in Geneva?"

"We know his wife suffered from rheumatoid arthritis. Our consulate in Geneva faxed a résumé to the FBI. It was forwarded to our sheriff's office, we got a copy yesterday. I reviewed it briefly."

Maggie looked over my shoulder as I removed the 8"x 12" brown envelope from my desk drawer and pulled out the sheet. In essence, it read:

> *Karl Hoffman—born to middle class parents—attended University of Heidelburg. Majored in economics—graduated 1972. Married 1975—no children—no criminal record—wife died suddenly eight months ago, age fifty one—no autopsy. Diagnosis on death certificate: Probable myocardial infarction.*

Maggie asked, "Do you think her death was the reason Hoffman wanted to see you?"

"Me? I haven't a clue. Why would he want to see me? And why was he so secretive? Perhaps we should talk to Mrs. Hoffman's doctor."

"If we're going to make further inquiries of the consulate's office, let's find out what information they can provide on the name, Soldato, and what organizations he belonged to."

A knock at the door interrupted our conversation. Elise entered with a copy of the *Desert Sun*. "Dr. Harrington, I thought you might enjoy this article in the Health Section of this morning's paper."

I read aloud the article outlined in red pencil.

> *Rancho Mirage doctor, Basil André Stuckley, receives Magna Pharmex Doctor of the Year Award In a ceremony attended by company officials last night at the Springs Hotel. Dr. Stuckley received the Golden Caduceus Award for clinical*

research studies on Dolorean β. The drug has remarkable,
proven pain-relieving properties for arthritic sufferers. Dr.
Stuckley declared that a new era in pain relief has been
achieved and many thousands worldwide would benefit.
A six-state speaking tour is planned in which Dr. Stuckley
will address doctors, nurses and other health providers.

A photo of Basil receiving a crystal bowl handed to him by Dr. Joachim Klaus Mueller appeared above the article.

I returned the newspaper to Elise. "That's quite impressive."

"I thought so." Elise turned and left the room. Maggie followed her backside as Elise closed the door.

"Why does she annoy me, so? What did you think of that news item?"

"That's paid advertising made to look like a news event."

"What do you mean?"

"That's the work of a public relations firm used by MP. They release so-called articles of public interest which are written to sound objective and newsworthy."

"Do I detect a note of cynicism?"

"You bet. Basil will deliver lectures complete with charts and graphs and other fol-de-rol to show the greater effectiveness of the new drug over others. He'll show how the drug remains in the blood stream for longer periods of time and provides greater pain relief. Health professionals may or may not believe Basil's well-rehearsed line of, excuse the expression, unadulterated bullshit, but at a company-sponsored banquet, the docs will pig-out on drinks and hors d'oeuvres, and they'll grab up little trinkets—pens, key chains, tote bags, visors, golf balls, all inscribed with the MP logo."

"Seems as though nothing has changed from the days of the snake oil hawkers—except for the amount of money spent hawking." Maggie said. "What does Basil get for his promoting efforts?"

"I don't know, I can only speculate. If you want to play with figures, let's try this: first-class travel accommodations, payment for loss of income while on tour, reimbursement for office expenses, all multiplied by a factor of two or three. And MP won't quibble over any expense sheet presented to them. All of that, mind you, is probably a conservative estimate."

"That's a great deal of money, Josh."

"Like a drop in the ocean to MP, there are millions, probably billions riding on that drug and word has to get out to prescribing docs everywhere in the world. The stuff may be no better than aspirin for relieving pain and may even be deadly—at least for some."

"Would you write a prescription for Dolorean β?"

"With what I know now? Only, with the warning: 'Take two tabs—then die.'"

TEN

After five painful hours in the office explaining my battered face to patients, I was eager for the Barcalounger and a Manhattan. Nearing our home, we surveyed the streets for unfamiliar vehicles. I touched my painful eye and lip gingerly and was reminded of last night's harrowing experience. I wondered if my assailant had been wounded by my gunshot and whether he had gone to an emergency room, where he would have been reported to the police. Secretly, I hoped he had sustained more than a superficial wound.

Maggie stopped at the door of each room and peeked in before entering. Once inside the den she commented that several pages had been disgorged by the fax. "Here's some information from the sheriff's office. It was sent today at noon." She scanned the sheet, "It's more information on Karl Hoffman." She read aloud:

> *Karl Hoffman aged 56, native of Geneva, well-respected citizen employed as banker twenty-one years. Married Clara Oldsmacher in 1975. No children. In 1991, wife was stricken with crippling arthritis with progressive disability. Multiple joint replacements. Functioned at low level until her death eight months ago. Medical treatment included steroids and gold injections plus other anti arthritic drugs. Mr. Hoffman had been involved with other lay persons seeking cures. They formed a group called, The Army Seeking*

A Cure over Arthritis, and were known by the acronym
ASCOA. Each member of the group identified himself or
herself as a soldier."

"Just as I thought, a soldier or Soldato, which is Esperanto for soldier."

Maggie cocked her head. "Arthritis isn't a cause of death, is it, Josh?"

"No, but it can set the stage for decreased resistance, anemia, poor nutrition, poor response to medication and intercurrent infections . . ."

With arms akimbo, Maggie walked slowly in a circle. "Supposing, Mrs. Hoffman had been taking Dolorean β and supposing Mr. Hoffman had learned that you were the only doctor critical of this drug."

"We don't know what she was taking. Do we?"

"Josh, just make the assumption she was taking Dolorean β. That seems to me to be the most logical reason for Hoffman wanting to see you."

"Go on."

"Hoffman may have believed you had the expertise to advise him on the lethal effects of Dolorean β, so he could pursue the legal ramifications of it."

"He could have picked up the phone, or e-mailed, or sent a telegram. Besides, he is, or rather he was, living in Geneva where the main office of MP Pharmaceuticals is located. He didn't have to come half way around the world to see me. Even if he had come to seek my advice, as you suggest, why wouldn't he tell me he was coming? There had to be some reason for the secrecy and urgency in his visit. As a matter of fact, the drug had been released in Europe two years before clinical trials were completed in this country."

"So, there was already a large body of information on the drug before you collected your data, right?"

"I would think so, but I never got any preliminary reports from Europe, certainly none that were negative."

Maggie with pursed lips said, "Supposing, the drug was responsible for a number of deaths in Europe and MP was well aware of that . . ."

"Okay, Maggie, say it. I know what you're thinking."

"You don't have to be an Einstein to figure out that MP might have attempted to squelch all the bad data. You said some time ago that Magna Pharmex was on the brink of making billions and a few, God alone knows how many, deaths would spoil the grand take."

"Are you saying all those who reported deaths or toxic effects had to be stopped?"

"Josh, for a really bright guy, whom I love dearly, you are so naïve about some things."

"Well, my Dear Ms Nightingale, you know that every dissenting voice can't possibly be muffled forever . . .'"

"Do you want me to name a few drugs that were in the grim reaper's arsenal long before anyone openly questioned their safety?" She was going to tell me whether I said yes or no.

"Remember, Thalidomide, Vioxx, Bextel?"

"Okay, your argument is convincing, now tell me precisely what all this has to do with Herr Soldato or Hoffman or whatever his name was who died in our office?"

Maggie was on a roll and became expansive. "We know Hoffman sought treatment for his wife who suffered from arthritis. While he was seeking a cure for her, she died. Let's make the further assumption that she was taking Dolorean β. He learned from some source that you had reported on suspicious deaths resulting from the drug, and he felt the need to talk with you."

"Why?"

"Because, if he could prove that this supposed wonder drug was a killer in disguise, the liability, the culpability, of Magna Pharmex might result in lawsuit settlements amounting to millions of dollars."

I could no longer deny Maggie's logic, she had a knack for cutting to the quick. "You're thinking that a murder-for-hire was contracted to keep Hoffman from bringing suit against Magna Pharmex?"

"Of course, I don't know for sure, but that seems like a reasonable possibility, doesn't it?"

The phone rang. Maggie pouted, "I hope that isn't the emergency room. The smallest fracture takes at least two hours of your time and we haven't had dinner."

Basil?—the sheriff's station?—yeah—sure—I'll pick you
up, give me about twenty minutes.

"What was that all about, Josh?"

"Basil was picked up along with others at his home and charged
with disturbing the peace, among other things."

Maggie, quick to latch onto phrases, asked, "Among *what* other
things?"

I hesitated, but knowing Maggie would wheedle details, I said,
"Lewd behavior and possession of illegal drugs." Before Maggie
could respond, I added quickly, "But he says he's completely innocent, unlike the others in his party. Anyway, he'll explain everything
when I see him."

"I bet he will, that con artist. Why do *you* have to pick him up?"

"Someone has to be responsible for his release, there's no one
else, and he needs clothes."

"Needs clothes? Oh, for the love of Pete! Take some of your old
clothes and try to hurry back." Maggie's tolerance reached the boiling point. She called out as I was leaving, "Find out why they didn't
book him into the Indio jail, and why they didn't keep him there,
where he belongs."

"Maggie, keep the doors and windows locked and don't answer
the door bell."

The Palm Desert Sheriff's parking lot was adequately lit but
eerily quiet with about one dozen cars in scattered parking slots. I
walked into the station to find a lone, pleasant, robust woman in a
starched uniform behind a glass panel. I handed her my professional
card and asked to see Dr. Stuckley, who was expecting me. I waited
in the small ante room for about five minutes.

"Jesus, Josh, am I ever glad to see you." Basil's almost nude
appearance stunned me. "This really isn't as bad as it looks," he
attempted to reassure me.

"Well, you're not dressed as though you're going to the presidential
inaugural ball. At least your shorts are clean, or are they?" In spite of
having an army surplus blanket thrown over his bare shoulders, he
shivered uncontrollably as he stood in his shorts, socks and unlaced

shoes. With hair disheveled, eyes blood shot. lipstick smudged around his mouth, he appeared as dissolute as the ultimate loser in strip poker.

I helped him dress in a pair of my too-long Levis and an over-sized sweatshirt since he was a size smaller than I. Then I folded the blanket and returned it to the officer behind the glass panel.

"Where's your royal entourage?" I asked.

"Huh? Oh, they were booked into the Indio station."

"Why were you spared that honor?"

Basil looked around to be sure we were out of ear-shot, "Our attorney got in touch with Captain Nelson in Riverside and told him of my importance in the community. I practically got an apology from the arresting officer."

"Yeah, right."

Basil sounded too glib and smarmy, and I had neither the patience nor inclination to challenge him.

"Why couldn't you dress before they hauled your butt down here?"

He appeared sheepish. "I guess I resisted the officers and became belligerent."

"Were you snorting, drinking, or both?"

"Aw, c'mon, Josh, I had a few boiler makers and inhaled a little snow. I was anticipating some glorious fucking . . ."

"Spare me the details. I'm taking you home. You can sleep off your screwed-up head. In the morning try to get back into your neighbors' good graces, if you were ever there to begin with."

I buckled him into the passenger seat where he soon collapsed like a rag doll. His head drooped on his chest, his body retained only by the seat and shoulder harness. Nearing his home, the community security officer approached and volunteered to help get Basil out of the car and into his house. We walked into the foyer, and I thanked the officer as he left.

Stunned at seeing the almost unbelievable chaos, Basil muttered, "Oh shit!" Disorder was rampant, furniture askew, partially eaten food and drink, soiled dinnerware and empty bottles were strewn about. The smell of stale beer competed with the mawkish sweetness of marijuana and cigarette smoke trapped in the fabric of the furniture, carpeting and drapes.

We entered the dimly lit master bedroom that oddly had been spared by the revelers. The mélange of garish decor defied classification, the mirrored ceiling, the four-poster bed perched on an elevated circular platform, walls covered with maroon velveteen brocade and paintings of exquisite reclining female nudes in the manner of Matisse and Goya were bordered by Victorian sconces that dripped with crystals. The furniture of some King Louis Period was adorned with billowy satin pillows.

My tired eyes, were playing tricks, someone appeared to be sitting in one of the dim corners. I blinked several times to accommodate to the subdued light. There materialized before me a pair of long shapely, crossed legs extending upwards from high heeled pumps over smooth knees to well contoured thighs. Details of the head and neck were obscured by shadows. The bosom appeared more than ample.

Basil wearing my too-long Levis and oversized sweatshirt which hung like a Mao-Tse-Tung garment stopped and stared at the figure in the corner. "Mimi?" He croaked.

A sharp female voice in a lower register rang out. "Well, if it isn't the dapper Dr. Stuckley. Aren't *you* the sartorial delight. Your charming outfit matches your character, loose and ugly."

Basil was bewildered. "How long have you been sitting there?"

"About an hour. I called the police station and was told you were being released and would be home shortly."

"Mimi, I, I, don't know what to say. Uh, how're you feeling, and the boys?"

"A lot you care, you fraud. You pompous ass. You poor excuse for a human being. I should have arranged for your murder and collected the insurance long ago! And your sons are completely disgusted with you. They know what a vile creature you are."

"Thank you for all your kind words." The usually confident, debonair figure had been reduced to a pathetic, cowering creature in the presence of this tempest. "Mimi, why didn't you tell me you were coming?"

"Hah! So, you could disappear again to avoid making child support and alimony payments? You miserable son-of-a-bitch, you haven't sent me a check in over two months. You've ignored my office calls, my e-mail, even my attorney's threats. Well, Mr. Fancy Doctor, I'm here to collect from you, right now. Sit your ass down at that pimpy French desk and write a check for $20,000.00, or I swear I'll tear this goddamned whore house apart and you with it!"

"Mimi, you don't understand, I've had extra expenses lately . . ."

"Listen to me, you creep, your extra expenses come from what you shove up your nose or for what you spend on a wiggling ass or betting at the casinos. I don't want to hear about any of that shit, I want what's coming to my boys and me. Hell, I'd confiscate this fancy cat house, if it weren't mortgaged for more than it's worth!"

Basil shuffled to his ornate desk, opened the drawer and removed a checkbook. He shook his head as though trying to focus. Mimi stood, straightened her skirt, squared her shoulders, then came towards us. "Mimi, you remember our old friend, Josh Harrington?" She gave me a condescending glance and walked by as though we had never met. Basil wrote the check and was about to hand it to her when she snatched it out of his hand. She waved it under his nose threatening him about further delinquencies. At about five feet seven inches, trim and immaculate in a Saint John's knit, with hair perhaps too blonde and lips too full, she presented a striking figure. Even her backside exuded sex, a well-defined behind undulated rhythmically as she stomped off.

Basil's eyes followed her until she was well out of the room. "Whew! I'm glad that bitch is gone."

"Why, may I ask, did you hold up her monthly checks if you knew she would carry on like this?"

"Josh, I'm over a goddamned barrel with my finances. It's like having your testicles in a vise and having someone tighten the screw."

"That check you just gave her, is that going to bounce?"

"Higher than a kite!"

ELEVEN

Maggie had fallen asleep on the sofa with the TV on. I tiptoed towards her and kissed her cheek. She opened her eyes and looked at her watch, "You've been gone such a long time. Dinner is cold, and I'm starving." Rising from the sofa, she ran her hands through her hair. "Tell me everything that happened and don't leave out any details. I'll reheat the food."

I gave a brief rundown of the scene at the sheriff's department, and Basil's encounter with his ex, Mimi. Maggie listened intently and interrupted only infrequently. "What do you think Basil meant when he said he was over a barrel financially?"

"His monthly payments must be horrendous, child support, alimony, house and car, recreational drugs, casino bets, and of course, women. Then, there are the usual business expenses."

"It occurs to me, Josh, that if Magna Pharmex ever hauled in his raft he'd sink . . ."

"Like a rock!"

"What are his obligations to MP?" Maggie did not wait for my answer. "I think he's their puppet. I'd bet he'd even peddle dirt for them to keep his retainer." She became pensive. "But he would report fatal drug reactions, wouldn't he?" She looked at me. I didn't answer immediately. "Well, wouldn't he?" she persisted.

"I would hope so."

"If he didn't, he'd be guilty of murder, as far as I'm concerned."

"I can't argue that. However, there are complicated philosophical, social and legal issues here. I'm not suggesting that I'm the one to settle any of them, but consider this, if a drug is developed which can relieve pain, cure cancer, fight infection, prevent blindness or whatever, but in some rare instances causes death, should those patients who benefit from the drug be deprived of it?"

Maggie sucked in her cheeks and did not respond.

"Sorry, I didn't mean to be pedantic or argumentative. The point I'm trying to make is that Dolorean β may have relieved many patients with intractable arthritic pain, unfortunately, a few have died. At what point, that is, how many deaths must occur before a drug should be declared dangerous and taken off the market? And, once again, would you deprive those patients who have benefited from the drug? Lastly, who's to make those decisions?"

Maggie shrugged, "I don't know. If adequate warning labels were placed on the drug containers, would that help?"

"Our main concern as doctors is the patient's well-being. Maybe it was Hippocrates who said, 'First do no harm.' That should also be true of the drug maker. How much good is a black box warning on the package if the patient dies? Supposing a patient takes two tablets and dies in less time than it would take an ambulance to get him to an emergency room."

"You mean if the patient develops something like anaphylactic shock?"

"Precisely. Then what value is a warning label? Another consideration is an effective and readily available antidote."

"Josh, is there any drug that's completely safe?"

"You mean from causing death? I can't be sure, but there are drugs that cause irreversible changes in some vital organs resulting in death. Consider the diet pills: Phen-Fen and Xenical . . ."

"Darling, that's all very interesting and sad, but my concern here is with Basil. If he should be dropped from MF's payroll would he be able to pay his share of office expenses—would you be responsible for his obligations too?"

"According to the terms of the lease, we are responsible separately or collectively for the monthly rental."

"So if Basil declares bankruptcy, you're left holding the bag."

"Right. There's no power in the world that could force him to pay his debts. And a good bankruptcy lawyer would see to that."

"Josh, I don't see how you can handle the expense of maintaining a double suite. We've got to find out where we stand in the event of his financial disaster."

"We could invite him to dinner and ask him direct questions."

Maggie took a deep breath, "I don't know if I can stand an evening with him, but it probably would be a good idea."

"Should we ask him to bring a friend?"

"For heaven's sake, NO! I want to talk to him without anyone interrupting. If he brought one of his airhead floozies, we couldn't talk seriously."

"Do you know how desirable you look when you're angry?"

Maggie's exasperation disappeared. She placed her arms around my neck, and gave me a long kiss. "Am I arousing any romantic urges, big guy?"

"You certainly are, but I'm not sure standing here like this is the best place for an interlude."

"Oh, Josh, I love when you talk sexy. Let's leave the dishes. Come to bed, and I'll show you how much I love you."

I could not remember whether my first honeymoon had been as exhilarating. Of course, that was long ago, but in these intimate moments, all comparisons paled.

At six twenty-two the phone rang. "I'll get it, love, finish shaving." Maggie picked up the cordless phone and brought it to me. With her hand over the mouthpiece she whispered, "It's Sergeant Mannheim."

Hello, Sergeant—it's just as I said—there was no way in the world—what was that?—no, I don't wear cuff links— Thanks for calling.

Maggie took the phone and looked at me. "What did he want? You're smiling, I can tell it's good news."

"The DNA studies from the semen found in Mei Ling in no way came close to matching mine." I patted my face with aftershave lotion. "I could have told them that." Maggie looked into my eyes with a triumphant glow, pinched my cheeks and kissed me. "You're not only a nice guy, you smell nice too."

"Mannheim wanted to know if I wore shirts with French cuffs. I told him I didn't."

"Why did he ask?"

"He said the crime scene investigators found one cuff link with the initial J under Mei Ling's hotel bed."

"And he thought that might belong to you?"

"If they found a second cuff link with the initial H they might have used that as an excuse to serve us with a search warrant for going through our home looking for anything else that might link me to her death."

Maggie remained silent for a moment, "You think they still suspect you?"

"Could be."

At six p.m. the front doorbell chimes rang. I opened the door to find Basil dressed impeccably in a light tan Brioni suit, with a cocoa-colored silk ascot and matching jacket handkerchief. I remembered his beggarly, pathetic appearance at the police station and thought this guy was more show than substance. He held a gift-wrapped wine box, which he handed me. "Welcome to chez Harrington." I said. Maggie came in from the kitchen and Basil pecked her cheek, then pulled her toward him, placed his arms around her waist and kissed her forcibly on the lips. Maggie took a quick step backwards, turned and walked to the kitchen. I was grateful she said nothing, but I knew she had exercised extreme restraint.

I removed the bottle from the box and could hardly conceal my excitement, a bottle of Lafitte Rothschild, Cabernet Sauvignon, 1976. I knew it cost more than my sport jacket. "Basil this is almost too good to drink."

"Nonsense! We'll have it for dinner." Basil snapped his fingers. He stepped into the living room and looked about. "This is quite cozy, quite charming."

"Not nearly as grand as your place," I said.

"What? That pretentious monstrosity is like a mausoleum when I'm in it alone. You can't possibly know the loneliness I feel. I'm like a damned hermit, considering how gregarious I really am."

"Basil, don't compare yourself to a hermit. Maybe you've forgotten that I saw one of your smoke 'n' poke parties, or at least the aftermath of one."

Basil tongue in cheek said, "Josh, that's a mere reaction to my monastic existence, at least five days out of the week."

"What about those other two days?" We both laughed. Maggie interrupted. "Fellas, come to the table, soup's on."

Basil watched as I helped Maggie into her chair. "Josh, you're an old fashioned gentleman, you really belong to a bygone era. Is he always this courteous, Maggie?"

"He is, he's one of the most considerate and gallant men I've ever known." Maggie turned towards me, smiled and touched my arm."

Basil asked, "Where did all this civility, all these fine manners disappear to? That's what's wrong with our society: we've lost concern, love, and honesty. We've forgotten how to do kind and righteous things. Instead, we're doing what is expedient and profitable."

"C'mon Basil, be realistic. Expediency and profitability are as much a part of modern man's character as his ability to walk, talk, and feed himself."

"Please, Darling," Maggie pleaded. "No lectures now, let's enjoy the food."

Basil stood and poured the wine. After making a display of holding it to the light, swirling it in the goblet, sniffing, tasting it and smacking his tongue, he said, "Here's to good friends, á votre santé." We clicked glasses. Basil sat and sipped the cream of asparagus soup. "Maggie your culinary expertise is magnificent. If you weren't saddled to this relic from the Victorian Age, I would steal you away."

"What makes you think I'd be a willing partner?"

"Few women can resist my charms."

"Does that include your ex?"

Without hesitation and without apparent offense, Basil responded, "Aha, she's the exception that tests the rule."

Basil followed Maggie's backside as she cleared the table. I thought, this guy is constantly on the prowl. After dessert we retired to the living room where he began to speak even more freely after his third glass of wine.

"Does Magna Pharmex have another project for you to promote?" Maggie asked. She was less concerned about Basil's sensitivities than I.

Basil hesitated, his tongue pushed against his left cheek while he stirred his after-dinner coffee slowly. "I was told by Herr Doktor Mueller," he emphasized the title with a mock German accent, "that I could be employed by MP as a sort of ambassador without portfolio to sing the praises of Dolorean β and any other drugs they were about to introduce in North America."

"How are you supposed to do that?" I wanted Basil to reaffirm the subtle and costly sales pitches made by the big corporation.

"Most of the early or preliminary studies are slanted to show a favorable response to a drug in a select group of patients."

"What do you mean by a *select* group of patients?" Maggie asked.

"These are patients culled from my own practice whose responses I can predict with some accuracy."

"All or most would respond favorably, right?" I asked.

"That's right. One of the company's favorite ploys is to buy TV time and have me interviewed by that guy who looks like a boys' choir leader. You know, the one who fakes those wide eyed responses to rehearsed answers."

"You mean an infomercial?" I said.

"That's right."

"What percentage of the company's resources are spent in advertising?" Maggie asked.

"I have no idea, and I doubt if that information is easily accessed."

"Do you have any long term concerns about continuing with Magna Pharmex?" Maggie's question made me a bit uneasy, but I was pleased she had asked.

Basil rose from the sofa and walked towards two hanging pictures of the desert painted by a local artist. He placed his hands in his back pockets then tilted his head from side to side. Was this a delaying ploy, or had he not heard Maggie's question, or did he just refuse to answer?

Basil turned towards us, "You may not be aware that some congressmen are challenging pharmaceutical firms for their so-called perks to doctors. A law in Vermont was passed in 2002 requiring drug makers to report to the state's attorney general all gifts of $25.00 or more given to doctors, hospitals or pharmacists."

"That should hardly be a concern of yours," I said. "It's the drug maker who would have to be concerned."

"That's the foot-in-the-door approach." Basil pointed his finger at me. "The next move by the state and then the federal government will be to tax the recipient of the company's largesse. In other words, doctors would have to report all gifts given them by drug manufacturers."

"You can't be talking about more than a few dollars in most cases," I said.

"How about a few hundred thousand dollars to some individuals," Basil said.

"Well, there's no legal problem if that income is reported," Maggie said.

"Your point is well taken," Basil countered, "but suppose the income is not reported?"

"That's simple, then you're guilty of withholding taxable income. Does that worry you Basil?" I asked.

He hesitated, "No, no, of course not."

"If the government demanded a full disclosure of the source of your earnings, would you be in difficulty?" I persisted.

He became defensive, "This conversation is deteriorating to complete idiocy. I resent any inference of unlawful activity on my part. My earnings are documented and come from well deserved efforts."

"Basil, relax, I'm not accusing you of anything. You're the one who suggested that the government auditors might be looking into some of these transactions."

"Screw them!" Let them look at my books. I have nothing to hide. What's more I'm too far down the food chain for that type of fraud."

Maggie looked at me. Basil was disclosing more incriminating activity than we had anticipated.

"In the event that you faced a catastrophic financial crisis—as for instance, if or when Magna Pharmex were to discontinue its physician promotion of new drugs, what would you do?"

"The likelihood of MP shutting me out is pretty remote. I've gathered enough incriminating data to . . ." He stopped abruptly.

"To do what?" Maggie asked.

"Oh, uh, nothing, nothing," Basil added quickly. Then looking at his watch, said, "I must be going. It's late, thank you both for a wonderful evening. Maggie, if you ever tire of this old relic, let me know."

Maggie responded, "Thank you Basil. Your kindness is exceeded only by your sincerity and lofty moral standards."

Basil bowed with a flourish and left.

Maggie looked at me, "Well, we know the game he's playing with MP pharmaceuticals. He can't be serious in thinking he can badger them into retaining him indefinitely. As soon as they believe he no longer serves their purpose, he's history."

TWELVE

News of Mei Ling's death and my presumed involvement had reached some of the personnel at Eisenhower Hospital. Nurses in the operating room were regarding me, I thought, with just a bit of coolness. The usual friendly chatter before a surgical procedure was missing and the relaxed conversation following surgery excluded me. I wanted to shout, "I'm innocent! Don't judge me falsely."

Not until the cause of Mei Ling's death could be established, would I be absolved of guilt. This guilt by association was damned unfair. I wondered if some of my patients knew about Mei Ling's death. Then I thought: of course they did. The homicide detectives had come into and gone out of our office a number of times while the office girls probably spread rumors and innuendos.

Whether people were actually shunning me or a kind of paranoia was enveloping me, I couldn't be sure, but even strangers seemed to ignore me. When I came into the office, Maggie, my anchor and soul mate, greeted me with her sweet kiss and walked with me to my consultation room. She inquired about the morning surgery and made small talk before handing me a report from the LA coroner's office. She read over my shoulder, "What does all that mean, Josh?"

I found the report to be as fascinating as the Indio coroner's. "He says Mei Ling died of an acute toxic poisoning of the liver and cardiac failure."

Maggie looked at me with knitted brows, "What troubles you, Darling?"

"This report is almost identical in content to the Indio coroner's report on Hoffman, the guy who died in our office. Maggie, get Hoffman's report from the file cabinet, and let's compare it with this one on Mei Ling." She laid out the reports on my desk side by side as though she expected to make a word-by-word comparison. As we started to read the histological details, we found similar wording in each.

"This is eerie, really weird!" Maggie ran her fingers across the reports and found exact wording in some phrases.

I said, "A twenty-eight year old gal doesn't suddenly die of liver disease without prodromal symptoms unless she is given a rapidly acting fatally toxic substance . . ."

"Just like Hoffman got?" Maggie asked.

"Yeah." We'd better notify the Indio and L.A. coroner's offices and have them compare their slides and autopsy findings on Hoffman and Mei Ling." I reached for the phone to call Dr. Thomas at the Indio coroner's office, when Maggie gently removed the phone from my hand and pointed towards the reception area where my patients were waiting.

"Josh, I'll call Sergeant Mannheim. Let him handle this matter. You don't have to do his work for him. It isn't as though he's been that nice to you."

Seeing sixteen pre-and post-op patients was exhausting but rewarding as well. When I took a history and did a physical, I attempted to do them in a manner that didn't give the patient the impression that he or she was on an assembly line being poked, prodded and pinched. The changing of dressings, the application or removal of plaster casts, even with the aid of an assistant, required time. My rewards came from the healing of painful fractures and worn-out arthritic joints that had been replaced with prostheses. The most rewarding were the skeletally deformed children who were made to look and move more normally.

Dashing from one examining room to the next left little or no time between patients. I had seen Basil briefly in the hall as he left one of his examining rooms. Following him closely, Elise carried charts and made hurried notes while Basil dictated. Just outside an examining room, Basil stood beside Elise, as she appeared to ask him something. I must have done a double take when I saw his hand reach behind her and squeeze her buttocks. Maggie had seen that also and rolled her eyes upwards, then shook her head, "That man is so-o uncouth! I can't stand him."

After seeing our last patient of the day, Maggie went through our exam rooms to check supplies and put equipment and medications away. She met me in my consultation room. She placed her hands on her hips and stretched her neck in a circular motion, then moved her head from side to side.

"Would you like to do anything special tonight, Darling?" Maggie's question brought a smile and a predictable answer from me, and I was sure she anticipated it as soon as she asked.

"Josh, you have a one-track mind—I'm grateful for it." Maggie's need for intimacy was as lusty as mine and intolerant of false modesty. When I became engrossed in other matters or failed to notice her gestures, she exercised a few womanly wiles. She took her sweater, blouse and skirt out of the office closet then closed the window blinds. She could have changed clothes in the washroom, but she knew I enjoyed watching her. She was quite right, of course, I always enjoyed watching her disrobe, especially when she got down to her bra that supported an ample bosom and made it appear even more voluminous and billowy. Her panties hugged the lower part of her hourglass shape with enough transparency to reveal the cleft in her rounded buttocks.

She teased with her come-hither glance that demanded my undivided attention. I walked behind her, folded my arms around her waist, then brought my hands to her bosom. I nuzzled her neck. She held my hands and pressed them deeper, then moved her buttocks from side to side against me.

"Maggie, you're the sexiest nurse in Riverside County."

"Oh, really? And how many do you know, intimately?"

"Since you've come into my life, only you."

"Good answer!" She slipped into her skirt and blouse and brushed her hair, using a mirror on the inside of the closet door. "Would you prefer me as a blonde?"

"I love you just as you are." I learned never to hesitate or qualify such answers.

"Do you think, if I were to put on that blonde wig I saw in Stuckley's closet last week, I would look more glamorous, more appealing?" Without waiting for my answer, she said, "I think I'll get it and try it on. If I look ravishing with it, you might just want to ravish me."

"Here? In the consultation room?"

In an attempt to be clever she said, "No silly, in one of the examining rooms."

"Our tables have no stirrups."

Maggie looked at me slyly, "Since when was that a necessity for you?"

"You really are becoming quite adventurous." I could not decide if Maggie was sincere about a quickie, or whether she was merely whetting my appetite for a romantic interlude at home. "Are you sure everyone has left the building? I wouldn't want the cleaning crew barging in on us."

She looked at her watch, "We have about a half hour until they come, but first I'm going to get that blonde wig in Basil's closet."

I called after her, "Maggie, come back here, stop acting silly." She had already gone and in less than a minute came running back.

"The wig's gone, darn it." She pouted like a child. "Do you think you'll find me as attractive without it?"

I laughed, held her closely and kissed her tenderly. Strange sounds were emanating from somewhere in the suite. I froze. "What the hell was that?"

Maggie released me and both of us headed for our examination rooms. All the rooms were open and empty. We went on to Basil's side of the suite; one examining room door was closed. Maggie, in front of me, tip-toed, then turned towards me with her index finger on her pursed lips. The sounds were vaguely like moaning.

Without forethought, I opened the door quickly. Maggie, standing beside me gasped, "Oh, my God!" Before us, on an examining table,

Basil lay completely naked, with a naked blonde on top of him, both copulating in the rhythmic crescendo of climax. The startled female looked at us and shouted, "Oh, no!" Quickly, they disengaged and grabbed their clothes from a nearby chair. All of this took place in seconds before I had the presence of mind to slam the door shut. We hurried to our consultation room. Maggie's response went from disbelief to amusement. She covered her mouth to stifle laughter like a little girl seeing something naughty then regaling in its forbidden nature.

"Josh, did you see that blonde?"

"You mean the gal with the wig? I did. At least we know who wears it."

"I can't believe what I saw. Elise, of all people." Maggie was almost breathless with excitement. "That night when we looked in his suite from the parking lot, I'm sure she's the one who was giving Basil a blow . . ."

"Practicing fellatio, my dear."

"I've always suspected that seemingly unsophisticated, namby-pamby was something other than what she appeared to be. Can you imagine that little tramp screwing around under our very eyes? Oh, this is more than I can take. Josh, you'll have to get rid of her now, for sure." Maggie took a deep breath, held it momentarily and exhaled noisily maintaining a brief silence until her next outburst. "Oh, that vile thing, that, that whore! How dare she . . ."

"Maggie, hold on! What you saw were two adults engaged in physical love, obviously by mutual consent."

"Don't trivialize this. This is entirely unacceptable in a professional office. Don't make excuses for her."

"Maggie, if they were married, would you have a different opinion?"

Impatiently, "Well, of course. That's an entirely different situation, but doing it in a doctor's office, even if they were married, I just don't know . . ."

"Weren't you considering a little intimate play here just a few moments ago?"

"Oh, I was just teasing."

"And weren't we intimate before our marriage?"

"Why must you try to justify what they've done? There's no way you can compare them with us. We knew we were going to marry."

"How could you have been so sure?"

Maggie's self-righteous attitude softened. She cocked her head and came close, putting her arms around my neck, "I loved you from the very first moment I saw you, thirty years ago when you were a bewildered intern on your first day at the Cook County pediatric ward. I came to your rescue, remember?"

"I certainly do."

"Do you know how many times I fantasized being in your arms?"

"No, tell me."

"More times than I can recall." With that, she closed her eyes and gave me a long opened-mouth kiss.

"Did you fantasize having intercourse with me?" I asked.

"I'm not about to tell you all of my secrets," she hesitated, "but now that you ask, yes I did."

"You knew I was married and had an infant daughter."

"Of course, I did. Didn't I knit a sweater for her? I loved you and could hardly wait for you to come on the ward every day."

"I remember you being friendly, well maybe being just a tad flirtatious, but I don't recall any overt attempts at intimacy."

"Josh, I knew you were a faithful husband and a loving father. I wasn't about to spoil anything. Besides, I wore that matronly starched nurse's uniform buttoned right up to my neck."

"If you had shown me a little cleavage, I might have been aggressive."

"I doubt that . . ."

A knock at the door interrupted our reminiscing.

THIRTEEN

"Just a moment, please." I opened the door. Basil was standing in the hall. He looked over my shoulder to where Maggie was standing and gave her a crooked smile, then asked to speak to me alone in the hall.

"Josh, I'm sorry you saw us in, in that position. Elise and I have been, well, intimate, for some time. She's a bit young, I know, but she's eager to please, and we do very well together."

"You needn't account to me for any of that." I studied him momentarily, "I'm curious, have you promised her anything? Have you told her you intend to marry her?"

Basil looked down both ends of the hall to be sure we were alone, cleared his throat and in a half-whisper said, "I might have dropped a hint or two in that direction. That way I get complete cooperation, I don't need to beg anymore. Anyway, that's just between you and me. Please apologize to Maggie for me. Tell her not to think less of me, or Elise."

I thought Maggie's opinion of him could not suffer much more, but now she had an even better reason for thinking about them as she did. "Jesus, Basil, you could have told us you were going to be in the office and spared us all this embarrassment. Besides, we could have left the building and turned on the security system while you were in it. Why didn't you take her to *your* home or *her* home?"

"I can't go to my home. I'm afraid I'll be served with papers, or that crazy bitch, Mimi will be waiting for me with a pistol."

"What are you telling me, you no longer go home? You're living in your car? Basil, you're not making sense. Besides, you could be served with papers right here in your office."

"So far, Elise has succeeded in telling the process servers that I'm not in, or I can't be disturbed, and my lawyer claimed that if Mimi's lawyer did anything to interfere with my right to make a living that would be grounds for non-compliance of payment obligation, or some such legal bullshit as that."

"Yeah, that's exactly what it sounds like, bullshit." Basil's explanations were illogical and given too quickly to be well conceived. Perhaps methamphetamine or some other mind-blowing drugs had altered his judgment. "Why didn't you have your little party at Elise's home or apartment or wherever she lives?"

"She lives in an apartment with other girls, and there's always someone around."

"You're telling me that in this whole Coachella Valley, there isn't a single place, not one hotel room you could use? Basil, please, don't insult my intelligence."

"It isn't that, Josh, going out gets expensive, and well, when I get the urge to knock off a piece, I don't want to wait. Sometimes Elise looks at me with those big calf eyes, and I don't know who needs it more, me or her?"

"You're like a depraved adolescent who can't keep his fly zipped up. You don't have the will power or the common sense to wait for a proper time or place. I'm not even sure about your choice of a companion, but that's your business. How in the hell do you go from your lofty perch as a medical researcher to a groveling womanizer without giving any thought to the consequences? You're a damned chameleon, a real Jekyll and Hyde. Just be sure you don't wind up the way they did, or rather, he did."

Basil made no immediate comment but placed his hands in his pockets, hiked his shoulders and looked down at his shoes. "Josh, I can't argue with you, you're absolutely right. I want you to know, I've made a decision: I'm going to change. I plan to see Dr. Killfoile, the psychiatrist, next week and hope to hell he can straighten out my head."

"Good. Maybe he can ratchet down your libido while he's at it."
As Basil turned to leave, I asked, "Are you leaving the building now?"

"No, I'm going to stay and finish some charts."

The phone rang in my consultation room. Maggie opened the door to tell me Sergeant Mannheim wanted to speak to me.

Yes, Sergeant, how can I help you?—As I recall, the doorman at the Palm Springs Hilton said Mr. Hoffman was picked up from the airport by the hotel limousine. The man already registered at the hotel got into the limousine when it went out to pick Hoffman up. The chauffeur said both men spoke in German and English. I see. Keep me informed

"What did Mannheim want?" Maggie asked.

"He said three men had registered independently into the hotel twenty-four hours before Hoffman's arrival."

"And?"

"There's the possibility that one of them could have slipped Hoffman the poisoned cocktail."

"The hotel has their names?"

"Yes, of course, but more than that, the security camera above the registration desk has photos that the police are reviewing. If any one of the three were foreigners, Interpol would be contacted and the photo would be wired."

"Josh, forgive me, I don't understand, what has all that to do with you?"

"You recall when we had dinner at Shame on the Moon, what is it two weeks ago? This guy sat across from us with his electronic recorder or whatever he had. Remember?"

"Of course, but . . ."

"Supposing, just supposing, he was also the one who met Hoffman at the Palm Springs Airport."

"Why would you think that?

"Why not? We agreed that the guy looked like a Northern European type with a blond brush haircut, dark suit and tie. The chauffeur reported that Hoffman and the guy in the limo were speaking

German, right? Ergo, the restaurant electronic eavesdropper and the guy in the limo could be one and the same."

Maggie shook her head, "That's a long stretch, isn't it?"

While driving home, Maggie turned in her seat to study me closely. That maneuver usually preceded a serious question or discussion. "Josh, what do you intend to do about Elise?"

"I don't know. I haven't given her much thought in the past thirty minutes." That flippant answer was not going to placate Maggie, and I knew a rebuttal was coming. I continued, "she seems to be pleasing Basil . . ."

"Josh! Stop trying to be clever! You pay half her salary, and I don't want her around. There's very little I ask of you, but this is one matter I won't tolerate! She's got to go!"

"Calm down, Maggie. It's possible that Basil would want to pay her entire salary and keep her employed as his personal . . . "

"Right! His personal slut." Maggie's emotions were mounting and not until they ran their course would she speak less caustically. My safest option was to say little or nothing and wait out the storm. In the garage and out of the car she slammed the door and marched into the house. The silent phase of her anger cycle was emerging and that was generally favorable since it preceded a more peaceful state.

We had changed into casual clothes when the phone rang. I was reaching for a bottle of wine from the cooler when Maggie picked up the phone. Her voice had returned to its usual pleasant and welcoming tone, for which I was grateful.

Hello, Harrington residence.

Her smile quickly disappeared. She put her hand over the mouthpiece and handed me the phone, "It's Mannheim. As usual, he doesn't sound cheerful."

Hello Sergeant. What's that? Yes, I'm sitting—what did you say? Would you repeat that? You can't be serious! Where? We were there just forty-five minutes ago. Damn!

"Josh, you're pale, you're trembling, are you all right? What happened? What did Mannheim say?"

"Basil's been shot!"

"Oh, my God! Is he going to be all right? Where is he?"

"He's dead."

"OH NO! NO! We just saw him. Where did this happen?"

"In his office, the cleaning crew found him slumped over his desk, a bullet hole in the back of his head, most of his face blown off."

Maggie dropped into a chair and started to shake and cry. She placed her head in her hands and sobbed convulsively. I placed my arms around her shoulders. She whispered between sobs, "This can't be true, it mustn't be true! It mustn't be!" She had to be in shock and riven with remorse. I stood and held her firmly as tears welled in my eyes.

FOURTEEN

At six-thirty the following morning, Maggie called Elise to have her cancel all patient appointments for the day. One of Elise's roommates answered the phone sleepily and said Elise had not been in the apartment and had not slept in her bed. Maggie called one of the other girls and asked her to come in early to cancel appointments.

The detectives were already at the office when we arrived at eight a.m. Mannheim with his sidekick, Hernandez, were about as welcome as two harlots in a convent. I understood the necessity for his questioning and probing, but Mannheim created an aura of intimidation, cynicism and distrust in the way he shifted his sunken, beady eyes as though suspecting any one of us as a murderer. His mouth formed a scowl that became more menacing when a response displeased him.

His pale, almost cadaverous face with its sunken orbits, thin lips and yellow, irregular teeth was in contrast to the robust, jowly-faced Hernandez whose ochre complexion offered a striking contrast with his brilliant white and uniform teeth.

Mannheim at over six feet provided the scarecrow frame on which hung a loosely-fitted black suit jacket which may not have been altered since it was taken off the store rack. Hernandez in his crisply creased short-sleeved shirt stood with bulging arms folded across a barrel chest and a conspicuously holstered pistol mounted on his right hip.

Mannheim, with usual deadpan, turned to me, "Did you have an argument with the deceased last night?"

The question took me aback. Why would he ask me that? Did he expect me to say yes and place myself under suspicion as the killer? The man couldn't be that stupid. "No, we didn't argue, we talked amicably."

Mannheim wrote in his notebook. "You own a gun, don't you, Doc?"

"Yes, you know I do."

Mannheim grunted and ignored my answer as he turned away briefly then turned back and stood about ten inches in front of me. His breath was offensive, and I backed away. "What time did you leave here last night?"

"Mrs. Harrington and I left at about five forty-five, give or take ten minutes."

"Did you know that Dr. Stuckley was in his office?"

"He said he was going to stay to complete some charts."

"Was anyone with him?" Mannheim's eyes locked onto mine as though he already knew the answer.

"Not that I know, but I can't be sure." I really didn't know whether Elise had left before Basil and I talked in the hall or whether she remained in the building and planned to meet him later. I was not about to speculate and have Mannheim grill me further about that. I expected Maggie to say something about Basil and Elise's affair, but she did not. When I asked her later, she said she took a cue from me and decided to say nothing since she did not want to involve Elise whom she thought was probably heart-broken.

"What time does the cleaning crew get here?" Mannheim asked.

"I think about six to six-thirty, I don't know for sure."

"And what time did you and Mrs. Harrington get home?"

"About six-ten."

"How long does it take you to get home from here?"

"About fifteen to twenty minutes."

"According to the coroner, the murder occurred some time between five thirty and six thirty." Mannheim looked up from under his bushy brows.

His repeated references to specific times were beginning to irritate me, "I hope you're not entertaining any ideas about me killing Dr. Stuckley. Even if your coroner's time slots are exact, and that's questionable, I had no motive, for God's sake, he was a friend."

Mannheim made no response. "What can you tell me about Ms. Sundstrom?"

"Who?"

"Elise Sundstrom, your employee."

"Oh, Elise. I know very little about her background. She was hired by Dr. Stuckley and worked primarily for him."

"You do have an employment application on her, don't you?"

"Yes, I think we should, but I don't remember ever seeing it."

Mannheim waited for me to say something additional. "Maggie, can you find the employee forms and bring Elise's here?"

"Did Ms. Sundstrom call you this morning? Do you know if she's sick? Is there any reason she's not here?" Mannheim asked.

"I didn't know she wasn't here," I said.

Maggie returned with a manila folder and was about to hand it to me when Mannheim intercepted it. He scanned the application and read aloud, "Birthplace Uppsala, Sweden, 1983. Parents, Berta Grunewald, housewife and Wilhelm Sundstrom, bio-chemist. Applied U.S. citizenship 1998." He set the application down. "No violations or convictions." Mannheim continued, "Can you tell me about Stuckley's family? Wife? Children? Lady friends?" We shook our heads. Mannheim looked at both of us, his scowl deepened. "Doc, he was your partner. You must know something about him, for christsake, a prominent citizen's been murdered, and we need to know who in the hell did it."

"Sergeant Mannheim, we're willing to help you as much as we can. Ask us direct questions, and we'll try to give you direct answers."

"Fair enough. Now what about his wife?"

I explained that he was divorced, and theirs was a fractious relationship. I mentioned that he was paying alimony and child support for two boys ages seventeen and fifteen. Mannheim made notes.

"Did he have a lady friend?" Mannheim's eyes bored into mine. I looked away and demurred, thinking I would avoid getting involved in any gossip. "Doc, you and the Missus here better tell me all you know, or I'm going to interrogate every one of your employees and tie up your practice tighter than a virgin's . . ."

"Okay. It's just that I, that is, we, feel squeamish about denigrating the memory of the deceased."

"That's very considerate, very decent, but you'll be doing a greater service to his memory by telling me everything. Just talk. I'll sort out what's important. Besides, you can't tell me anything that will shock me. I've heard it all and seen it all. Now, tell me about his lady friend. Did they show any animosity towards one another at any time?" We shook our heads. "Is there a chance that the girlfriend is pregnant?"

Maggie exasperated, took a long breath and exhaled noisily. "Sergeant, is that important to the investigation?"

Mannheim gave Maggie a condescending look. "Yes, ma'am. If the biological father openly rejects the unborn child as well as the mother-to-be, she could get awfully mad, or one of her relatives could get damn mad."

"I can assure you that Dr. Stuckley and Elise were anything but hostile to each other last night."

Mannheim's head jerked up from his writing pad. "Care to explain that?"

Maggie managed with remarkable restraint to say only that Basil and Elise appeared to enjoy each other's company.

Mannheim kept writing and made no outward response. "Do you know if Doc Stuckley had any enemies, unhappy patients, anyone who would want to kill him? Do you know if he made any shady deals? Did he have big debts, gambling IOUs?" We shook our heads again and shrugged almost in unison.

"Can you tell me if he ever spoke of financial troubles?"

"He might have mentioned that at some time. Many of us have those problems."

Mannheim looked up from his notebook and nodded. "We're checking into his bank accounts now." The detective seemed to have found a topic of greater interest and was about to plumb Basil's finances. He sat on the corner of my desk, flipped the pages of his spiral notebook and prepared to take more notes. Most of the questions regarding Basil's spending habits I could not answer. Mannheim became visibly annoyed but persisted. "

"That house of his in Clancy Lane—I bet it cost between one and a half to two mill." I shrugged and said nothing. He slid off the corner of my desk and pulled the seat of his trousers out of his behind. Closing his spiral notebook, he said, "Doc, did you pick up your revolver from the station yet?"

"Yes. I picked it up three days ago."

"We never did get any hospital E.R. reports of a gunshot wound on that break-in at your home. You probably just grazed the guy, and he never got medical attention." He headed for the door with Hernandez behind him. "If you should see, what's her name . . ." He flipped the pages of his notebook, "Elise Sundstrom, before we do, would you have her get in touch with me?" He hesitated again at the door and turned around while Hernandez stepped aside.

"One more thing, Doc: Do you know if Stuckley had any relatives, any heirs, anyone who could inherit anything from him? I remember you said he was divorced. How about children?"

I started to tell him, again, about Basil's two sons when he put up his hand to stop me. "You're right, Doc. You did tell me, I remember now, sorry about that." He and Hernandez left.

Maggie looked at me. "Josh, do you really think Basil's sons could possibly be involved in killing him? I wonder if they were even named as beneficiaries in his will."

"I don't know, but strange as it may sound, I had that very same thought just before you asked."

"What would be their motive for killing their father?"

"You mean besides the inheritance, if it even exists?"

"How would those boys justify murder in a court room?" Maggie asked.

"Hypothetically, they could claim severe abuse, physical, mental and sexual, with salacious details provided by a conniving lawyer who would coach the boys into giving vivid descriptions of their father's depravity and terrible temper which led to their beatings and sexual assaults."

"I can't even imagine that. These are terrible allegations you're making."

"You're right, but the act of killing a doctor at the height of his career has to be the act of some demented maniac . . ."

"Or the premeditated, calculated job of some hired goon," Maggie countered.

Looking at the stack of unpaid bills on my desk, Maggie pulled one out and gave it a cursory glance. "What do we do about something like this, the monthly rent? You can't afford to assume responsibility for this entire suite and pay all the employees."

"Fortunately, Basil and I had Key Man life insurance policies on each other, and what I'll collect from the policy will more than take care of the added expenses, at least for a while. The problem will be getting word out to Basil's patients and directing them for care elsewhere. As for the office girls, we'll have to let at least two of them go, which reminds me, where is Elise?"

"One of her roommates said her bed hadn't been disturbed. Neither one of them had any suggestions as to her whereabouts," Maggie said.

"We should go through Basil's file cabinets and desk drawers," I said.

"We can box his old records for storage and keep the current ones available for those patients wishing to see other doctors."

"Did you get clearance from the sheriff's department?"

"I did. They've already made a survey of everything they considered important, and CSI has been here also."

Maggie started in on Basil's file cabinet. "There are three file cabinets full of Magna Pharmex communications."

"Let's start on the most recent ones."

Maggie studied one letter, the cadence of her voice slowed as she read aloud, "Here's one dated two weeks ago that sounds a little ominous." She glanced at the bottom of the page. "It's signed Dr. Joachim Kurt Mueller, Chief of New Products Division."

"What does it say?"

"The first paragraph sounds innocuous, but this last paragraph disturbs me. Listen to this. 'We have enjoyed a mutually beneficial association for five years. You are about to accept a position with another fine, well-established pharmaceutical firm, and we wish you well. We ask that you not make public any statistics on Dolorean β to which we are not privy regarding its efficacy and safety. A violation of this request could result in serious consequences.'"

Maggie raised an eyebrow and repeated the phrase, "Serious consequences? Serious enough to result in murder?"

FIFTEEN

Maggie went from Basil's recent files to another cabinet that held correspondence dating back twelve years or more. Manila folders heavy with yellowing sheets bound with thick rubber bands were labeled, 'Proceedings from Los Angeles Superior Court'. She attempted to remove one of the old rubber bands when it disintegrated.

"That's ancient stuff and shouldn't concern us, Maggie."

She protested, "Since we're looking at everything else, why not this?"

"Court proceedings are long, detailed and unless you have a lot of time and a legal-type mind they can be utterly boring."

Maggie held the folder in both hands as though weighing it. "Do you know what this is all about?"

"I think so. It probably concerns Basil's early days of practice in L.A., before he came to the desert." I hadn't planned on expanding on the explanation, but Maggie was not about to accept that without further elaboration. "Basil was involved in some serious errors in judgment about twenty years ago when he occupied an office on Wilshire Boulevard in a building occupied by high-priced Beverly Hills specialists.

"How do you know all this?"

"Over the course of our relationship Basil confided in me and there were others who were eager to relate gossip. He had a flair for embracing the unusual, the avant-garde, the less conservative methods of practice, not all of them bad but some of them of questionable value. At one point, he fancied himself a guru in the treatment of stress, which he claimed led to headaches, depression, bowel irregularity, night sweats, sexual frigidity, etcetera. There was enough in the literature to substantiate those claims."

"You're saying he proposed cures?"

"Yes, and that's when he got into trouble. He said he could treat those problems with specially formulated medications and hypnosis."

"Hypnosis? How did the medical community react to that?"

"Most doctors would have nothing more to do with him and his unorthodox methods. Truth is, they regarded him as a sort of quack, and he lost his referral practice. After all, he was board certified in Internal Medicine and should have had a good referral base."

"So he lost that part of his practice?"

"That's right. When I asked him about that years later, he said his plan was to by-pass referring doctors and to carry his healing campaign directly to the public."

"How did he do that?" Maggie sat on the edge of her chair.

"Basil started one of the early M.D. TV infomercial programs where he made his pitch to housewives within a radius of a hundred miles. He had plotted a program with a young fellow, Rick Salazar, a used car salesman. This young man had so impressed Basil that he bought a junker from him. Basil claimed the guy could have sold air conditioners to Eskimos, so Basil conspired with him to produce a TV infomercial.

"He reasoned that women who suffered from headaches, constipation, and excess gas were eager for relief and would listen to a sincere professional, a real doctor. During his TV interviews, Basil would assume a professorial dignity and answer the scripted questions. The questions and answers were, of course, rehearsed so there were no glitches, no amateurish delays or responses."

"Did the L.A. medical society or Board of Internal Medicine sanction that sort of thing?"

"Of course not. However, from a legal point of view, they could do little. Remember the face of medicine was changing. The age old advertising taboos had fallen like a stack of dominos. If the guy was unethical, one could argue that was a judgment call, and if some thought he was a pariah to conventional medical practice, Basil couldn't have cared less, he had all the patients he could handle."

"Did he ever take in a partner?"

"I asked him that at one time. He had difficulty attracting doctors to share his type of practice. Two or three tried working with him but quit after a short time. His wife, Mimi, certainly didn't help matters, but that's another story."

"He probably became quite wealthy."

"He did exceedingly well, but not by his patient practice alone, that is, not by seeing one patient at a time."

"Really? How did he do it?"

"He wrote several books or rather had those ghost-written, books on achieving good health in ninety days, or some such drivel, exhorting the reader with proper-eating, daily exercising, mental cleanliness, whatever that meant, all the old saws that grab the attention of those looking for quick fixes. There's so much malarkey driving the health-book market by people who claim to have secretive solutions. Basil had a stepladder approach to treatment. If the patient wasn't helped through reading, he or she could take the next step upward by making an appointment to see him personally. The next step was to place the patient on a diet that included vitamins, minerals, thyroid extract, hormones and ephedrine in costly containers available at ridiculously high prices. If that didn't work, the patient could take a *super* prescription to the compounding pharmacy. Basil received kick-backs on those prescriptions. In fact, he was a major investor in the pharmacy."

"Why did he do all those unethical things?"

"Like others, he equated success with money."

"All right, we know he was a charlatan, but apparently he worked just within the law, so he couldn't be arrested or forced out of practice."

"On his diet regimen three people died and two law suits followed. Full investigations were made into those deaths, but Basil's defense team prevailed, and he was not held responsible but given a reprimand by the judge. Subsequently, he abandoned his weight loss program.

"You mentioned that his wife didn't help matters. What was she like?"

I paused long enough to recall our early days in practice. "I met Mimi for the first time when we were all newly-married, about twenty-five years ago in L.A. Mimi was a good looking gal, still is. She became the driving engine for Basil's medical business, although she had no appreciation for the sanctity of the profession, or for Basil's earlier commitment to it. Once the dollars started rolling in, she assumed the role of the Wicked Witch of the West. Although she had come from a wealthy family, her father, a building contractor, doled out an allowance to her while she lived under his roof. For the first time in her life, she took possession of some *real* cash and spent it on herself, her kids and her home.

"She wasn't about to permit Basil to have a partner, one who could compromise her *take,* so she drove any prospective partner out of the office disdainfully with a holier-than-thou attitude. Actually, for all her covetousness, she was the ideal partner for Basil's practice. She hired a public relations firm and nagged them about getting Basil on the Larry King show or the Oprah program. She became almost delusional with greed."

"All right, so Basil was unethical, and his wife was a bitch on wheels, but he was raking in mucho dinero. What happened?"

"The guy became obsessed with his power over female patients, especially those with dependent personalities, and there were plenty of them. He saw himself as an iconic figure, one who could assert his sexual prowess on any woman.

"Some of those gals who submitted to his hypnotic treatment discovered after coming out from under his spell that they had been molested. He faced the inevitable, a growing number of law suits from women who charged him with rape. Despite enormous defense costs and a time-consuming court trial which he lost, his license to practice in L.A. was revoked."

"He was really an S.O.B. Did he serve jail time?"

"No, but he paid dearly just to slink away with his tail between his legs."

"You said some patients died while on his weight-loss program?"

"Yes, three women. Although they were morbidly obese and had other medical problems that were aggravated by the medication he gave them."

"What do you mean?"

"All three had elevated blood pressure and two were diabetic."

"What was in the medication he prescribed?"

"For one thing, amphetamines which, as you know, can raise blood pressure, causing a stroke or acute coronary failure. As weight loss occurred, insulin requirements changed, a fact that was not always considered. The point was simply that these patients had not been properly monitored, if they had, some of those tragedies might have been averted."

"Why weren't they watched closely?"

"In a practice that virtually becomes an assembly line, the doctor may not see every patient on every visit. Often the responsibility of getting information will be assigned to a physician's assistant, a PA. Many of them are well trained, but some are neither licensed nor certified and know only what they have been taught by the physician for whom they work."

"Are you saying that the P.A. might not even know how to take a blood pressure reading?"

"That's not as far-fetched as you might think. In a super busy practice, mistakes are not unusual. A patient on a diet program might come in for a weekly injection of multi-vitamins or some nostrum like pregnant mare's urine, get on a scale, have her weight recorded, buy some canned diet food and then told to return in a week or two. Hundreds of patients can be processed that way, if a few hypertensives or diabetics slip through the cracks, well, so be it."

"Josh, you make that sound as though that type of practice is acceptable."

"Far from it! That kind of medicine only reflects the deterioration of a noble profession. Some docs feel the only way they can stay afloat is to see as many patients as they can. Medicare, as you know, pays painfully little and state insurance programs pay less. Then there are the mountains of paper work. In some cases we actually lost money because of the time spent trying to get permission from the insurance carrier to do the surgery that paid little to begin with."

"What's the solution?"

I shrugged,"God only knows."

SIXTEEN

Four days had passed since Basil's murder, and still the police had no clues, at least none that they shared with us. Along with the murder was the disappearance of Elise Sundstrom who seemed to vanish with only the clothes on her back. An APB failed to locate her, and Interpol had nothing to offer. According to reports, her parent's home in Switzerland had been under constant surveillance but nothing suspicious had been reported.

"That Elise just vanished," Maggie said. "Do you really think she's involved in Basil's murder?" Before I could answer, Maggie continued, "Of course, I thought she was a country bumpkin from the start until I saw her performing those sexual gymnastics on Basil right here in his office." Maggie shook her head. "What a shameless tart she turned out to be, a heck of a lot more worldly than I imagined!"

"Maybe she was acting under orders," I suggested.

"Right! Basil's orders."

I looked at my watch, 5:10, the last patient left ten minutes ago and our two remaining front office girls knocked at the consultation door to say goodnight. Almost immediately after, there was a second knock.

"Come in." Standing in the doorway was his dark eminence, Detective Sergeant Mannheim, my favorite harbinger of sad tidings and his strong but silent partner, Officer Hernandez. Their appearance always evoked a twinge of apprehension. Mannheim's stony expression gave no clue as to what he was thinking, or what he was about to say.

"Sorry to disturb you at this late hour, Doc and Mrs. Harrington. Can we have a word?"

I pointed to the two chairs in front of my desk. Maggie sat in a corner chair on my side of the room. "To what do we owe this honor, gentlemen?"

Mannheim spoke, "Do you think there is any connection between the murders of . . ." He looked at his spiral notebook, "Karl Hoffman, the guy who died in your office and Doc Stuckley?"

I shrugged. "Why do you ask? There was similarity in the autopsy findings of Hoffman and Mei Ling Bolton. Both had acute liver poisoning as the primary cause of death, whereas, Doc Stuckley was killed by a gunshot wound to the head."

Mannheim raised his head slowly from his writing pad and stared at me with his deep set eyes. He seemed annoyed. "I know all that, Doc, but I'm wondering whether Stuckley suspected a link between the death of that China doll and that Swiss banker and was about to make a statement or reveal something . . ."

"I wouldn't know. Tell me what you're thinking, so I can follow you better."

Mannheim continued to play his cards close to his chest and was not about to divulge any information unless it came back to him tenfold. He did not respond immediately but pushed his tongue against his sunken cheek, first on one side and then the other. He looked at his notes again.

"The poisonous stuff that killed that Chinese dame and that Swiss gnome was manufactured originally by the, ah, excuse my pronunciation, A.G. Schussenhausen Chemische Fabrik in Essen, Germany in 1913. It was formulated as a paint solvent but was found to be too toxic and killed a number of workers who handled it. It was poured into non-corrosive barrels and stored in an underground warehouse at the factory."

I was unsuccessful in stifling a yawn since I was dreadfully tired from working on a 4:00 A.M. emergency fracture at the hospital.

"I hope I'm not keeping you up." There was unadulterated sarcasm in Mannheim's comment but his droning monotone was almost unbearable.

"No, no, please forgive me, go on. I'm tired, but I'm really interested."

Mannheim returned to his notes, "The chemical company was bought out by a Swiss company after World War I for pennies on the dollar or rather deutschmark when Germany fell bankrupt."

I folded my arms across my chest and glanced at Maggie, who I was sure, had been concerned about my falling asleep. I felt my head nod twice. I jerked it up, opened my eyes and stared at nothing at all until my lids felt heavy again.

Maggie had anticipated my napping and interrupted, "Detective, forgive my abruptness, but where are you going with this history lesson?"

"If you'll just bear with me a while longer . . . the Swiss Company that bought the German chemical factory in 1921 moved everything, lock, stock, and barrel out of Essen to Geneva."

Mannheim's recitation was like a powerful soporific. I found myself shaking my head to stay awake. His monotone continued, "The company in 1923, adopted the name Magna Pharmex and produced basic drug preparations for the US market as well as for Europe and South America under different names and different price structures."

"Detective, you seem to know a great deal about this company. What prompted your research?" Maggie asked.

"We did a review of Doc Stuckley's banking statements and found monthly deposits made directly into his account from Magna Pharmex Corporation, that is, until one month ago. I want to know what Doc Stuckley did to get those fat checks."

That piqued my interest.

Mannheim may have expected me to reveal some sort of privileged information, but I had none to offer.

He wasn't pleased, "I don't know what he did for Magna Pharmex, but he sure as hell collected a lot of moolah. More importantly, I learned that the poisonous crap, that paint solvent that killed those factory workers in Germany during World War I was included in that shipment to Switzerland in 1921."

"Meaning?"

Mannheim's bushy eyebrows arched, and he sighed impatiently. He spoke slowly, emphasizing each word, as though he were instructing an idiot. "Meaning someone at Magna Pharmex had access to that stuff and probably used it to knock off the China doll and the Swiss doughnut."

"Good! Now all you have to do is find the SOB," I said, "and determine why he wanted to kill them."

Later that evening at home, Maggie looked at the obituary column of the *Desert Sun*. "Josh, here's an article on Basil."

I was fast approaching unconsciousness as I lay on the sofa. "Why don't you read it to me?"

Maggie reached for her glasses. "Murder of prominent Rancho Mirage Doctor continues to baffle police. Dr. Basil André Stuckley of Clancy Lane was found shot to death in his Monterey Avenue office on May 18. Dr. Stuckley was the recent recipient of the prestigious Magna Pharmex Doctor of the Year Award. He was known for his clinical research studies that launched a number of drugs. His latest assessment of the drug Dolorean β was expected to create a worldwide demand for the pain-relieving medicine, especially for arthritis sufferers. He was appointed honorary chairman of the local Arthritis Foundation for the past three years and had lectured extensively across the USA, Canada, and South America. He served as head of the arthritis department at the Eisenhower Hospital and attended at the John F. Kennedy . . . and so on."

Maggie continued reading, "He is survived by his two teenaged sons, Mark and Basil Jr. His divorced wife, Mrs. Mignon G. Stuckley resides in Beverly Hills with her sons. Memorial services will be held at the Palm Desert Presbyterian Church Saturday morning at 10:00 a.m."

"Those obit notices sure make a guy seem great."

"You're planning to be there, aren't you, Josh?"

"Of course. Pastor Lewis called and asked if I would say something nice."

"Will you find that difficult?" Maggie asked, tongue in cheek.

"Don't be unkind to the memory of the dearly departed. Basil did many good things."

With hands on hips, Maggie commented defiantly, "Really! Name two, no, by golly, name just one."

I was clearly at a disadvantage, "As far as we know, he loved his sons, he also loved Elise."

Maggie silently formed the word "bull" with her lips. "You mean he had intercourse with Elise. I doubt that he could really love anyone but himself. Your eulogy is going to be the quickest and most meaningless one on record. I can't wait to hear what you'll say."

"I was sort of hoping you'd write it for me."

SEVENTEEN

An imposing architectural triumph, the Presbyterian Church presented twin sculptured concrete spires like arms reaching towards the heavens. On its fastidiously maintained grounds, a flowered area encircled a life-sized bust of Dwight D. Eisenhower whose bald head served as a repository for bird droppings.

We arrived a half hour before funeral services, just as a white Lincoln hearse with landau irons pulled up to the entrance of the chapel. The whiteness of the vehicle glowed in the mid-morning sun as two men in gray uniforms emerged from the driver and passenger sides. We parked among the mourners then ascended several steps to the anteroom of the sanctuary. A robust young woman wearing a Scottish tartan complete with tam and knee-length socks was playing *Amazing Grace,* on bagpipes.

A second set of glass doors separated the anteroom from the church proper. At least four hundred people were seated in remarkable silence. The subdued lighting seemed to brighten the image of a pleasant-looking Basil on a fifty inch television screen, as he might have appeared ten or fifteen years ago. Above and behind the screen rose an awesome unadorned cross, back lighted by an enormous gothic-arched, stained-glass window with vivid panels that gave a sunburst effect. The room had *a* serene elegance, almost breathtaking in its solemnity, a structural tour de force of darkly stained wooden beams carved and curved gracefully like the keel of a ship set upside down. Polished organ pipes on either side of the stained glass window gave further emphasis to the height of the altar.

An abundance of flowers adorned the bier and the coffin. Pastor Lewis, upon seeing us, waved us forward. I introduced Maggie. He held her hand and bowed. "Thank you for coming." He informed us that we would be sitting behind the family and close friends of the deceased to the right of the coffin. "Doctor Josh, you'll speak after I deliver the memorial address."

"Will Mrs. Stuckley, that is, the former Mrs. Stuckley, say anything?" I asked.

"Oh, I should hope not. She's not scheduled to say anything. We have a tight program, and only the good Lord knows what she might want to say."

"Nothing flattering, I'm sure."

We sat in the row behind those seats reserved for family and watched as the mourners arrived. Despite an outside temperature approaching one hundred degrees, most men wore black suits, some with black shirts and ties. Maggie, who had craned her neck to see the arrivals, gave me a poke in my ribs. "Is that she?"

I turned to look. "That's Mimi, all right. Those two handsome boys must be her sons. One looks like Basil, only taller, the younger one looks more like Mimi." As Mimi and the boys approached, I stood and offered my condolences. Mimi, striking in a black dress, black broad brimmed veiled hat, black stockings and black high-heeled shoes looked at me but said nothing. She gave Maggie a perfunctory glance and passed on with her boys in tow.

"Friendly sort," Maggie mumbled.

"Oh, oh. Look who's coming down the aisle."

"Who?" Maggie was no longer whispering since the organ music had started.

"Some of the *doktorum* from Magna Pharmex." Leading a group of three was Herr Doktor Mueller, the inscrutable. I was sure he saw me but did not acknowledge my presence. The triumvirate sat on the left side of the aisle like programmed robots, upright and uptight. I glanced again at the back of the chapel, "Look who else just came in."

"Who?"

"Scarecrow and Lion: Mannheim and Hernandez." Mannheim paused to look at the guest registry, then surveyed the room. In his usual funereal suit, Mannheim looked appropriately like any another mourner. A small folded pamphlet with Basil's picture had been given to each mourner, a program of dedication and worship. Services began as the Reverend J. Lewis delivered the eulogy without referring to notes. When he concluded, he announced my name as the departed's dear friend who would say a few words. At the lectern, I put on my reading glasses and unfolded my notes.

"Dear friends: Basil Stuckley and I met twenty-five years ago when we were young doctors, new to the LA area. I remember him as an eager, hard-working internist who had a passion for clinical research. His significant work was published in the Journal of the AMA as well as other publications. Pharmaceutical firms, impressed by his work, solicited him to test new products. He established a relationship with the giant Swiss corporation, Magna Pharmex, and as they say, the rest is history. His research helped bring a number of new products on line, products that are now household names. He has been taken from us much too soon, and he will be sorely missed by his family, his friends and the medical community the world over."

Maggie put her hand to her mouth to suppress the smile as I returned to my seat. She leaned over and whispered, "You would have been a wonderful politician, you said nothing controversial then stretched the truth a bit. Let's hope Saint Peter believes you."

After the hour of service had concluded, the coffin was wheeled up the middle aisle with pallbearers on either side. The Scottish lass who preceded the entourage to the hearse played a postlude. About four hundred mourners followed in an orderly procession. News cameras flashed and TV cameramen came in close as the casket was placed in the hearse.

A veiled figure standing about twenty feet off waved then dabbed her eyes, further obscuring her face. Maggie elbowed me again and nodded towards the figure that appeared vaguely familiar. I left Maggie to approach her. At that moment, Mimi followed by her two sons, caught my attention and walked towards me with extended hands.

"Josh, I want to thank you for giving that lovely eulogy. Please forgive my initial rudeness; I just didn't appreciate what a good friend you were. You know I resented Basil and thought his friends were of the same ilk, I was certainly wrong about you."

"Mimi, this is my wife, Maggie." The women greeted one another politely, and Maggie was properly contrite. Mimi and her sons left, while I looked for the veiled woman. Where did she go? I scanned the parking lot—at a distance of about thirty feet, a door to one those expensive sport coupes, a Mercedes or Lexus, closed on the passenger side, and the car sped out of the lot.

"Did you see her?" Maggie asked.

"Mostly her back side, but I don't know for sure who that was, do you?"

"I thought possibly, Elise. Did you get the license number?"

"No, but the more I think about it, the more I'm inclined to think that was the sport coupe that sped out of our office parking lot and the same one that sped away from our home several weeks ago. Did you see where Herr Doktor Mueller went?"

"I saw him talking with Mimi, but then I lost sight of him too." Walking towards our car, Maggie continued, "Let's concentrate on someone who would benefit from Basil's death."

"To the exclusion of Hoffman and Mei Ling's deaths?"

"Yes, it would be convenient to link all three, but that may be difficult. Do we know if Basil had any assets?" Maggie asked.

"He told me he was in hock up to his eyeballs, but he might have had something stashed away or an insurance policy naming beneficiaries."

"Would an insurance policy pay off if he was murdered?"

"Yes, providing the beneficiaries were not the murderers."

"Are you still thinking his sons might be suspects? They're kind of young to inherit any money, aren't they?"

"Depends on the terms of the policy. Basil probably designated an executor for his will. If he didn't, the court would appoint one. Anyway, his attorney should know all that."

"Who's his attorney?"

"A mutual acquaintance, Roscoe Ulysses Farquhaar, Esquire."

Maggied sighed, "You can't be serious."

EIGHTEEN

Roscoe U. Farquhaar's office was located in a two-story building behind some high-end restaurants, art galleries and beauty salons off El Paseo. It was in one of those pink and beige stucco-faced buildings built about twenty years ago providing minimally spaced offices. They preceded the elegant shops that would appear some dozen years later to make El Paseo the Rodeo Drive of the Coachella Valley.

At either end of the long building were two elevators. We entered one at the east end, the door opened with squeaking complaint. It was in need of paint and air freshener. Odors of cigarette and cigar smoke were trapped in the fabric-lined walls along with the mawkish smell of marijuana, and if one had a keen sense of smell, the odor of inexpensive after-shave lotion and perhaps a tell-tale whiff of flatulence.

The elevator ground to an unsteady halt, and the door opened haltingly. Maggie held my arm firmly. "Let's use the stairs when we leave."

Roscoe U. Farquhaar, Attorney at Law, was written in gold leaf lettering outlined in black on a frosted glass door reminiscent of post World War II decor. In the low-ceiling anteroom, a fifty-plus-year-old secretary in a muumuu sat behind a green utilitarian metal desk. Along the walls were unmatched metal file cabinets. Several folders lay on her desk with a computer. Crumpled papers around the wastebasket missed their mark.

"Can I help you?" she asked as she studied our faces then looked at an appointment book. "Dr. and Mrs. Harrington?" We nodded. "Mr. Farquhaar will see you now." She pointed to a closed door to her left.

A small office dominated by a desk with an almost unbelievable amount of clutter occupied the center of the room and made the secretary's quarters by comparison appear clinically clean. Seated behind and almost obscured by an irregular stack of files, Roscoe U. Farquhaar stood to greet us. A bespectacled, balding man with a rosy, chubby face and a bulging abdomen that hung over a hidden waist line extended his hand, "Hello, Joshua, good to see you again, yes, good to see you again. This lovely lady must be Mrs. Harrington?" He pumped Maggie's hand. "Please have a seat," he looked at the two chairs piled with papers, then hurried to clear them so we could sit. "Terrible, terrible about Basil. Why would anybody want to kill that lovely man? Why? Why?" Roscoe repeated words and phrases.

"We were hoping to get some help from you."

"Certainly, certainly, how can I help?"

"Did Basil have a will? Did he leave anything to anyone?"

"Are you thinking about yourself?"

"No, no. I'm thinking about his sons, Mark and Basil junior."

"Mark and Basil junior, yes, yes. Well, Joshua, you know all that is privileged information: I couldn't possibly divulge any of that without the consent of . . ."

"Of whom?" I interrupted. "According to Basil, he hadn't been in touch with his relatives on the east coast for thirty years. Roscoe, think about this: a prominent citizen who happened to be your friend and mine has been murdered, and the cops don't have a hope of a clue. You know they're going to sit you down with a court order and ask you questions till your hemorrhoids bleed."

Maggie looked askance. "Josh, please."

I knew that he knew he was under no legal obligation to tell me anything. Yet, I had hoped, because of our long friendship, he *would* help.

Roscoe cleared his throat, "I know I can trust you to be discreet, most discreet." With elbows on the desk and hands folded in front of him, Roscoe leaned forward and in conspiratorial tones announced,

"Basil had a life insurance policy; his wife and sons were beneficiaries. When Mimi divorced him, he removed her name from the will and policy."

"But the boys were retained as beneficiaries?" I asked.

"Yes. At age twenty-one, they'll inherit the money."

"How much would that be, Mr. Farquhaar?" Maggie asked.

In a half-whisper he said leaning forward, "Quite a bit, quite a bit, a million dollars apiece."

Maggie whistled low, "A lot of people would kill for less."

"Basil junior won't be eligible to inherit that amount for at least two or more years and Mark for two years beyond that," I said. "Could Mimi act as executor if those funds were disbursed now?"

"That possibility exists." Farquhaar closed the file and stood.

"Roscoe thank you for the information, if . . ."

He interrupted, "I was not only Basil's attorney, I was his confidante, yes, his confidante. I know quite a bit more about him."

"Anything you care to share with us now? Anything that would bring us closer to finding his murderer?" I asked.

Farquhaar looked like the personification of the Cheshire cat. His secretary knocked at the door, and announced that his next client had arrived.

"Thanks, Roscoe; what do I owe you for your time?"

"Not a farthing Joshua, however, I'll tell you what you can do, invite me to lunch and the three of us can talk with less time constraints, yes, less time constraints." We left Farquhaar's office and walked down the stairs to the parking lot.

"Who is this character, Josh? Why in the world did Basil use him as an attorney? He appears to be anything but high class and from his office not very successful."

"He's an iconoclast, a seeker of justice, an anachronism in our time, but known to get down and dirty when necessary. Many years ago when the three of us were starting out, that is, Basil, Roscoe and I, we met at a young professional's gathering in LA. I've forgotten the occasion. Roscoe was a handsome, young, bright guy and like Basil was Harvard trained. Basil and he got along famously. Whenever Basil needed legal advice, he called Roscoe. As a matter of fact, I did the same. After leaving the east coast, Roscoe went to work for a large law firm in Century City, and I thought his career would really take off."

"What happened?"

"Roscoe was convinced that any lawyer who trained west of Boston couldn't possibly be as sharp or as astute as he. He had a sort of superior air and remained aloof from the California group. He never became a true player."

"If he believed that, why did he leave Boston in the first place?"

"I asked Basil that very question. He said Roscoe had a problem with gender preference."

"You mean he was homosexual?"

"Yeah, I think that would be fair to say."

"Today, that would hardly be considered a transgression."

"Twenty-five years ago, the professional environment was less tolerant, especially in staid old Bean Town. One day, one of the senior partners walked into the corporate men's room to find Roscoe and another male partner kissing and fondling each other. Roscoe didn't even wait for the corporate 'dear john' letter, he cleared out his desk and took off for the west coast where the issue of gays and lesbians was more relaxed."

"So it *was* his homosexuality that got him fired from the Boston firm."

"I'm sure that was a big factor, but it wasn't the only one."

"What do you mean?"

"Roscoe was a dyed-in-the-wool New England Democrat, and an ever-loving FDR, JFK admirer who espoused the Democratic Party line among that bunch of hard-nosed Republicans. To them, he was a political pariah. When the bosses passed the hat for Reagan's election campaign, Roscoe not only refused to contribute but openly objected, going into a tirade about wealth and privilege. Like I said, he was not a player, he just lacked political savvy, you know, finesse."

"But he had to be capable if Basil stuck with him," Maggie said.

"His legal skills were never an issue, and what's more, he was compulsively and passionately honest, and that was another factor that rankled some in that Boston office."

"How so?"

"When he submitted fees based on time spent preparing for a case, he made sure charges were based on actual time doing research and not some trumped-up charges made by the front office. Once when he saw a front office copy of fees that were sent to his client, he had an unholy fit and demanded the office manager make adjustments. He was advised by his superior that charges had to be modified because of the firm's losses due to pro bono work and cases taken on consignment that failed."

Maggie shook her head, "Poor Roscoe, he may be a slob, but I guess he's an honest slob." She continued, "Do you think he knows anything more about Basil that could help us?'

"He hinted as much. We'll take him to lunch and pump him."

One week later in mid-June, Maggie was placing patients' charts on examining room doors when I approached. She handed me a chart, "Josh, you recall this patient with the Charcot knee? Well, wait until you see him walk with his prosthetic leg. He's doing beautifully, and what's more, he's clean-shaven and wearing a natty polo shirt and golf slacks. The prosthesis has changed his personality. He thinks you're wonderful."

She smiled, sidled up to me, gave me a kiss, and then asked, "Who's going to have a birthday tomorrow?"

"Maggie, you needn't remind me of my age."

She put her arms around my neck and looked into my eyes. "You're aging like a fine wine. What would you like for your birthday?"

I looked down the hall in either direction to be sure we weren't being watched, "Besides you? Nothing! You're the best gift I could possibly imagine." Gently, I squeezed her derriere then slid my hand around to the side of her breast.

"Easy sailor, save all that for tonight and tomorrow."

"Can't we send these patients home and have a little party now?"

Maggie, ever playful, pushed her pelvis against me, "Tell your friend down there to behave, we have work to do."

Coming rapidly around the corner then stopping abruptly, Carmenita, breathless, apologized. "Oh, excuse me. Detective

Mannheim would like to talk to, Dr. Harrington." She handed me a cordless phone.

Maggie rolled her eyes. "What again?"

Detective, how can I help you?—Yes—yes. I'll bring it to the office tomorrow afternoon.

I handed the phone back to Carmenita. "What did he want?" Maggie asked. "Ballistics would like to do more tests on my revolver."

"Did he say why?"

"No, and I was in no mood to talk with that peculiar bird."

NINETEEN

Roscoe U. Farquhaar's seersucker jacket probably could not have been buttoned for the past decade. His blue and white broad striped shirt seemed to emphasize his girth and bay window as it dipped below the belt. A panama hat reminded me of the portly Sidney Greenstreet as he appeared in reruns of *The Maltese Falcon*, filmed in the late 1930's.

"Maggie, Joshua, good to see you both again." With both of his hands, he took our right hands individually and shook them vigorously. "Thank you for inviting me to this lovely restaurant. Pacifica is one of my favorites, yes, it's a lovely restaurant." Roscoe signaled the waiter whom he obviously knew, then looked at us, "Will you have some Chardonnay? Good—good. A bottle of Kendall Jackson, please, Mitch." Roscoe obviously had no intention of observing proper decorum by allowing me, the host, to select the wine. With a broad smile, he rubbed his hands in anticipation, then reached for a slice of warm sourdough bread and slathered it with butter. When the waiter opened the bottle and poured an ounce into Roscoe's goblet he murmured with closed eyes, "Heavenly, just heavenly." He proposed a flowery toast, gulped his wine and reached for a refill.

Before Roscoe's memory faltered with wine consumption, I thought it best to remind him that he had been invited to lunch to give us information on Basil, information which he had hinted might be important.

"Yes, yes!" Roscoe reveled in having an audience as much as he reveled in eating. He became completely animated and like Falstaff, held court, waving a fork for emphasis. He washed down another piece of bread with wine and began, "Basil had an internship at Massachusetts General Hospital. A fine hospital, a fine hospital."

He mopped his brow with his napkin then reached for another slice of bread. While chewing, he continued, "During his residency, Basil's acquisitive nature pushed him beyond his regular duties, and he managed to moonlight in a small community hospital where he took care of indigent patients whose medical bills were paid by local health agencies and pharmaceutical firms."

"Pharmaceutical firms?" Maggie asked. "

"That's right. The patients volunteered to go on experimental drug programs and were offered a stipend."

I must have had a dubious expression because Roscoe assured me that the program was quite legitimate, the patients were warned of possible drug reactions or side effects, and in addition, they signed waivers of responsibility. "Even at that early stage in his training, Basil had a penchant for running protocols on new drugs for a profit. He was quite enterprising. In some cases, he reported startling improvements in patients with end-stage illnesses such as: uncontrolled diabetes, leukemia, cancer, etc. His findings were published, at least when the results were good."

"That implies that some of his results were not good," Maggie said.

Roscoe brushed his mouth of crumbs and with the same napkin swiped the tablecloth clean. He held his knife and fork upward as the waiter delivered our salads. Maggie looked at Roscoe, expecting a response to her comment. Looking up from his plate, Roscoe realized that he was expected to respond.

"Basil was never a fool, no never a fool. He knew that good drug responses brought much more in the way of gratitude from the drug manufacturers, so he sometimes skewed his findings to satisfy the drug maker. His charts showing cures and improvements earned him bonuses which he came to expect and then relied upon, yes, he relied upon them."

The waiter refilled Roscoe's wine goblet, emptying the bottle. Maggie and I had hardly sipped ours. "Roscoe, how do you know all this?" I asked. The salad dishes had been removed and the entrées were being served. Roscoe attacked his entrée with the same gusto as he had the salad.

"Remember, I was Basil's confidante. He told me all about his activities, and was eager to share his successes, yes quite eager."

"So what happened? If everything went so well, why did he leave the Boston area?" Maggie asked.

"Excellent question, excellent question."

"About that time, drug manufacturers started advertising their new products directly to the public through magazines, newspapers, and TV ads. Oh, big TV ads! Of course, the ads said you had to see your doctor for a prescription. Well, the docs had no experience with these drugs that the patients were clamoring for, but many prescribed them anyway. The same techniques are used today with celebrities touting the drugs."

"That's a sure prescription for trouble," I said.

"Quite so, quite so. Basil prescribed one of those advertised drugs, a type of antibiotic, but made his own interpretation for indications and dosages." Roscoe stopped to sip his wine.

"Please continue," Maggie said.

"Well, several patients became quite ill, and what is even worse, two died, one was a teen-aged boy, an ethnic high school football player who sustained a leg injury which became infected, and the other was a pregnant woman in her sixth month. After the antibiotics were given, their conditions worsened. Lab studies showed a failure of the body to make certain white cells to fight the infections."

"Probably an agranulocytosis, a toxic suppression of . . ."

Roscoe interrupted and went right on, "There was a tremendous outcry from the close-knit community, followed by incriminating questions. Why had this doctor prescribed those terrible drugs when so little was known about them? People wanted Basil's hide and they were going to make him and the hospital and the drug company pay and pay and pay. Basil's picture appeared in every local newspaper and on TV. He was portrayed as evil for having used patients experimentally. He was sued for millions, that is, his malpractice carrier was sued. In two separate trials that lasted several weeks, he was found guilty of malpractice along with the hospital and drug manufacturer."

"What happened then?" Maggie asked.

"The father of the teen-aged football player swore vengeance, and boasted he would kill Basil one day. I recall a newspaper photograph of an angry father and his younger son who stood with clenched fists. The father was a brutish, hard-drinking ship welder who made his threats when he'd been drinking. The husband of the pregnant woman who left a two year old behind was inconsolable and promised that he too, wouldn't rest until Stuckley suffered as he did." Roscoe had taken the last slice of bread from the basket and swirled it around his plate to sop up the gravy. Two drops fell on his shirt, which he did not notice. He continued, "Basil figured his future in the Boston area was as murky as a cesspool, and he left for the Promised Land, the West Coast. Actually, Basil's far-thinking, optimistic risk-taking personality was anathema to the conservatism of staid old New England.

"We both left Boston at about the same time and remained fairly close. Of course, Basil married and I never did."

"After thirty years, you think those two men in Boston would still pose a threat to Basil? Do you seriously believe they could be responsible for his murder?" I asked.

"If you're thinking otherwise, I'll let you in on something: every year on the day of that teen-aged boy's birthday, Basil would receive a kind of terse note which said, 'We'll never forget.' It was never signed, but he knew who sent it."

In my peripheral vision, I saw the faint outline of a figure approaching our table. Thinking it was our waiter, I placed my hand out, anticipating the bill for the lunch. Instead, a bony hand was placed in mine. Reflexively, I pulled mine away and looked up. Standing like an unholy specter was Mannheim and Hernandez standing behind him.

"I hope you're here as a guest and not here to hassle me," I said.

"I can't afford to eat lunch in such fancy places," Mannheim said dryly.

"How did you know I was here?"

"I called your office. Your receptionist told me."

"I'd invite you to join us, but we're ready to leave. What was so urgent that you had to track me down?"

"What I have to say may be best said in private."

"Anything you have to say can be said in front of Maggie and Mr. Farquhaar, my attorney."

Mannheim's deep-set eyes bored into mine. He spoke in his usual deep monotone, "The bullet that killed Doc Stuckley was fired from your revolver."

A numbing second or two followed. "Did you say what I thought you said?" Mannheim nodded slowly. I asked, "Okay, what's this crazy story about?"

"Not much Doc, except that your weapon seems to be the one."

Roscoe who sat blinking with his mouth agape smacked his lips, bolted upright and blurted, "Wait just one minute. What kind of drivel are you spewing, officer?" Then he looked at me, "Joshua, don't say another word. These charges are utterly ridiculous. Not a word of this is believable. Have your lab techs run more tests. My good friend here is no more responsible for killing that man, than I am."

"Well, Counselor, maybe you should be questioned too. Anyway, Doc, we'd like you to come down to the station and answer a few questions." Suddenly the restaurant became deadly quiet, and diners at nearby tables stared.

Roscoe confronted Mannheim, "He's going nowhere without me."

"Suit yourself." Mannheim turned his back to Roscoe. "Doc, you can leave your car here. We'll drive you down to the station. When we're done there, we'll drive you back." This sounded more like a command than a request.

Maggie paled and appeared apprehensive. "Well, I'm certainly going too."

Mannheim surveyed the three of us and paused at Roscoe. "You'll be tight in the back seat, but then again, you just might enjoy that."

TWENTY

The ride to the Palm Desert Sheriffs Department on Fred Waring Drive was a long ten minutes of crammed hip and knee discomfort. Mannheim walked with us to his office, then left saying he would return with another chair. Hernandez followed him. I stood as Maggie and Roscoe sat in the stark, block-walled office. Maggie was about to speak when Roscoe pointed to a desk lamp, put his index finger to his lips, then to his ear. A possible bugging device? I wondered if Roscoe might have been a tad too suspicious. On the other hand, who knew?

Mannheim returned with a chair. Hernandez looked in the doorway, saw the crowded conditions and walked away. Seated at his desk, Mannheim opened a drawer and removed several black and white 8 x 11 photos of magnified rounds that had been fired and showed us distinct markings on the casings. "This was recovered from Doc Stuckley's desk after it went through his skull, brain and face." Mannheim used a pencil to indicate specific markings. He compared the round fired in the laboratory with the round recovered from Stuckley's office and showed us similarities in the ridges which he said were practically identical. "When the Riverside County Lab made its study, there was some doubt, but a local lab ran additional tests that corroborated our findings."

Something sinister had been concocted by Mannheim, I suspected, as he set the photos down on his desk then looked at me, "The ball's in your court, Doc."

Roscoe seething, stood, pointed at the pictures and stammered, "Those goddamned pictures don't mean a fucking thing as far as my client is concerned, not a fucking thing!" His round face became scarlet and his eyes bulged, "Don't you go accusing him of anything, you hear?"

Mannheim, imperturbable, continued in his deliberate manner, "And, Doc Harrington's prints were on the gun."

Roscoe shouted in a higher octave, "Of course they were! It's his gun, you idiot!"

"I'll just let the facts speak for themselves. Meanwhile, I believe we're entitled to know a few things about Dr. Harrington's whereabouts at the time Dr. Stuckley was murdered."

"Are you charging my client with *murder?*" Roscoe shouted.

"No, we're just engaging in a little fact-finding here, that's all."

Roscoe stood, "Josh, we're out of here! This bozo is on a fishing trip hoping you'll indict yourself with some misinterpreted comments."

This scene that had started out amicably was spiraling into a vortex of suspicions and accusations. I felt a wave of frustration. "Just a minute, both of you. I know I'm absolutely and completely innocent. I'm not going to sit by and listen to anyone impugn me. Detective, what exactly is it that you want to know?"

Roscoe was displeased but did not argue.

"All right, Doc, tell me where you were when Stuckley was murdered that evening?"

"We went through all of this before . . ."

"Humor me, Doc, tell me again." Mannheim stood, taking notes.

I went through a thorough accounting of Maggie's and my time in the office while Basil was still there and then our time at home later in the evening.

"Do you know if that gal, Elise, was still in the office when you left?"

"I don't know."

"Do you know if your gun was where you left it in the house?"

"Of course not. I don't check on it every day I might not see that thing for weeks or months at a time."

Mannheim pushed one end of his pencil against the desk top then reversed the pencil and did the same thing several more times.

"Could someone have broken into your house, taken your gun, shot Stuckley, then returned the gun?"

Maggie was clearly annoyed, "Detective Mannheim, really! We never found signs of forced entry . . ."

Poker-faced Mannheim showed no emotion. "Could someone have a duplicate set of keys to your home?"

Roscoe broke in, "Is that a probability question? How would you like that answered? In percentages?"

Mannheim turned to face Roscoe. "You want to talk in terms of probabilities and percentages? All right, here's something you can bet on, I'll tell you what I think, and what the prosecutor's office is going to think. Doc, here, is a likely suspect for killing Stuckley. He had the opportunity, he had the weapon . . ."

"And what about the motive?" I interrupted. Now *I* was mad! "What the hell would be my motive? Do you have any idea how stupid all this sounds? Christ Almighty! What put that crazy notion in your head?" I could feel the heat rising at the back of my neck.

Roscoe and Maggie tried to calm me, "Josh, dear, relax."

Creepy, unemotional Mannheim turned towards me again. "We received a phone call from a gal two days ago who said you and Stuckley were sworn enemies and . . ."

"Hold on!" Roscoe became more belligerent and glowered at Mannheim. "Either you're lying through your goddamned teeth, or some misbegotten bitch is filling your head with bullshit! Anyway, that's all hearsay crap."

Mannheim remained unfazed. "I'm just reporting what happened."

Maggie faced Mannheim, "Would that call have come from Elise?"

"Don't know. She hung up before we could trace the call. Then turning towards me, Mannheim said, "You recall, Doc, when your keys were returned to you the morning Mei Ling was found dead in L.A.?"

Maggie turned her head swiftly towards me, "What is he talking about, Josh?"

Aware that I might have failed to mention this detail to Maggie earlier, I spoke slowly and calmly so as to defuse any further suspicions or anger Maggie might have had. I related that my key ring had been discovered in Mei Ling's purse after she was found dead. I could not offer an explanation, and I certainly didn't appreciate the fact that Mannheim broached the subject, nor did I know what he had in mind.

Mannheim pushed his tongue against his cheek and looked down his nose at me. He said he had a possible scenario; my keys might have been taken by someone who had duplicated them before the L.A. homicide detectives discovered them.

"Wait a minute. Those keys were returned to me the day Mei Ling was found dead. When did anyone have time to duplicate them?" I asked.

Mannheim shook his head, "I don't know, but someone could have."

"Do you have any other questions for my client, Detective? If not, we're leaving." Roscoe with a flourish handed Mannheim his card. "If you need anything from my client, call me first."

"Yeah, I'll be sure to do that."

"Now, be good enough to drive us back to our car."

TWENTY-ONE

At six-thirty a.m. on the first Saturday in July, the predicted high temperature for Palm Desert was one hundred ten to one hundred fifteen degrees. Although the weather pattern was normal, one had to be protected from extended sun exposure and remain well hydrated, facts we full-time desert residents knew well. Maggie slipped out of bed, put her robe on, turned on the coffee maker, and then brought in the morning paper. I lay in bed thinking about the day's chores, grateful that my patient load in the hospital was small as it usually was in mid-summer when about half the population left town for cooler climes.

Maggie brought me a cup of coffee and set it on the nightstand beside me. She leaned over and kissed me. "Good morning, lover, did you sleep well?" Coffee on her breath was like an aphrodisiac. I slipped my arm and hand under her gown and felt the smooth, inviting skin of her buttocks. I brought my hand around to her silky, slightly rounded abdomen, and let it drift downwards. "Easy, Sailor, that kind of exploring might lead to something seriously good."

"Would you deny this lover his reward for being faithful and hopelessly enchanted by your feminine pulchritude?"

"My, such fancy words, more feminine than Mei Ling?" Maggie had that naughty, mischievous look.

"Now don't go spoiling my moment of anticipation by being snide. Mei Ling, God rest her soul, was a mere nymphet compared to you."

"Is that good or bad?" Maggie laughed.

"Lie down on top of me, and I'll demonstrate."

Maggie threw off her flimsy robe and brought her nightie up and over her head to straddle me. She had never indulged in false modesty, nor had she ever given a hint of being coy. Best of all, she never deprived me of gratification and was always a willing and eager partner. With deftness, she untied my abbreviated pajama bottoms and slid them off to feel my tumescence. "Ah, that's my boy," she smiled, then with open mouth kisses darted her tongue on mine. Having a partner with no inhibitions was more glorious than words could possibly describe, one who revels in the same kind of exploration, desire and sexual fulfillment.

Maggie moved forward to allow her perky ripples to be suckled. She moaned softly and moved more rhythmically as I entered her, squeezed her buttocks and assisted in the to and fro motion.

After minutes of frenzied activity, she collapsed on my spent body and murmured, "You're such an animal, and I love it." After several more minutes, I asked, "Do you mind if I get up?"

"Not just yet, not until I'm sure he's through." Maggie savored every moment of physical contact as though it were the most precious sensation in the world, which it really was. Maggie rose. I watched her magnificent backside as she moved towards the shower. I remained enamored of her narrow waist and the rounded buttocks that defined the essence of her female form.

Once in the shower, she called out for me to join her, "Come on in Sailor, the water's fine!"

"Aren't you afraid I'll molest you?" I shouted above the noise of the shower spray.

"Honey, you're good, but not that good."

At the kitchen table, Maggie started to clear the dishes. I volunteered to help, but was told to sit and enjoy the morning newspaper. I scanned the sports page, looked at the local news then the business section. One article caught my eye, "Here's something interesting, love, two giant pharmaceutical firms, have tendered offers on controlling shares of Magna Pharmex."

"Really? That's interesting. What else does the article say?"

"It says, the eighty-three year old drug giant with main offices in Geneva, Switzerland announced, through one of its officers, the need for a financial infusion to sustain its research and development program. Corporate profits were down twenty-two percent in the last quarter as compared with a year ago. One of the firm's officers who requested anonymity suggested that an invasion of the company's financial safety net by impending law suits had sparked the need for a takeover to cushion the possibility of bankruptcy proceedings."

"It seems that Magna Pharmex is walking a pretty tight rope," Maggie said. "Why do some companies flourish while MP reports loses?"

"I think a great deal of hope and money had been placed on Dolorean β, and if that were to fail, and nothing promising was coming down the pipeline that could be their death knell."

"So why do other drug companies do well?"

"Not all of them do, that's one reason there are so many mergers. The successful companies may offer higher salaries and bonus incentives to their creative staff members—from their CEO's down to their researchers and their detail personnel."

"Do the CEO's have a background in medicine or pharmacy?"

"They could have, but they're often pirated from another industry. They're usually people with successful managerial track records. The end point of success in any business is being able to sell a product, even if that product is represented by false claims. It's the same old snake oil hawking we see repeated over and over on costly TV ads . . ."

"That's just crass commercialism."

"That's not the worst of it. How many drugs have actually caused deaths, even while the manufacturer was receiving reports of those deaths, but continued to advertise them? And how many suicides have been triggered by psychotropic drugs that are claimed to cure a neurosis or psychosis?"

"I have no idea."

"Neither do I, but I know there are some."

Maggie tilted her head and looked at me, "How much do you think Basil made every time he spoke to an audience and pitched one of MP's products?"

"Rumor has it that the tab on one of the lectures netted him ten to fifteen grand. Ironically, some of those lectures were accepted by the AMA as credits for continuing medical education."

"Do you think given the proper circumstances, you could have done what Basil did? The lecture circuit was certainly profitable for him."

"Maggie, I don't know what you mean by proper circumstances. I was trained as a surgeon, and that's what I do and that's what I enjoy. I wouldn't condemn Basil for what he did, if in fact, he was sincere and never touted anything that he knew was harmful or dangerous."

"Are you thinking that Basil's murder was in any way connected to MP pharmaceuticals?"

"I just don't know."

"We know he lost his contract with MP and was about to represent another drug firm. Do you think he had any secrets, any information that would be damaging to MP?"

"I'm sure he didn't have any chemical formulas in his head, especially of a defunct and dangerous product like Dolorean β. Anyway, who would want it?"

Maggie remained thoughtful for a moment, "Supposing, just supposing, a trial was held in the case of someone suing MP for the wrongful death of a loved one who took Dolorean β and supposing the prosecution got Basil to admit that he knew the drug, in at least some instances, caused death. MP certainly wouldn't want him to testify, would they?"

"Maggie, that's an awful lot of supposing. Besides, Basil would have had to incriminate himself"

"Not if he'd been granted immunity."

I shrugged, "That scenario isn't convincing."

"Is it your feeling that Magna Pharmex was *not* responsible for Basil's murder?"

"As I said before, I just don't know, but I sincerely hope not."

"Well, what about Mei Ling's death and that Mr. Hoffman who died in our office?"

"Even if I were to guess that Magna Pharmex was somehow responsible, it would still only be a guess. Why would a giant corporation get involved in the murder of three, two, or even one person?"

"Josh, think about that for a moment, if there were millions, possibly billions of dollars riding on the sale of one drug . . ."

The phone rang.

Dr. Harrington, this is Millie at the exchange. I have a man on the line who wants to speak to you. He says it's important and thinks you'll want to talk with him. Is this a patient? *No, he's not He said it's a personal matter and one that concerns you. Okay, put him through. Dr. Harrington? My name's Bolton, Doctor Robert Bolton—Mei Ling Bolton's father. I'm calling from Berkeley. I've read the police files regarding her death, and I talked with the homicide officers in charge at LAPD. I have some correspondence you might be interested in. I've given copies to the police. I doubt they'll share that information with you. Why don't you come up here and we can talk about this? Give me your email address. I'll send directions.*

Maggie had been listening on the extension. "Are you going to see him?"

"I feel I ought to, I'll be gone only one day."

"Not without me, you won't. You know what happened the last time I let you go alone."

TWENTY-TWO

"Dr. Harrington," Carmenita's voice came through the consultation room intercom. "Mr. Farquhaar is on line one." I motioned to Maggie to pick up an extension phone.

> *Joshua, dear boy, listen carefully. I have it on good authority that the State Attorney's going to file a complaint against you in the case of Mei Ling Bolton's death (Pause) Hello?— Hello? Are you there Joshua?*

I broke out in a clammy sweat. Just about the time, I thought I was rightfully free and clear of any involvement, Roscoe dropped the hammer. In a subdued voice, fighting a parched throat, I responded, "Yes, I'm here. What do I need to do?"

> *You don't need to do anything Let me explain a few things: the State Attorney, Harry Horsleigh, known in the profession as Handsome Harry Horseshit is a first class prick who's going to play this case for all the voting publicity he can get. He's got his eye on the governor's mansion. Is he going to impanel a grand jury? He would if he could, but he doesn't have squat. No sir, he doesn't have squat. All he has is someone's eyewitness account or maybe a film clip from*

a surveillance camera showing you carrying Mei Ling to her room. According to the timer on the camera, you were in her room for ten minutes. The DA's report says there was no evidence of a struggle, no blood, no hair, no marks on her body except for that ankle sprain, and remember the semen found in her, didn't match your DNA. Most of all, you had no motive, no motive at all, and that miserable jackass, Horsleigh, knows that. He's grandstanding for the voter—don't you worry. That miserable bastard probably pulls down one hundred twenty-five grand, but spends one mill on campaign advertising, lives in a five mill mansion in Holmby Hills, has a chauffeur-driven Jag and wears custom made suits. Those statistics require some creative accounting. Yes sir, some fancy figuring indeed. I'm conferring with my accountant, Bud Burns, who will reveal all this more graphically in court, if necessary.

Who does Horsleigh present his case to?

Some judge in the criminal court. I know a number of them, and I can argue the law better in front of them than the D.A. or any of his snot-nosed assistants. Will I have to make an appearance in LA? Not if I can help it. I'll go down there and clean up this mucked-up mess, once and for all. Roscoe, I thought I'd have to have a criminal lawyer handle . . . *Joshua, my boy, I am a criminal lawyer—all lawyers are criminals, don't you know? It's just a matter of degree. Ha, ha. Yes, just a matter of degree. Truth is, criminal law is what I like best. The piddly civil stuff I've done for you and Basil, God rest his tormented soul, didn't amount to a gnat's ass. Criminal activity is rampant among the white heads around this retirement playground, and the con artists who steal from them. Every once in a while one of those conniving investment wizards will get his comeuppance. A half-crazed geezer will blow the son-of-a-bitch 's head or balls off. Yes sir, right off. Then I go to work.*

Roscoe, what about the police's claim that my revolver was used to kill Basil?

One problem at a time, my boy. I know you're innocent and all that really matters—you've got me on your side. They'll be using any flimflam, any bullshit they can dredge up to nail you. Yessir, it's the same old stupid conundrum. Where the hell is the motive? Can you hypothesize any situation that would give you the advantage if Basil were dead?

No, I . . .

Did you owe him money? Did he owe you money? Was there a bitch involved that you were fighting over?

Roscoe was on a roll engaging in rapid-fire questioning without waiting for answers.

Did you own anything in common that the survivor would get?

Roscoe, you know damn well, the answer to all that is an emphatic NO! We may have had small disagreements in office procedure but nothing else.

That's good. Now, I want you to think hard, unconventionally, as the expression goes, out of the box. Who would benefit from Basil's death? Did he owe anyone a ton of money? Did he have dealings with the mob? What about that little filly he was screwing? What's her name—Alice—Alicia?

Elise

Oh, yes, and how does she figure in all this?

Roscoe, I just don't know. These are the same questions the detectives have asked. As for Elise, I believe, she's still missing.

A jilted lover like that, might have whacked him. But where in the hell would she get your revolver? If it was your revolver?

Forensics says the projectile pattern matches . . .

Never mind what the hell forensics said. There isn't a lab test that we can't challenge or raise enough doubt about to create confusion in a courtroom. Do you remember those medical experts with fancy credentials in the O.J. Simpson trial who strutted, bedazzled, side-stepped, withheld information and slung so much shit that the jury didn't know what the hell they were listening to or what to believe? My boy, in that case, the favorable verdict went to the highest bidder. Yes sir, the highest bidder. But you don't have to worry about paying a fortune to any silver-tongued, belly-crawling, shysters, because I know you're innocent, and I'll prove it Yes sir, I'll prove it without demanding a lien on your home.

Despite Roscoe's bombast, he failed to convince me that proving my innocence was going to be a mere formality. I felt a queasiness, which was only partially relieved after Maggie set the phone down, walked towards me, placed her arms around my neck and begged me not to worry. For the rest of the afternoon, even while seeing patients, I was preoccupied with the injustice I felt about the Mei Ling case and the stupid and cruel games the law played with innocent people.

Sleep came fitfully that evening but by five-thirty a.m. I leapt out of bed to prepare for the morning surgeries. Like many surgeons, I rehearsed the operative procedures in my mind and had dismissed all negative thoughts.

At noon Maggie, approached me as I walked into the office back door from the parking lot. "How did surgery go, dear?"

"Fine. Mrs. Van Offing has a new knee and Mr. Barry, our arthritic wrist patient, had his fusion. And, I my dear, am dragging my tail. Before I see my first patient I want to sit, put my feet up on my desk, have a cup of coffee and listen to what my lovely wife has to tell me."

On the intercom, Maggie requested Carmenita to bring two de-caf coffees, one with and one without cream. As I settled into my chair, Maggie came to my side leaned over and kissed me gently on the lips. I brought my arm around her hips, looked up and asked if she knew how much I loved her.

She smiled coquettishly, "Care to demonstrate?"

"Not here, but sit on my lap and I'll give you a preliminary showing."

Maggie sat on my lap sideways, placed her hands around my neck and kissed me when a gentle knock on the door announced Carmenita's arrival. Maggie jumped up, opened the door, took the two coffee mugs and thanked her. I took a sip, closed my eyes, placed my hands behind my head, and leaned backwards. Ten minutes must have passed before I awakened. Maggie, sitting in the chair opposite me, smiled. "Feeling better?"

"Much. Now what's on the docket?"

"Mister, or rather, Dr. Bolton called, asked when you had a free day. I suggested Wednesday, the day after tomorrow, and he said he'd be happy to meet us at the San Francisco Airport, then drive us to the Berkeley City Club."

The flight on United out of Palm Springs took a pleasant hour and a half. Maggie indulged in fanciful guessing about what Bolton would be like as well as what he was going to tell us. I remembered from Mei Ling's description that he was a tall New Englander who towered over his petite Chinese-American wife.

"Do you think he bears ill-will towards you, Josh? Do you think he suspects you were somehow involved with her death?" Before I could respond, Maggie continued, "I sure hope not. He must know you're an honorable guy. The police reports would have indicated that, wouldn't they?"

"Maggie, I doubt that Bolton would want to see me if . . ." An announcement over the PA system requested all passengers to take their seats and prepare for landing.

I took our overnight pull-type luggage out of the overhead bin, walked up the aisle to emerge into another massively crowded airport. A commercial sameness existed in the corridors, the chain-store emporiums of souvenir items and clothing with baseball and football logos, book and magazine stalls, fast and semi-fast food eateries, beer and ale pubs, coffee bars and a predictable repetition of those groupings. Even the restrooms were spaced at regular intervals, one side then the other. Yes, it was the same everywhere, and yet there existed an excitement, a promise of something different outside those walls. I liked the beat, the rhythm, the pace of hurrying people. We walked outside to the pedestrian island, stopped and looked around expectantly. Five then ten minutes passed. People on either side came and went. Maggie had an anxious expression, "Josh, are we waiting in the right place?" Another worrisome five minutes passed.

"I'll call him on my cell phone." At that moment, a tall, slightly bent man with a cane came towards us. His hobbled gait suggested knee disease. As he neared us, we could see he was neatly dressed in an academic gray herringbone jacket with leather-patched elbows. A full head of white hair and a thick white mustache gave him a commanding tutorial appearance. Squinting through dark horn-rimmed glasses he asked, "Dr. and Mrs. Harrington?" Switching the cane to his left hand, he extended the right and gave me a firm shake.

"Welcome to San Francisco, I'm Bob Bolton. Sorry to have kept you waiting. Getting around with this game limb takes a while. I'm pleased you could come. My wife was unable to join us and sends her apologies. She's taking Mei Ling's death rather poorly and has been in an awful depression, she remains at home in deep mourning."

Dr. Bolton's car was a massive twenty-year-old Cadillac Sedan de Ville that despite its size barely accommodated his long stiff leg. Like other old cars, this one bore the stigmata of age, the ingrained soiled, cracked leather seats, the smell of stale gasoline and fumes that were forever buried in the interstices of the fabrics and the worn and permanently stained carpeting.

He turned towards me as I sat next to him and then towards Maggie in the rear seat. "I thought we might enjoy a bite at the Berkeley City Club. We can have a leisurely lunch and discuss Mei Ling's letters." He pointed to an old worn leather briefcase on the back seat of the cavernous interior. "The letters and papers, I believe are quite revealing and may account in part, at least, for her tragic death."

TWENTY-THREE

The Berkeley City Club, a California State Historical Landmark, defied architectural classification but exhibited definite elements of Moorish and Gothic influences reminiscent of the Hearst Castle at San Simeon. Like typical tourists, we gawked at the vaulted beveled-wood ceiling.

We entered the dining room and were approached by a waitress whose name tag read, "Mandy."

Dr. Bolton pointed his cane to a corner table, "Something quiet and secluded, dear." Walking towards the table, Bolton said, "Mandy is my god-child. Her father and I were classmates in Ante Diluvium times." At a corner table for four overlooking the magnificent garden, Bolton set the briefcase on a chair next to him. He remained standing while I pulled Maggie's chair out for her to be seated. While he unbuttoned his jacket he looked benignly at both of us. "Shall we imbibe in some *spiritus frumenti?*"

"I'd love a vodka gimlet," Maggie said enthusiastically.

"I'll join you," I said.

"Mandy, make mine the usual, 'Johnny Walker, Black Label,' on the rocks," Bolton requested. He reached for the briefcase, and then seemed to change his mind. "I should tell you something of our families' backgrounds before I show you Mei Ling's letters. Her mother, Liu Song, my wife, was a student in my class when I was a teaching assistant at Berkeley years ago. After six months of dating, we were married by a justice of the peace without the blessings of my parents. Liu Song's parents accepted this round-eyed giant with reservations. Mei Ling was born a year after our marriage and was the absolute joy of our lives, a good and obedient child even after the arrival of two siblings within four years."

"I'm curious, Dr. Bolton, how did you resolve differences in religion and customs?" Maggie asked.

"I hope you'll not be offended when I tell you we were a family without the constraints of formalized religious practice. Ours was a sort of loose pantheism where an ethereal Being was manifest in the beauty all about us. Forgive me for sounding pedantic, but I have difficulty explaining such things more simply. You mentioned customs? We had no trouble, Liu Song was born here and wished to be thoroughly American. She did not cling to any Chinese customs except for keeping some magnificent recipes that she inherited. And for her belief in a strong family unit.

"When Mei Ling was eight years of age her mother and I brought her east for the first time to meet my Boston Brahmin family. The younger children remained with my wife's parents.

"My wife was raised in the relatively liberal climate of northern California and later in the egalitarian surroundings of Berkeley. She was terribly dismayed by the cool and snobbish reception of my tightly-knit clannish Yankee family.

"Mei Ling who even as a child could charm the most unfriendly person had difficulty breaking down the barriers of my family's social ostracism of both her and her mother. I don't want to bore you with my perceptions of the psycho-dynamics of Mei Ling's personality development, but it was my impression that her encounter with my unfriendly boorish family, made her aware for the first time that she and her mother were unacceptably different, it scarred her delicate and innocent psyche. Perhaps she thought that money was another factor separating our little family from those horrible snobs, that's my term, not hers.

"As an instructor in psychology, I made a frightfully poor salary and Liu Song augmented our income by writing book reviews and submitting Chinese recipes to a local newspaper. As you might have guessed, we weren't living in the lap of luxury.

"Mei Ling as a beautiful doll-like child had developed into a stunning adult with many suitors, I might add. She learned to navigate through a field of ardent would-be lovers." He leaned back in his chair and put his hands in his pockets. "As much as she admired me, she swore she would never marry a poor, underpaid academic." Bolton chuckled and shook his head, "For that, I couldn't blame her." Our drinks arrived and we toasted to good health.

Bolton continued, "She talked of becoming a doctor or a lawyer or a CEO, any position that would give her riches and power. She graduated magna cum laude and was granted a full scholarship for medical school here at Berkeley. She did splendidly through her second year when a pharmaceutical firm offered a prize of ten thousand dollars for original research. I believe it was for antihistamine development. Well, that kind of money was more than Mei Ling could resist. She teamed up with her pharmacy instructor, and predictably, the two of them shared the first prize.

"The pharmaceutical company learned that the lion's share of the original research came from Mei Ling. She was approached by the drug manufacturer and offered a salary of fifty-thousand dollars a year with the stipulation that if she worked for three years, then wished to return to medical school she could do so and her salary would be continued until her graduation. With her fertile mind, she brought to market two other successful drugs and her salary and bonus money lured her into levels of costlier living. Her value to the company was inestimable, but she became restless and felt confined in a position with limited upward mobility."

"Dr. Bolton . . ."

"Please call me 'Bob.' And if you have no objections, I'll call you Josh."

"That's fine. Now tell me why Mel Ling was detailing drugs when I met her for the first time less than a year ago? Surely, that job hardly compared in salary to what she had been making."

Bolton signaled the waitress and pointed to his empty tumbler. "Mandy—refill, please. You're quite right, Josh. Mei Ling took a cut in income to become a detail person, but it was part of a grand plan sponsored by the drug company. They hoped to groom her for much bigger game. However, there were four obstacles that had to be overcome before she could assume the reins of high powered management as she explained to me. Number one, in a field dominated by men, she would have been an unwelcome interloper as viewed by the old guard. Number two, she was not a Swiss citizen in a Swiss company with strong nationalistic pride. Three, she was exceedingly young, and four, she had no experience in retail marketing."

"You're talking about Magna Pharmex?" Maggie asked.

"Yes, of course."

"How did she plan to overcome these obstacles?" I asked.

"Most of them simply seemed to have vanished after she advised Herr Doktor Mueller, her supervisor and sponsor, that she had received an attractive offer from Pfizer. MP would overlook three of the four obstacles, but the board members insisted she go on the road as a detail person, to experience first hand the problems of promoting drugs and obtaining M.D.'s concerns in prescribing." Bolton sipped his whiskey, placed the tumbler on the table and made small slow circular movements with it.

"How well did she know, or rather what was her relationship with Mueller?" Maggie asked.

Bolton looked up quickly, "He was head of the new products development division and knew intimately of Mei Ling's work."

"Didn't he want to keep her in research where she could help develop new products?" I asked.

"Yes, I suppose he did, but she had her own agenda for success and that didn't include being isolated in a lab."

"Forgive me for being direct, Dr. Bolton," Maggie's tone was less than apologetic, "but did Mei Ling have an affair with Dr. Mueller?"

Bolton suppressed a smile. "Leave it to a woman to be perceptive and incisive in matters of the heart. Your question is well taken, and I believe some of her letters will clarify your concerns." He reached for the briefcase. "Fortunately, Mei Ling made copies of all correspondence including those of hers which were hand-written."

"Why was that?" I asked.

"She was highly methodical and wanted complete records, both verbal and written of all transactions, plans and promises with dates, names and places. She was much more circumspect than I. The letters and communiqués are gathered in chronological order, so I'll start with the earliest ones. Interrupt me if there is anything you don't understand."

Bolton removed a packet of letters bound by a thick rubber band that he removed and placed on his wrist. "Some of the material is technical and quite frankly beyond my comprehension. I'll take the liberty of reading what I understand."

"Do you mind if I make notes?" Maggie took a spiral notebook from her purse.

"Not at all. The first letter from Dr. Mueller dated two years ago this month stated that he intended to present to the president Mei Ling's request for a transfer to the North American Sales Division for the promotion of MP drugs with the stipulation that her basic salary be maintained."

Bolton replaced the letter in its envelope and put it face down beside the bundle of letters. Reading from the next letter which was from Mei Ling to Mueller, Bolton said that she thanked him profusely and was indebted to him."

"Was Mueller married?" Maggie asked.

"Allow me to read from a few more letters and you'll learn." Bolton glanced through several letters quickly, then folded them and replaced them in their envelopes. "In this letter, Maggie, I believe we'll find the answer to your query. Mueller started out by saying that he planned to be at the San Francisco, Mark Hopkins on July 8th and would be delighted if Mei Ling could join him for dinner at the top of the Mark. Mrs. Mueller would not be joining them as she was visiting friends in Millbrae."

"Interesting." Maggie interjected.

"A follow-up letter from Mueller stated that he enjoyed the evening with Mei Ling and wondered if he might have the pleasure of meeting her again for an evening dinner cruise on the company yacht where they could discuss some classified information on a new drug."

At that point, I had hoped Bolton would not go through each letter but rather refer to those he had earmarked as important. "Bob, are you going through each and every letter?"

"No, of course not, forgive me, I get carried away. Sometimes I want to read every word she wrote. I loved her so very much." He took a handkerchief, dabbed his eyes and wiped his nose.

I berated myself for having said something that was obviously painful to him. Maggie glared at me. "I'm sorry, please read whatever you wish."

Bolton regaining his composure, smiled weakly. "I become emotional when I think about her. A parent should never have to bury a child." He opened another letter. "This one comes from the office of the president, Dr. Herman Gerstner, and is dated August 20th. In it he tells Mei Ling how pleased the board members were with her work on project number TRO-129, code name, Dolorean β." Maggie and I shared surprised glances but made no comment. "He goes on to say her performance under the tutelage of Dr. Mueller had been exemplary according to the doctor's reports."

"So Mei Ling was working under Dr. Mueller?" Maggie asked.

"Yes, I thought you understood that. He was her boss and his name appeared first on all new and experimental drug reports."

"Was that a point of contention in their relationship?" I asked.

Bolton folded the letter and placed it in the envelope among the letters already reviewed. "Well, you'll see how things developed in these later correspondences."

Maggie interrupted before Bolton read the next letter. "Dr. Bolton, can we make the presumption that Mei Ling was intimate with Dr. Mueller?"

Bolton did not answer immediately and the conversation stopped when the waitress, Mandy, with pad and pencil asked for our luncheon orders. "The crab Louis salads are our specials this afternoon and they're served with warm garlic sourdough bread and a non-alcoholic beverage of your choice." Maggie and I opted for the salads while Bolton after looking briefly at the menu requested sand dabs.

"Mandy, dear, bring me another," Bolton handed her his empty whiskey tumbler.

"Dr. Bolton, are you sure? You've already had two."

"As sure as I am that you are my favorite god-child and once one of my better students." Mandy pulled back her head, smiled and looked askance, "So if I was one of your favorite students, what am I doing here as a waitress?"

"Don't blame me, my dear. I advised you not to marry that ne'er-do-well who saddled you with three children then took off for parts unknown."

The repartee sounded rehearsed and good-natured.

Mandy leaned into the table and in subdued but well articulated wording said, "That son-of-a-bitch taking off for parts unknown was the best thing he did for me, that, and giving me three good kids."

Bolton looked after Mandy's matronly backside and sighed, "Why do some women make such stupid choices when they themselves have so much to offer?"

Maggie looked at Bolton, "Doctor, do you have Mei Ling in mind when you say that?"

Bolton hesitated before responding, as though to select his words carefully. "Mei Ling's choices were not entirely to our liking, and yet, because she succeeded in almost everything she ever did, we were seldom, if ever, critical."

"Recalling some of Mei Ling's comments about Mueller, I thought she regarded him as a rather boorish, anti-social character," I said.

"Josh, surely you understand the aggressive behavior of career women who try to move heaven and earth to gain their ends. Some wag once said there was not a successful actress in Hollywood who did not perform sexually at the pleasure of those who could further their careers. Perhaps that dictum holds for some women seeking success in the arts, industry, or politics. And who are the virtuous souls seeking to criticize these women? Upstanding men who are eager to stick their promiscuous cocks in every female orifice?" He looked at Maggie. "Please excuse my vulgarity."

Mandy returned with Bolton's third whisky. He gave her a perfunctory thank you and started to sip. I worried about his sobriety and ability to read and discern the important points in Mei Ling's communiqués. But he continued without apparent impairment.

"In this letter, dated a little over a year ago, Dr. Herman Gerstner, the president of MP pharmaceuticals, thanked Mei Ling for a wonderful evening in which important information was exchanged.

Gerstner stated that he was grateful to have been informed about the friendly rivalry between her and Dr. Mueller. Furthermore, if he had to make a recommendation for advancement in the department based on physical appearances alone, he would have chosen Mel Ling in a nano-second because her body was the loveliest and most sensuous one he had ever had the pleasure . . . and so forth and so on."

TWENTY-FOUR

Our food arrived. Bolton carefully pushed the envelopes to the side of the table before the waitress set his plate down. He sniffed his sand dabs, looked up at her and said, "Good, they smell fresh."

"Do you think a rivalry had been forming between your daughter and Dr. Mueller?" Maggie asked.

Bolton's cheeks were mildly flushed, and again I was concerned about his ability to drive after two and a half drinks, but he gave no sign of confusion nor was his speech impaired. "My daughter and this Mueller fellow apparently maintained some type of relationship, but her letters suggested some disenchantment with him. In a letter dated approximately one year ago . . ." Bolton riffled through several letters before finding a hand-written note. "Here it is, I'll read the last paragraph which contains the essence of Mueller's comments.

> *While I still find you enormously desirable, my little kit-ten, I believe more than ever, that you are competing for my position, and quite frankly, I would rather see you dead before that happens. Please remember I am still capable of promoting your status in this company if you continue to grant me favors. By the same token, I hold your position in my power and can influence the board to demote you or fire you or even bar you from the industry permanently.*

Maggie set her fork down and stared in disbelief as Bolton read. She looked at me briefly, and gave me the elbow to be sure I understood what he had said.

Bolton continued, "In the next several weeks, Mei Ling made excuses for not seeing Mueller and advised him in telephone messages that her new responsibilities as a detail person covering central and northern California allowed no time for socializing."

"What was Mueller's response?" Maggie asked.

Bolton opened another letter from Mueller which was a venomous diatribe on Mei Ling's ungrateful attitude considering everything he had done to further her career and to remind her of the risks he had taken spending time away from his wife and family just to be with her. He asked her to rethink her attitude because he did not take rejection lightly. Bolton folded the letter and placed it in its envelope then gathered the rest of the letters and stacked them in chronological order. He took the thick rubber band from his wrist and placed it around the stack.

Maggie's eyes flashed. "Imagine the nerve of that lecher threatening Mei Ling."

"Bob, do you believe Mueller was responsible for your daughter's death?" I asked.

"I think he's the strongest suspect. What do either of you think?"

"I certainly agree. Mueller is the most likely."

"Have you heard from the LA police?" I asked.

Bolton took a deep breath. "Not in quite some time, and I don't know why. I think their moving painfully slowly, perhaps they want to be sure they have a solid case . . ."

"Against whom?" I asked knowing full well from what Roscoe Farquhaar had told me about the LA prosecutor attempting to indict me.

"Josh," Bolton looked around as though to be sure no one was eaves dropping and in a subdued voice said, "Harry Horsleigh, the State's Attorney, spoke to me some time ago and asked me to maintain absolute secrecy as to the nature of our call. He tried to convince me that he was making a strong case for your indictment. When I asked him on what basis, he said that the information was confidential and could not be divulged."

"Did he make any reference to the communications you sent him regarding Mei Ling and the men from Magna Pharmex?" Maggie asked.

"When I saw Horsleigh, he said he could find little to incriminate them, and furthermore the telephone conversations were merely hearsay, not admissible. Then he made some slanderous remarks about Mei Ling's promiscuity, and I told him he had no right making such statements, especially to me, and unless he apologized, the conversation would end, and he could expect no further cooperation. I was seething, and the more I thought about him, the less I wanted to cooperate. I read the police report including your statement regarding the events preceding my daughter's death. There was nothing to link you to her murder, and now that I've met you I'm more convinced than ever of your innocence."

"That's one thing you can be absolutely sure about," Maggie said.

"Did the police interrogate Mueller?" I asked.

"How do you confront a polecat who's hiding four thousand miles away and denies knowledge of anything?"

Mandy approached and inquired about desserts but had three negative responses. "How about some strong coffee?" She directed her question at Bolton. Before he answered, Maggie chirped, "All the way around, please."

"What are the facts other than those letters or communiqués that would positively link her murder to Mueller?" Before Bolton or Maggie attempted a response, I continued, "Here's what we've got: number one, we suspect that the hepatotoxin, the liver poison, exists only in the Magna Pharmex warehouse in Geneva. Number two, a gold cuff link was found under Mei Ling's hotel bed, and I know that Mueller wears cufflinks."

"With the letter 'J'? Maggie asked. "His name is Kurt Mueller, isn't it?"

"Something about that name bothers me. Let me look, I have his professional card in my wallet" I found his card which read, 'Dr. Joachim Kurt Mueller, Chief Biochemist Department of Research Pharmaceuticals.' "As I recall he wore French cuffs."

"The crime lab has samples of the vaginal semen, don't they?" Maggie asked. "Why don't they compare it with Mueller's DNA?"

Bolton interjected, "He's got to cooperate with the police Investigation, and while he's taking refuge behind the thick walls of the drug factory, he's not about to ejaculate, spit, or surrender any of his precious epithelial cells for our convenience or his conviction." After two cups of black coffee Bolton stood with difficulty not because he was inebriated but because of his arthritis. When Maggie and I attempted to help him, he became defiantly independent and waved his cane in a limited circle. "No, no, I'm fine, thank you." He carried the old leather briefcase and started towards the men's room.

"Please allow me to hold your case while you're occupied," I suggested.

"Thank you, Josh," he said as he handed it to me. "I trust you with it, and besides, you know all about the contents."

Mandy approached with the bill and looked about for Bolton.

"I'll take that, thank you," I said.

Deplaning at Palm Springs always gave me a warm welcoming feeling, but with Maggie holding on to my arm the sensation was even more pleasurable. The giant white canvas-roof tops like enormous tents provided an informal plein-air atmosphere I would think about tourists arriving in winter and reveling in the magnificent warmth of this semi-tropical land. We walked across the street to the convenient parking area and our SUV.

Once outside the airport parking facility, Maggie said, "There are certain facts regarding Mei Ling's murder that should be explored further, or that moron DA, Horsleigh, is going to try to pin that rap on you."

Without taking my eyes off the road, I asked, "What do you suggest?"

"We know she was alive and well when you left her. Someone was either in the room at the time you brought her into it or gained access to it after you left, then poisoned her."

"Go on."

"There had to be more clues other than someone else's semen and a gold cufflink."

"Such as?"

Maggie hesitated, "I don't know. Maybe finger prints on a glass or on a doorknob, maybe clothing fibers or fallen hairs . . ."

"You think something that CSI didn't pick up?"

"Maybe. That DA isn't going to bust his butt to find the real killer while you're a convenient target. What better publicity can he get than trying to nail a doctor who had a wild night on the town away from his wife?"

"Are you suggesting we hire a special investigator to go over the CSI findings?"

"Precisely. Or better yet, go beyond their findings. Josh, I'm not going to sit by and watch the love of my life sacrificed by some rotten, lying, publicity-seeking SOB."

I glanced at Maggie out of the corner of my eye, her jaw jutting and her mouth set in firm determination. She declared, "I'm going to have Roscoe hire a private investigator, and when he collects enough evidence we're going to yank that complacent, smart-ass Mueller out of his Swiss vault and try him for murder."

"Do you know about Swiss extradition laws?"

"Well, no, but I assumed . . ."

"We can't assume anything until we know for sure. As a matter of fact, Mueller could slip across our northern or southern border and be saved by their extradition laws."

"Our primary job is to get you off the hook. What Mueller does with his worthless life will be someone else's problem."

"I patted Maggie's thigh to get her out of her dark mood and to remind her that I appreciated her loyalty and concern. She placed her left arm around my waist. "You poor dear," she smiled, "you've been under so much pressure, maybe I can fix that tonight."

We headed north on Ramon Road towards the I-10 freeway ramp east bound. Twilight had partially obscured the access, but I was familiar with the approach and had no difficulty melding into the fast lane after looking quickly to the left, to the right and the rear-view mirror. "Maggie, did you mention our trip to San Francisco to anyone?"

"Yes. The girls in the office were told. They had to know in case of an emergency, and we told Roscoe Farquhaar, remember? Why do you ask?"

"There's a sport coupe that's been on our tail for the past half mile or so. I think it's the same one that tried to force me off the road a couple weeks ago. When we approach the Cook Street cutoff, I'm going to gun it and swerve sharply to the right."

"Josh, don't do anything crazy. I'm frightened!"

"Keep your head down. I'm going to cut in front of those semis in the right lane at the last minute, and we'll lose that bastard."

"We may lose our lives, don't do it!"

"Hang on." I glanced in the rear-view mirror. Not twenty feet behind, the sport coupe was advancing to our left. I swerved to the right amid screeching brakes across three lanes and found a niche between two semis. Air brakes whooshed among a cacophony of blaring horns. I roared off the Cook Street ramp at over 100 miles per hour, weaving around traffic. I exhaled, "Whew! That was exciting." I eased off the accelerator and stepped on the brake.

Maggie, her head and shoulders flexed below her waist asked excitedly, "Did we make it?" Lifting her head slowly and showing no sign of amusement, she said, "That was the dumbest, most stupid thing you've ever done! We could have been killed."

"Believe me, I thought this guy meant to do us in, and I wanted desperately to lose him."

"Well, you lost him all right and almost lost us. Nothing justifies what you did. Don't you ever do anything like that again." Maggie was not to be mollified, and I was not about to argue. Perhaps she was right, and my paranoia might have killed us.

"Forgive me, Darling, you're right, I shouldn't have done that." As we approached our garage, I looked around, no familiar or unfamiliar vehicles parked close by. In the garage, I jumped out of the car and hurried to open her door. She looked up at me with a sort of half smile that I interpreted as a sign of partial forgiveness, although she said nothing.

The trip to and from San Francisco was tiring and the freeway caper unnerving. I went to our bedroom and started to undress. I turned on the local TV news channel then turned my back to it as I removed my tie to hang on the closet rack, then removed my shoes and unzipped my trousers. The TV announcer said there was a late-breaking news story, just minutes ago another I-10 freeway chase east of Cook Street ended when a costly sport coupe crashed after striking a semi near the Jefferson Street off ramp. The driver who attempted to evade a California Highway Police patrol in pursuit ran after his vehicle came to a stop. He was seen throwing a gun in the roadside brush.

I whirled around to watch the TV. There were no pictures, of course, since the incident was too recent.

"Josh, did you watch channel 3?" Maggie asked excitedly, "I was watching the kitchen TV. That guy who had the gun may have been the one . . ." She ran towards me and held me tightly, "Oh, Josh, please forgive me. I never should have doubted you. You probably saved our lives." Frightened, she held me closely and buried her head in my shoulder. "Darling, I'm really scared."

In our pajamas, we watched the 11:00 o'clock news from the living room sofa anticipating film of the patrol/car chase. After twelve agonizing minutes watching international, national, local news and what seemed like interminable inane commercials the chase scene appeared.

"That's it!" Maggie jumped up, pointed at the TV screen, "That's the car that was tailing us! I can't believe what I'm seeing."

"Sh-h-h, we'll miss the details." The CHP camera caught the sport coupe crashing into the rear of the semi and almost running under the trailer. When the truck came to a stop the driver of the coupe emerged but was limping towards the edge of the freeway where he tossed something, presumably a gun, into the brush. Four CHP officers behind the open doors of their vehicles had guns aimed at him and ordered him to halt with his hands raised. He limped backwards towards the officers and was ordered to lie face down spread eagle.

"Were you able to see his face?" Maggie asked.

I shook my head. "The guy was bald, white, medium height, somewhere between forty and fifty years of age, I would guess."

"Did they release his name?" I shook my head. "I'm going to call Roscoe and have him get information on that guy."

"Isn't it a bit late? It's almost eleven-thirty."

"By morning, this guy might be bailed out by some hotshot lawyer, and God only knows where or when we'll hear of him again. If Roscoe can't get down to the sheriff's station, he can send his special investigator."

In bed, Maggie remained too edgy to concern herself with anything other than our near catastrophe. She placed her left arm on my waist, and even though I was dreadfully weary, I did not dare fall asleep or remain unresponsive. I knew she wanted to talk.

"Josh, are you awake?"

"Uh, huh."

"Why would anyone want to shoot you?"

"Probably a hired gun."

"Who hired him and why?"

"Someone who figures I know too much."

"About what?"

"If I promise to tell you in the morning, will you go to sleep now?"

"Absolutely not! You tell me everything you know, this very minute." She shook me until the need for sleep vanished.

I turned on my back and Maggie bolted upward, hovered over me and expected conversation. "When Mei Ling came to my hotel room, her original intention, she said, was to seduce me and draw all the information I had on the toxic effects of Dolorean β. She wanted to know about the autopsy reports, and what I intended to do about submitting them for publication."

"How did she learn about your secret files and the autopsy reports?"

"One possible source is Basil who may have talked with someone. You recall I mentioned that I had confided to him. As for the autopsy reports, I mentioned them in my communiqués to Geneva quite some time ago. They never followed through, at least not to me."

Maggie thought a moment. "So someone at Magna Pharmex wants to kill you?" Before I could answer, she asked, "And why was Mei Ling killed?"

I sat with my back propped against the headboard. The tired, weary feeling had vanished as I recalled the events to an even more alert Maggie. My rising adrenaline titre made the telling easier. "You may recall, or perhaps I failed to tell you, Mei Ling had a sudden change of heart from her original intention of milking information from me. She realized I was a decent and honest guy, probably one of the few who didn't want to get into her, and she didn't want any harm to come to me."

"What did she mean, she didn't want harm to come to you?" Maggie sounded anxious.

"Well, the price I might have to pay for what I had done or planned to do was quite high, possibly my life."

"Your life? What exactly did she tell you?"

"Magna Pharmex was having difficulty sustaining its research and development program since its sales had plummeted.

"Now tell me what it was that she told you, word for word." She was insistent.

"Several giant pharmaceutical firms are in a price-bidding war for the take-over of Magna Pharmex. The mechanism for the acquisition, stock options, buy-out, partnership, or consolidation—I don't know, and anyway it's not important to the story. The important part is that the companies vying for the take-over are hoping to get their hands on Dolorean β and all its positive hype promising enormous sales profits world-wide."

"I understand all that. Get to the point: tell me where *you're* involved."

"Don't you see? I have case records that strongly suggest—hell no, they positively implicate the toxicity of Dolorean β. Any company competing for the purchase of MP Pharmaceuticals certainly would want to know that this potentially spectacular product has caused the deaths of a number of people. No company would willingly assume the litigation possibilities of a product like, say, Vioxx."

"Josh, you've already advised MP of your findings as well as the FDA."

"I feel like a lone wolf baying on a barren hillside with no one heeding my warning."

"Then what is your concern?"

"Sooner or later some patient-advocate group or team of lawyers is going to discover my findings and send this drug firm crashing on its glass behind."

"If you don't say anything more about the drug, or publish any-more papers, wouldn't they let you alone?"

"Maggie, my precious love, I know you're concerned about me, but I also know that you would not tolerate my ignoring a deadly drug."

Maggie remained pensive for a moment, "You're right, Josh. It's just that I feel such frustration and worry about your safety. When I think how vulnerable you are, I could cry. That damned DA is trying to pin Mei Ling's murder on you, and the local police are looking at you crossed-eyed because they think your revolver killed Basil . . ."

I reached over and kissed Maggie. She was in no mood for affection. "What about Mei Ling's death? That certainly hasn't been resolved," she said.

"Someone, must have known she was about to reveal MP's secret to bury criticism on Dolorean β before the proposed sale of the company and wanted her snuffed."

"Why would she have a change of heart? She was so ambitious, so aggressive."

"Possibly two reasons, number one, pangs of conscience, number two, fear of implication in a conspiracy of silence preceding a hor-rendous law suit."

"I was under the impression that you were the only one she had confided in. The fact that she had some Champagne that night might have loosened her tongue and the fact that she couldn't bribe you with additional grant money . . ."

"Someone may have been listening to our conversation—some-one may have been in her hotel room at the time or had planted a listening device."

"Josh, I'm not sure this is all believable, a giant firm like MP killing people . . ."

"Maggie, there are millions, probably billions of dollars riding on that drug. The lives of several individuals can be sacrificed as easily as that," I snapped my fingers. "Anyone who threatens the profits of giant industries is disposable. People have disappeared mysteriously or have been *accidentally* killed. There was the case of Rudolph Diesel, for instance, the inventor of the diesel engine who disappeared while on board a ship headed for America from Germany. His invention was perceived as a threat to the profits of the petroleum industries, and there was the case of the Celanese manufacturer whose product threatened the silk industry, he disappeared from a plane . . ."

"You've made your point. It's just that I'm so terribly naïve. I'm afraid I'll never understand the unimaginable evil of some people." She snuggled against me, "Hold me tight. I feel safest in your arms, never let me go." Maggie's rhythmic, relaxed breathing indicated that she had finally fallen asleep before I could assure her that her love and concern gave me the same feelings of security.

At six a.m., the phone made a jarring ring.

Hello? Roscoe?—Yes, we'll meet you at the Coffee Bean on El Paseo at eight—no, I have no surgery this morning—just hospital rounds.

I patted Maggie's derriere. "Up and at 'em, love, we've got a date with Roscoe."

At eight, El Paseo was predictably quiet during the offseason summer months. Several window washers with extended poles, brushes and squeegees were at work. A maintenance man hosed down a nearby sidewalk taking care not to splash the few curbside vehicles. We pulled up behind an old black Saab sedan in need of washing and dent repair. A soiled license plate read, RUF ONE.

Seated at a small round table at the far end of the coffee shop, Roscoe dominated the scene with the roundness of his head perched on the larger roundness of his chest and abdomen. His welcoming smile on a florid face, one that did not tan, just reddened and his emphatic hand wave directed us as though we might have missed him in this otherwise empty café. "Please sit down, sit down," he waved us to the other two chairs. He signaled the waiter, ordered a double something-or-other mocha latte and an oversized bran muffin which he was quick to assure us was not made with lard, as though that negated all the other calories. Maggie and I ordered regular coffees and shared a croissant.

"What did you learn about that freeway maniac?" I asked.

"For one thing, I'm glad you decided to lose him in that chase. I think he had every intention of killing you, yes sir, every intention."

"What did he say? Who is he? What did he want?" Maggie pressed.

Roscoe bit into his muffin and sprayed a few crumbs as he attempted to answer before chewing completely. He took a gulping swallow of his latté, "Ooh, that's hot!" He fanned his tongue and continued, "That bastard said precious little before demanding to see his attorney."

"What's his name?" Maggie persisted.

Roscoe reached into the inner pocket of his rumpled seersucker jacket and pulled out a small blue spiral notebook. He moistened his thumb and index finger on his tongue and turned the pages. "Here it is, Jacob Eisenmacher, E-I-S-E-N-M-A-C-H-E-R, age forty-two. Address somewhere in the Andreas Hills, Palm Springs."

"Who does he work for? What does he do? Maggie demanded.

"Don't know. He clammed up and insisted on talking to his attorney."

"What did he sound like? Is he American or foreign?"

"Good question, Joshua. He spoke like a European who learned formal English either in school or from a tutor; you know the kind of English that is too precise."

"Describe his appearance," Maggie said.

"Medium build, about five feet ten inches, bald, a few bruises and scratches on his face and arms, a swollen right ankle that was obviously painful and at the time still untreated."

"Was his weapon recovered?" I asked.

"Yes, yes, I believe the officer said it was a Clock or a Glock or something like that. Frankly, I detest the sight of those things and know nothing about them." Roscoe shook his head in disapproval.

Maggie leaned into the table. "You said Eisenmacher's first name is Jacob?"

"Yes, as I understood it, yes."

"That's another 'J' initial for the cuff link found under Mei Ling's hotel bed," she said.

I paid the bill then Maggie and I headed to the office.

TWENTY-FIVE

Carmelita approached. "Dr. Harrington, the last patient has left, is there anything you would like me to do before I leave?"

"No, thank you, goodnight."

I looked at my watch, five-twenty-five, the end of a tiring day. My upper back and shoulders ached. Maggie had already changed clothes when the phone rang. "Josh, dear, it's Roscoe."

Joshua, my boy, I would beseech thee to hie unto my office after yon working hours.

The stilted, antiquated language Roscoe effected from time to time usually amused me, but at this hour I was patently annoyed.

Roscoe, I'm bushed. Can we delay this for another day?— No? You won't object if Maggie comes along?

The question I thought, rhetorical, but Roscoe surprised me when he said that he preferred seeing me alone. I would understand why at the meeting. One hour would be more than sufficient time for the meeting, he thought.

Maggie assured me that she felt not at all slighted, and since she had her own vehicle there would be no inconvenience. The extra time at home would permit her to prepare dinner.

At six-ten p.m., El Paseo was almost as desolate as it was at eight a.m. except for the curb-parked cars of those diners who sought "early-bird" dinners, a favorite among the budget conscious retirees. The outer door to Roscoe's office was locked but a light within revealed a slender male approaching it. "Dr. Harrington? I'm Marvin Korbin, special investigator." With that, he extended his right hand and shook mine firmly. "Roscoe and I have worked a number of cases together over the last twenty or so years." The man resembled a young Robert Redford at about six feet with a shock of gray-blond hair that fell boyishly over one side of his forehead. An affable smile and demeanor suggested a hale-fellow-well-met personality. His well-defined five o'clock shadow suggested a day that had started quite early.

"Did you say Korbin?" I studied his handsome face. "Any relative of an uncanny mechanic working in a Chicago auto impound?"

"Ah hah! So you met my old man?" he smiled. "The guy with the computerized mind? I've been told I've inherited the curse of his memory for minutiae."

We walked into Roscoe's cluttered, musty office and there like a laird of his Welsh-Scottish ancestry he dominated a fiefdom of law tomes and journals. Upon seeing me, he stood up and over an irregular tower of books and briefs, raised his arms like Abraham to welcome the prodigal son. "Joshua, my poor beleaguered Saw Bones, so good of you to come to my humble office. You've already met the incomparable Marvin Korbin, a fine young man, a fine young man.

"Marvin spent the day in L.A. reviewing with his extraordinary expertise the evidence collected by the CSI, the State Attorney's office and the coroner. His discerning eye and ear for detecting alterations and fabrications of so-called facts and uncovering discrepancies in released reports concerning the late Ms. Mei Ling Bolton are invaluable, most invaluable." I felt a sudden sense of relief, appreciation and curiosity. "Let me clear those chairs of legal dross, so we can all sit and listen while Marvin holds court, and we may commiserate."

Marvin had already removed his jacket, loosened his tie and unbuttoned his shirt collar. He rolled up his sleeves to reveal muscular forearms, covered with tanned blond hair.

From an inner pocket of his jacket resting on the back of his chair, he removed a small spiral notebook.

"I talked with Dr. Joyce Wade at the coroner's office, who conducted the autopsy and reviewed the files on Mei Ling Bolton. She placed the DNA patterns on a viewing box and stated categorically there were no groupings of identical bands in the studies of the semen found in the victim's vaginal vault and those found in Dr. Harrington's sputum sampling."

"Marvin, we were apprised of that fact previously," Roscoe said.

Korbin ignored the comment and went on, "The period of intercourse extended over a relatively long while, that is probably over an hour or more."

"How do you know that, and why is that important?" I asked.

"The amount of ejaculant found in the vagina probably represented the effort of an initial series of thrusts—that is, when the semen was in greatest quantity and arousal time was shortest." Korbin looked at both of us. "Look guys, these were the doc's words, not mine." He continued, "A period of physiological rest or refractory period followed which may have lasted from fifteen or twenty minutes to an hour or more depending on age, vigor and the participants' state of health."

Roscoe suppressed a yawn, "Get on with it Marvin, what's this leading to?"

"The supposition is that at least a second episode of arousal occurred when the penis ejaculated smaller amounts on the victim's, abdomen, hands, breasts and face. This usually indicates mutual participation, a consensual relationship."

"I'm not sure that follows necessarily. That woman may have been forced by whatever means to participate, or for all we know she may have been already dead."

"So you believe this was someone Mei Ling knew well?" Roscoe asked.

Korbin continued, "The examining doctors believed that the two people willingly consummated the sex act. No screaming was reported, no thrashing observed, no signs of struggle, but, Korbin paused for emphasis, "there were two short hairs found under the victim's fingernails that were not hers, coarse hairs presumably from a male chest, arm pit or pubic area."

"Meaning?" Roscoe asked.

"Someone had left his calling card, twice, and the assumption is that the murder took place sometime thereafter."

"Aren't we forgetting that there was a surveillance camera in the hall? Didn't it show anyone else coming or going into Bolton's room?" I asked.

"I reviewed the tape for the entire day and night at a fast forward speed, of course," Korbin said. "The next person to enter that room was the maid, after she knocked at the door at eleven a.m. and got no response."

"This is ridiculous, my boy. You're saying there was no one other than Joshua, Mei Ling, or the maid who entered or came from that room until the next morning? Are you sure you looked at the entire surveillance film?" Before Korbin answered, Roscoe stood and stretched, tucked his shirt into his trousers, hiked them up and belched. "Sorry, lads, I don't buy this."

"Like I said, I looked at the entire film, but there is a problem, a serious problem."

"Now what the hell are you talking about?" Roscoe's demeanor changed.

"The surveillance film was interrupted for about twelve minutes during the early morning hours," Korbin said.

Roscoe glared at Korbin. "What kind of bullshit is this, like another eighteen minutes of missing Nixon tapes? Who was the bloody bastard who fucked with that film, do you know?" Roscoe's jowls quivered.

"I talked with three guys at the hotel who handled this film," Korbin explained. I was told that film interruption was not unusual. Kids and even adults will cover a camera lens just to be ornery."

Roscoe was not appeased. "This could destroy a good part of our defense, yes a good part of our defense." He plopped into his chair, ran his hand over his bald pate then asked, "Well, do you have any other helpful news?"

"Yes, I gained access to the room and looked about . . ." Korbin hesitated with a knowing grin as though he held the winning card and was about to slam it on the table.

Roscoe searched Korbin's eyes, "Okay, Mr. P.I. what marvelous discovery did you make?"

"Ms. Bolton's room had a door that connected to an adjacent room."

"Aha!" Roscoe rubbed his chubby hands. "Now we're getting somewhere. Who occupied that room? Is it anyone we know?" Roscoe was practically breathless. "Come, my dear fellow, who occupied that room?"

Korbin smiled knowing he had information Roscoe wanted dearly. "I went to the hotel registrar, gave her a room number and a date, she typed in a few keys on the computer and, voila!"

"Then what?" Roscoe could not contain his excitement.

"The room was one of a block of rooms reserved by Magna Pharmex six months previously."

"Korbin, damn you! You're toying with my patience, stop this nonsense! Tell me, who occupied that room?"

"Easy, Roscoe, this is no time to have a stroke. The room was registered to a Dr. Mueller, J. Kurt Mueller."

"I knew it! I knew it!" Roscoe jumped up, snapped his fingers and did a little jig, a kind of Highland fling executed with the grace of a Disney hippo. He stopped suddenly, "Did you say J. Kurt Mueller?"

Korbin looked at his notebook again, "That's right. J.Kurt Mueller."

"Yes, I knew that. I made the assumption that you knew that also. Mueller with the gold cufflinks. "Another J."

"I was unaware of that, my boy. Now that I know, I'm calling the D.A. this minute."

"Roscoe, I hardly think that's enough of a clue to hang a murder rap on this guy, but I think it's helpful." I looked at my watch. "It's after six. He can't possibly be in his office."

Roscoe wagged his finger. "No, no. I can always reach him. Handsome Harry and I go back a long way. He clerked for me when he was a neophyte. I have his home number and a lot of personal information he probably wishes I didn't have." Roscoe referred to a

Rolodex then punched in the phone numbers and waited impatiently. "Come on, you big stiff, pick up the phone."

This is the Horsleigh residence, how may I help you?

Tell your eminent boss this is the Internal Revenue Service, and we have a few questions for him.

Mr. Horsleigh is dining just now, can this matter wait?

I'm afraid not. Roscoe winked and placed a hand over the mouthpiece. "Old Harry will probably choke on his filet mignon when he gets the message."

Hello, is this handsome Harry Horsleigh? No, this is not the IRS. This is your old mentor and nemesis, Roscoe U Farquhaar. Harry I don't want to detain you, however, in the matter of the State of California versus Dr. Joshua Harrington regarding the death of Mei Ling Bolton, I thought you ought to know one or two facts had been concealed or altered, most probably by your department. Some later CSI reports differ from the original ones. As an example, the victim's lipstick was found in the adjacent room occupied by an acquaintance of hers, Dr. J. Kurt Mueller . . . Just a moment, please. I'm not quite finished. Her lipstick was found on a Dunhill cigarette, the kind smoked by Dr. Mueller. Another fact, the coroner's report on the toxic substance found in Ms. Bolton's body was a product found in the warehouse inventory of Magna Pharmex where Dr. Mueller is a company official. As soon as we get DNA studies from that guy, we're going to blow your case wide open. Furthermore, I might accuse you of withholding exculpatory evidence . . . . What's that? Of course, I'm not going to reveal anything to the news media. I wouldn't think of doing anything as nefarious to an old friend, but someone else might.

You maintain none of that will influence your decision to go ahead with what you believe is a compelling case against Dr. Harrington? Harry, my boy, what I am about to tell the world is too good to divulge at this stage of our pre trial proceedings. I would love to have a jury hear what evidence we have that would expose your miserable, cheating, arse to the American Bar Association, to the judge and jury and to the legal profession in general . . . you think I'm bluffing? Listen closely: within seventy-two hours your sorry mug shot will be plastered on the front page of the L.A. Times for one whole week and your illustrious career will be tossed in a city dumpster where it belongs. You can't imagine what I'm talking about. You had better prepare for your own legal defense. Sorry to have interrupted your dinner. Enjoy the rest of the evening.

Roscoe returned the phone to the cradle with a wide grin and faced us. "Well, boys, did we take care of old Harry Horseshit? If that son-of-a-bitch gets an hour's sleep tonight, he'll be lucky. Marvin, my boy, that was a brilliant move on my part, just a brilliant move. Joshua, you can forget about appearing in court on charges of Ms. Bolton's murder. The D.A. will be preoccupied with saving his own worthless arse, and the case hasn't enough merit to be taken on by any assistant D.A."

TWENTY-SIX

"Josh, is that you? How did the meeting go?" Maggie called from the kitchen as I came in from the garage. The unmistakable pungency of sautéed onions, garlic, peppers and tomatoes teased with oregano and other spices filled the house. Maggie concocted her own combinations of Italian, French, and Mexican cooking and did not refer to any written recipes. She was an intuitive cook, this was her version of spaghetti puttanesca, one of my favorite dishes. My stomach growled with anticipation as I sidled up to her while she prepared a salad. The essences of spices and vegetables clung to Maggie's hands, hair, and apron.

"You smell good enough to eat," I whispered in her ear. She turned and with an exaggerated fluttering of her eyes said, "We can talk about that after dinner, or if you feel an uncontrollable urge, I can put the meal on a low simmer and . . ."

"I thought about you most of the day until that meeting with Roscoe and his special investigator."

Maggie turned and looked at me, "Don't think for one minute that I've forgotten about that meeting. I want to hear every word that was spoken and by whom." I picked up the glasses of wine, handed her one and made a toast she had heard almost daily since our first date in Chicago, "To my love." We clicked glasses, then kissed.

"Let's enjoy our wine in the living room for a few minutes, and you can tell me about your meeting." Maggie listened intently as I gave her the details and was thrilled when I mentioned that Roscoe said there would be no trial involving me with Mei Ling's murder.

"Why do you think Roscoe told Horsleigh he had to be concerned with his own legal defense?"

"I don't know, but it may have something to do with illegal funds. It's the same old BS, money and all the privilege and trouble it can buy."

"I'm so glad you're not that way, Josh."

"My biggest vice is loving you too much."

"Never!" Maggie set her wine glass on the cocktail table then took mine and placed it next to hers. She leaned towards me, placed her arms around my neck and gave me a long moist kiss. "That's just for openers." She stood and led me to the table. "You're convinced Dr. Mueller is the one who murdered Mei Ling?"

"He's the most likely suspect, and Roscoe's of the same opinion."

"If the DNA of the sperm found in Mei Ling matches the DNA of the mucous found on Mueller's cigarettes and champagne flutes in Mei Ling's room, doesn't all that add up to a strong case against him?"

"That would be my take on the situation, but Mueller's nowhere to be found. Roscoe thought he might have left the States for Switzerland, and Korbin the investigator, was assigned to check the international airline passenger list."

"If Mueller were in Geneva, couldn't he be brought back here by extradition laws?"

"Roscoe explained to us: to begin, there is no proof that he is or was responsible for the murder. Secondly, if he were the murderer or an accomplice, the extradition laws can be as complicated as a nuclear reactor and frustrating beyond comprehension. The average time for getting a known criminal back to the scene of a crime can be anywhere from two to four or more years, providing the guy doesn't take a powder in the meantime. Roscoe said there are about twenty-five hundred cases where fugitives wanted by the U.S. are believed to be in foreign countries."

Maggie said, "Supposing the Geneva newspapers were informed that an apparent, respected Swiss citizen associated with a famous pharmaceutical house had been a suspect in the murder of a U.S.

citizen and was hiding out or refusing to cooperate with the crime investigating authorities. What would that publicity do for Magna Phamex's image and sales?"

"We would have to be extremely careful about incriminating the company or any individual, or we'd run the risk of a defamation law suit."

"Josh, there are ways of couching phrases that are not openly offensive or legally condemning, and heaven knows there are lawyers and editors who use those tactics every day." Maggie's argument for publicity was intriguing. She continued, "If a story like this is turned down by a reputable newspaper what would you think about letting a tabloid run with it?"

"I'll bet there are publicity photos showing Mei Ling and Mueller together. In fact, now that I recall, an L.A. Times reporter and cameraman were at the L. A. Towers Hotel interviewing MP big shots and taking pictures that night. Maybe there's one of Mei Ling and Mueller together."

I started to help Maggie clear the table and placed the dishes in the dishwasher when the front door chimes rang. I looked at my watch, eight-forty five. "Who'd be calling at this hour?"

Maggie removed her apron and headed towards the door when I gripped her arm and pulled her back.

"Maggie, stay here," I whispered.

"I will not!" Her whispered response was louder. She stood firmly at my side, "If it's another fake Fed Ex guy he's going to have to deal with both of us." Perhaps thinking that I failed to notice her, she picked up a paring knife and held it at her side.

"What do you intend to do with that?" I continued in a whisper.

"Level the playing field."

"Put that back, please."

"Why do we have to open the door at all?" She asked in a hoarse whisper.

"Because whoever it is, knows that someone's home, all the lights are on." The door chimes rang again.

"Just a minute!"

"Who's there?"

From the outside came a familiar voice, "It's Marv Korbin, the investigator. I've brought someone I think you'll want to see."

Maggie looked at me and raised her eyebrows then motioned with her head towards the door. Standing before us was Marvin and a female with dark glasses, a scarf covering her head and an upturned collar obscuring her lower facial features. She turned her face upwards to look at us then lowered her head quickly.

Marvin asked, "May we come in please?" The mystery woman advanced slowly. Maggie and I watched as she removed her head cover, lowered her collar and brought her glasses forward and down. "Elise!" Maggie shouted, then reached for her arm. "Where have you been?" Elise had difficulty making eye contact. When she wasn't looking at the floor. She glanced around the room to avoid our gaze. Her apparel, a smart pantsuit was a distinct improvement over her typical office attire, usually an uninspired print dress. Maggie said, "You know the police have been looking for you since Dr. Stuckley's murder."

Before Elise could respond, Korbin extended his hand and introduced himself to Maggie.

Sensing that Elise needed time to recover from her nervousness and diffidence, I directed my comments to Korbin. "You've had a busy night. I was with you just two hours ago. How did you find Elise?"

"I knew her whereabouts for several days," Korbin said.

"How did you locate her when the police couldn't?"

Maggie interrupted and persisted. "Elise, for heaven's sake, where have you been? You've been gone for three weeks." She took Elise by the arm and led her into the living room.

Korbin stepped back outside, looked up and down the street then moved into the hall and shut the door.

Elise sat stiffly on the edge of the sofa, her hands fingering a small handbag. "I, that is, we, Basil, I mean, Dr. Stuckley and I had a romantic affair . . . as you know, we were quite intimate. I wanted him . . . I loved him so much, he promised to marry me every time we had, well, you know, made love."

"Tell us what happened that evening," I asked.

Elise looked down and began haltingly, "We were making love in that examining room when you opened the door, I was terribly embarrassed."

"Incidentally, why the blonde wig?" Maggie asked.

"Basil had a thing, a sort of fetish for blondes, I guess. Getting the wig was his idea."

"After your affair that night, what happened?" I asked.

Elise cleared her throat, "We returned to his consultation room where he sat at his desk and started to go through some charts. He ignored me, just like I didn't exist, even though I sat on the other side of the desk. I waited for him to say something, anything. Finally, I got enough courage and asked if he was serious about getting married and if he had made any plans. Without looking at me he said, 'Can't you see I'm busy? Don't bother me now."

"Were you angry enough to kill him?" Maggie asked.

Elise pouted, "At that moment? Yes, I guess I was."

"Did you shoot him?" Korbin asked.

"Oh, no! For heaven's sake, no. Even when I was mad, I loved him. I would never do anything like that. I just sat there waiting for something, I don't know what. Then he said still without looking at me, 'It's getting late. Why don't you go home now? I'll see you tomorrow."

Maggie studied Elise. "What did you do then? You didn't go to your apartment. One of your roommates said you hadn't slept in your bed that night."

"That's right. I felt terribly depressed when I left Basil and knew I would be miserable enough to keep my roommates awake with my crying. I decided to go to Basil's apartment where I visited with him occasionally, I had my own key. I thought I could talk to him when he came there later that evening, and maybe we could clear things up. If he wasn't going to marry me, I was going to give him an ultimatum, I would leave him immediately. But he never showed up." Elise began to sob and took a Kleenex from her purse.

"When did you learn he was murdered?" I asked.

"The following morning, I jumped into my car and drove on the freeway, just to be alone and to think, I was just so heartsick. I stopped at a roadside café for a cup of coffee and called the office on my cell phone. I disguised my voice and asked to speak to Dr. Stuckley. I talked to Carmenita who didn't recognize my voice. When she told me the shattering news, I must have screamed into the phone. I became dizzy and nauseated. I ran out and jumped into the car where I just sat and cried and cried until I couldn't cry anymore."

"Where were you living? How did you get along?" Maggie persisted in her interrogation.

Elise seemed more at ease after taking several sips of the Chardonnay Maggie served. All eyes focused on her as we waited for an explanation. If we expected a direct answer, we were denied. She started a circuitous explanation of how she stayed with friends, but her details were vague and contradictory. She mentioned that she did part time work using a false name and otherwise evading detection.

"Didn't you know the police were looking for you?" Maggie asked.

"I knew they would be, and I just needed time to think. The thought of being held in custody and having no good defense was more than I could handle. I just didn't know what to do."

"Well, what did you do, where are you living now?" Maggie wanted direct answers.

"I met this kind Swiss man who unfortunately is no longer able to provide for me." Elise stopped and when no further explanations were forthcoming, Maggie started in again.

"What man? Where were you living?"

Elise responded slowly, choosing her words carefully. "I'm sorry I can't give you his name or whereabouts." The confessional was brought to a halt and further coaxing seemed useless.

"You know you'll have to turn yourself into the police," I said.

"I'm ready for that now, I have a lawyer."

"Really? Who's been advising you?" Maggie asked.

Elise sipped her wine, and looked about the room with a detached smile. "What a lovely home. Did you do your own decorating?" She chose to ignore Maggie's questions and arose signaling to Korbin her intent to leave.

Maggie's frustration was palpable. She stood, raised her head and in a less than cordial manner asked, "Didn't we see you at Basil's funeral service? Who were you with?"

Elise hesitated. "Forgive me for not answering your questions. I've been told not to discuss certain things." She walked towards the door. "I wanted you both to know how sorry I am about Dr. Stuckley and to assure you that I had nothing whatever to do with his murder."

Korbin opened the front door and preceded Elise, again checking the street to the right and left. He opened the passenger side for Elise then turned to us and shrugged. "I'll be in touch."

Maggie turned to me, "I wonder if our little Prudence Penny has morphed into a bona fide professional?"

"You mean a lady of the evening?" I smiled.

"You could call it that if you insist on being polite."

TWENTY-SEVEN

At the office on the following morning I put in a call to Roscoe.

*Hello Roscoe—Maggie suggested a way of smoking Mueller
out of his Geneva hideaway—you what?—Maggie will be
happy to know. Keep me informed—no, I haven't seen the
L.A. Times today. Yes, I'll be sure to read it.*

Maggie walked into the consultation room as I placed the phone
on the cradle. "I just spoke to Roscoe who was positively ebullient, he
was too excited to talk at length, but this is the gist of what he said:
he got in touch with the FBI in L.A., they persuaded the authorities
in Geneva to obtain a sample of Mueller's DNA for comparison with
what was found in Mei Ling. However, Mueller insisted that a lab of
his choice would make the test."

"How smart is that?" Maggie asked.

"Perhaps not smart at all. We'll just have to trust that the doctors
conducting the testing are honest. We're at their mercy."

"How is the DNA comparison made?"

"As far as I can tell, a photo screening of the semen DNA pattern
found in Mei Ling will be sent electronically to the lab in Geneva
and a comparison will be made with Mueller's DNA. Do you realize
what that means? As soon as the study is completed in another two

or three days Mueller will be held to a murder charge that he'll find pretty damned hard to beat."

"That S.O.B. deserves to be hanged." Maggie took a folded L.A. Times from under her arm then spread the front page on my desk. She looked at me and then pointed to the paper. "Josh, I think things are beginning to look brighter." On the front page in the right hand column a byline read:

> State Attorney Harold C. Horsleigh charged with accepting bribes. Indictment imminent. Complete meltdown of long career seen as campaign contributions total hundreds of thousands, possibly more. Among those who contributed are . . .

A list of corporations was mentioned. One Maggie had underlined with a yellow marker read: *Magna Pharmex.*

"Oh boy, is this ever a revelation. Now I know what Roscoe was talking about."

"Josh, why was Magna Pharmex giving the D.A. campaign money?"

The question stopped my enthusiasm long enough to make me think why an excessive bribe would be given. "Obviously to stop the investigation in the murder of one of their employees, Mei Ling, by one of their own officers, I would think."

"And what about the investigation of the man who died in our office?" And the guy with the listening device in the restaurant?" Maggie did not wait for my answer. "And what about the theft of our office records on patients receiving Dolcrean β and the attempted robbery in our home? And what about the murder of Basil?" Maggie's questions came in rapid fire order.

"All that took place outside of L.A. County," I added.

"But Horsleigh is the State's Attorney, all those unsolved crimes could come under his jurisdiction if he chose, couldn't they?"

"Well, he's not going to get the opportunity. He's out on his butt, and his successor is going to have to put up with the thorny likes of Roscoe U. Farquhaar, like it or not."

Carmenita's voice on the intercom interrupted, "Dr. Harrington, Sergeant Mannheim and Officer Hernandez are here and would like to talk with you, if you can spare a moment or two."

Maggie raised a brow, "Since when did they become so polite? As though they care whether you can spare a moment or two? They'd interrupt you in surgery if they could."

Two short raps on the door preceded their entry. "Sorry to bother you Doc and Mrs. H.," Mannheim morose as usual, advanced into the room and in his monotone added, "We'd like to examine your car, Doc."

"You'd like to do what?"

"We'd like to go over your car to determine if it was wired."

"Wired? Wired for what? What are you talking about?"

"That wild bugger we picked up on the freeway, the one who planned to gun you down confessed to one or two tricks before his hot shot lawyer got to him. We figure he was high on something like 'ludes or amphetamines."

"What kind of tricks was he talking about?"

"He said he planted radio-controlled explosives under your car that would detonate from a control point at about a hundred feet. Fortunately, he screwed up and the explosion never came off. Whether this guy was telling the truth or hallucinating we don't know, but he was running off at the mouth like he had a prod up his ass. Excuse my vulgarity, Mrs. H."

Maggie was more frightened than offended. She clutched her chest and turned ashen. "You mean he planned to blow us up?"

"That's right. If what that maggot says is believable. Do you mind if Officer Hernandez takes a quick look at your car?"

I handed Hernandez the car keys while Mannheim remained with us in the consultation room. Maggie overwhelmed by the enormity of Mannheim's disclosure just sat and stared as we spoke. After Hernandez left, I asked Mannheim if he was going to assist him. Mannheim shook his head, "Naw, he knows a hell of a lot more about electronic stuff and explosives than I do. I'd just be in his way. If he suspects something, we'll impound the car and our mechanics will go over it with a fine toothcomb. Chances are he'll be able to tell us in a few minutes whether anyone tampered with the car."

"He must be quite capable in his quiet, unobtrusive way," I said.

"Yeah, smart as a whip and a memory like a steel trap." I commented," Not at all like the prejudicial, archetypical concept some Anglos have of Hispanics."

Mannheim glared at me. "Hernandez is not a wet-back, if that's what you're thinking, Doc. His ancestry is Spanish and Indian, dating back to the Conquistadors of the sixteenth century who explored the southeastern states. According to him, his forebears were Spanish as well as Creek and Seminole Indians who managed to survive and migrate to the north and east sectors of the country. Actually, he's a first generation Californian who doesn't consider himself primarily Hispanic, but rather a Native American. He says his ancestors have been screwed by edict for two centuries by our benevolent government. In spite of that he is a loyal cop and a solid tax-paying citizen."

Hernandez returned wiping his hands in a handkerchief. "I couldn't find anything in the engine compartment, and as much as I could see with a flashlight there was nothing under the chassis. But to be safe I would suggest putting the car on a hoist and checking the under-carriage."

"When did that moron have an opportunity to mess with our car?" Maggie asked.

"I don't know that he did, for sure, but if he did, he could have done it in a number of ways: acting as a parking lot or garage attendant, a gas station serviceman, that kind of job doesn't take long. Anyway, you decide whether you want to drive it home cr whether you want us to haul it to our garage where we can inspect it better."

"That's no option. I'm not going to ride in *that* thing until I know it's safe." Maggie was adamant.

"Keep the car keys, we'll take a taxi home after office hours," I said to Hernandez.

Near the close of the day, Carmenita announced that Mr. Farquhaar was on the phone and would like to speak to me. I took the call in my consultation room.

*Hello Roscoe—yes—what? You've got to be kidding. How
could that be? Someone posted a $250,000 bond?—but
the guy tried to kill us—of course, he would deny it. No
priors—a verifiable weapon registration—trial date set for
two months from now? Roscoe, that guy can put a bullet
through me and be out of the country before then. Who put
up the bail bond?—some L.A. law firm—that figures. I'll
have to keep looking over my shoulder. Don't tell me the
guy's going to be on surveillance—you know better than
to expect me to believe that.*

Maggie came into the room and heard the last part of our conversation. "What was that all about?" I explained what Roscoe had said.

"That's terrible! How can they do that?" Maggie's eyes were flashing. "We're going to be targets for that lunatic." She folded her arms,
paced the consultation room, shook her head and sighed. "Who in
the hell is behind all this?" She looked at her watch. "I called a cab,
they'll be here in twenty-five minutes."

Maggie changed her clothing then sat and looked out the window
but was too angry to engage in conversation. The sound of a door
lock turning made her jump, we looked at each other.

"Probably the clean-up crew," I said. I hurried into the hall to find
them filing in, one man and two women who partially bowed as they
passed me with their supplies. Only one woman, Yolanda, appeared
familiar to me. The frequent turnover in workers was a source of mild
irritation because the cleaning routine had to be explained each time.
I asked Yolanda where Charlie was, the old boss.

Whether she comprehended fully seemed doubtful, then she
cocked her head. "Eh? And smiled, "Ah, *si, si.* Charlie, he work no
more *aqui.*" I nodded to let her know I understood, but pursuing a
dialogue would have been distressful for both of us.

A knock at the front door was followed by a shout, "Taxi!"

Maggie held onto my arm as we approached the ten-year old
capacious Lincoln limousine. The driver opened the rear door for
Maggie, and as I was about to go to the other side she reached out and

held my arm commanding me to enter on her side. Maggie's distrust of strangers had become apparent. She studied the driver's face then as she sat on the worn and shiny black leather seat she stared at the mounted chauffeur's license as though memorizing ID numbers.

My cell phone chimed.

Yes Roscoe—in your office tomorrow morning at seven—see you then.

"What did Roscoe want?"

"He thought I might want to get the forensic pathologist's report first hand from the Swiss lab regarding Mueller's DNA tests. Roscoe's confident the findings will support a conviction of Mueller."

Before stepping out of the cab in front of our home, Maggie looked around.

"All clear?" I asked.

She nodded without assurance. I paid the cabbie, and we walked briskly towards the front door.

"Josh, I have an awful premonition. I just wish all these bad people would go away. Can't you negotiate with them? Tell them they can have anything you've got. Just leave us alone."

"Maggie, we've been through all this before. I don't even know who there is to talk to. No one has come forward to claim responsibility for all this craziness nor has anyone wanted to talk with me. We've got to hope the police will find enough evidence to put an end to this."

Maggie approached the front door with trepidation even though we had recently installed a security system. She tiptoed into the vestibule, disarmed the alarm, then peeked into the den. Finding that room orderly she walked through the rest of the house with less apprehension.

After dinner, I sat on the sofa with the newspaper and felt my shoulders slumping and my eyelids flickering. Maggie removed my shoes, brought my legs up and placed a pillow beneath my head. My world was made more comfortable and endearing by this lovely woman. I was about to fade when I saw the lower section of the front page, "Beleaguered State's Attorney Horsleigh says all cases on docket to be pursued despite current indictment problems." Somehow, the threat of his office no longer carried a sting, but a lingering concern remained. I couldn't be as sanguine as Roscoe: he always seemed to manage supreme confidence in the face of impending doom.

TWENTY-EIGHT

"Come in you lovely people, come in!" Roscoe's cheerful salutation brightened the dismal disarray of his office. "So pleased you could come in at this unholy hour. As soon as my secretary honors us with her presence we'll have coffee and perhaps a delectable treat from the doughnut shop. I do like those goodies." He patted his belly. "Yes, I do."

No sooner had he said that, when Millicent came in with an oil-stained bag and a carafe of coffee. She had torn sheets off a roll of paper towels and handed two to each of us—one to be used as a plate, the other as a napkin. Roscoe ripped open the bag to display six varied doughnuts including two jelly-filled. "Please help yourself," He beseeched us. Before we made our selections, he took a jelly-filled and held it with his thumb and index finger. His bite spread jelly and sugar on both sides of his mouth. With his other hand, he cleared the jelly from his face then licked his fingers.

"Marvelous taste, marvelous taste," he cooed. "Well, mustn't waste anymore time." He pushed the intercom button, "Millicent, call the pathologist in Geneva." He placed his hand over the speaker, "It's a bit after four in the afternoon there. Those burghers don't put in extra hours like we industrious Americans.

"Joshua, pick up the other phone, so that we can both listen to the professor. This is one of those calls that fills me with tingling anticipation. It's as though we are about to receive the keys to the kingdom." Roscoe swiped his mouth with a paper towel and took a gulp of coffee.

Hello, Professor Hegel, what news do you have for us?

Roscoe listened for several minutes, his face darkened, a frown transformed his mouth, his head drooped, and he groaned.

There is no mistake? Did you have your colleagues verify your findings? You're sure the specimen came from Herr Doktor Mueller? Wait please, there's a doctor on another line here. Perhaps you can explain that to him.

The information from the Swiss forensic pathologist was explicit, there were only two identical markers in the DNA strips. Not nearly enough to suggest that the semen found in Mei Ling came from Mueller.

Roscoe was utterly crushed. In a barely audible voice, he thanked the Swiss doctor. With his elbows propped on the desk, he held his head in his hands, "I don't understand it," he muttered then pounded the desk. "It doesn't make sense. Who in the sanctified name of the Lord could have deposited his filthy seed in that sweet little girl and then killed her?" Roscoe glanced at us, "Joshua, Maggie help me understand this unholy conundrum." Our dejected faces offered no solution. Then in his finest theatrical mode, Roscoe's visage and body English turned one hundred eighty degrees. With a flourish he announced, "Don't you two worry, this is only a temporary setback. Yes sir, only a temporary setback. We're going to redevelop and redefine our investigative procedures and get the son-of-a-bitch who has thus far eluded us." Ignoring the intercom he took a deep breath and roared, "Millicent, get me Marvin Korbin!"

"Dr. Harrington, one of the sheriff's officers returned your car. He said to tell you it was safe to drive. I placed the keys on your desk," Carmenita informed us as we entered the office. "He said Detectives Mannheim and Hernandez would be in touch with you later."

"That's just what we need: more bad news from Mutt and Jeff," Maggie said.

"I can't believe what I heard from that Swiss doctor. I was sure Mueller would be involved . . ."

"We still can't be sure that he isn't," Maggie said.

At three-thirty, that afternoon, Carmenita escorted Sergeant Mannheim and Officer Hernandez to my consultation room, not that they needed to be shown where it was, Carmenita did not want them to loll around the reception room.

"Fellas, what cheerful news do you bring from our esteemed sheriff's department?" I extended my hand to shake theirs. "I understand our car had no hidden bomb devices, that's a relief."

"That's not true, Doc," Mannheim said in his unemotional monotone.

"What? Carmenita told me the officer who returned the car said it was safe to drive. You're telling me it *isn't?*"

"Hold on, Doc, I didn't say that, it's safe to drive, now." Mannheim paused after his cryptic remark.

"Forgive me. I'm not following you . . ."

"After we got the car onto a hoist we found an explosive device hidden on the inner side of the left front frame rail. It was removed, of course, and we got some pretty good finger prints," Hernandez said. "That was the good news."

I knew there had to be a yin to this yang. "So?"

"They belong to our freeway mayhem cowboy, Mr. Eisenmacher," Mannheim said.

"Did you bring him back in?" I asked.

"We would, Doc, if we knew where the hell he was."

"Dammit! I knew something like this would happen. Didn't anyone think he was a flight risk? They could have placed an ankle detector on him. This bastard is probably planning to gun me down again."

"That's really what we came to talk to you about, Doc." Even when he was about to propose something helpful, Mannheim looked sinister. "We'd like to give you round-the-clock protection, or suggest that you take a quick vacation, get out of town until we catch this son-of-a-bitch."

"You've got to be kidding! I can't leave, I have patients in the hospital and patients scheduled for surgery. I could ask Dr. Weiss to see my office patients or even make hospital rounds, but there is no way I can postpone scheduled surgery at the last minute, patients make arrangements with their families and at their jobs. "

"We'll do our best to protect you and the Mrs. We figure we should be able to haul this guy's ass in if he's still in the country," Mannheim said.

"Why is it that I take little comfort in what you're telling me?"

A single knock at the door preceded Maggie's entrance. She looked at each of us. "Josh, you're flushed, what's going on?" She cast a baleful eye at Mannheim. When I explained what the detectives revealed, she blanched and guided herself into a chair.

"Let us know, Doc, what you plan to do," Mannheim said as they left. Maggie was sobbing softly and dabbed her eyes with a Kleenex. I walked to her side and placed my arm around her shoulders.

"Darling, please don't cry. This whole thing will blow over as soon as the police haul this guy in." Maggie held my arm but seemed to take little solace in what I was saying.

"Josh, tell me again: why would anyone even think of killing you? Is it because you reported fatalities with Dolorean β? Why would a corporation as large as Magna Pharmex even consider something as terrible as that?" Maggie squeezed my arm and with her large blue eyes searched mine for an explanation. "Can't you promise them that you'll stop . . . ?"

"Darling, I can't undo what's been done. The big guys at Magna Pharmex in sales and promotions know about my clinical research, someone there wants to be sure I don't get any more publicity and make no more speeches or write more articles for the Journal. Besides, they're negotiating a stock deal with one of the other big pharmaceutical houses, and if MP's so-called promising new drug is found to be lethal to some—well, their bargaining position will be badly compromised."

"Other companies have had troubles with some products, but they don't kill people who criticize them, do they?"

"Let's hope not. One of the primary differences between the other drugs and Dolorean β is that it has not been released for generalized distribution, whereas other drugs have been available for months or years with sales amounting to many millions and even billions of dollars. For example, Prempro has been reported to cause breast cancer, Ortho Evra, a birth control patch may cause clots and Neurontin used for seizures may cause suicides . . ."

"So your saying once a drug has a foothold in the market place it's more difficult to dislodge."

"That's right, especially if it's known to help many more than it harms. But deaths attributable to a new or experimental drug, that's different, and they present a pretty hard rap to beat. The entire industry is facing the problem of mounting lawsuits. Some lawsuits are frivolous. Others, like class action suits give the law firms a bundle while the individual plaintiffs get a pittance. I didn't intend to lecture, but I think you can begin to see some of the ramifications of the drug business, and I've only discussed a few.'

"Are you sure this Eisenmacher is working for Magna Pharmex?"

"I think so, but I wouldn't bet my life—sorry, I said that."

"Josh, why don't you call Roscoe to tell him of these latest developments?"

We saw our last two patients and Maggie appeared emotionally and physically drained. "Let's eat out. I don't think I have the stamina to prepare dinner."

"Fine. How about some Mexican food in Indio?" Maggie changed her clothing while I sat tired but ever grateful and appreciative of her lovely womanly form. I was reminded of our first intimate encounter when she disrobed in the Chicago hotel room. I couldn't believe then how wonderful the visual and tactile sensations were. Even the delicate scent of this woman stirred me and her movements evoked carnal cravings. Our preoccupation with dreadful events in the past several days had discouraged intimacy, but I felt a sudden resurgence, a need for holding and caressing her. Before she slipped into her dress, I hugged and kissed her then pressed against her. Only her bra and panties sheltered her from complete and magnificent nudity.

"Oh, Josh, I needed and wanted that for the longest time. I was beginning to wonder if we would ever make love again."

"That's one thing you can count on, Baby."

As we approached the I-10, we were keenly aware of the immediate surroundings and looked for suspicious cars. I glanced frequently in the side and rear view minors while Maggie sat in a kind of sidesaddle position looking to the left and turning her head towards the rear. Almost simultaneously both of us spotted a late model red Corvette with a hard top traveling at excessive speed in the fast lane.

An uneasiness gripped me as I maneuvered the car towards the right lane. Only a mile of freeway lay ahead before the off ramp, but the Corvette was already crossing lanes and moving towards us.

Panic seized Maggie. "Josh, what are you going to do?"

"I'm going to get into the far right lane and hope to hell some vehicle will shield our left side. Release your seatbelt and cram yourself under the dash!"

The Corvette was approaching our lane and would be abreast of us in a few seconds. Who in the hell is in that car—that goddamned madman? Jesus, I didn't want things to end this way. I reached over and touched Maggie's head gently as she was crouched below, "If I lose control of the car, try to reach the steering wheel then stomp on the brake. The advice was desperate and impractical, but I wanted Maggie to have a chance at survival. The Corvette neared the lane next to ours, when a horn blasted and a third car sped next to us and like a wedge forced the Corvette to move left. We turned off the freeway and the car to our left followed closely. On the street, I pulled over to the right and stopped. The car behind us did also. Trembling with fright, Maggie asked, "Are we all right? Josh, are you hurt?"

"I'm okay, just a little nervous." At that moment, the driver from the car behind was standing beside my door.

He shouted, "Open the window, Doc. Are you both all right?" It was Marvin Korbin. "Roscoe called and told me to keep a close watch on you love birds. Glad I did."

"Who was in that Corvette?" Maggie asked. He shrugged. "We'll know soon. I called in the license number. There were two in that car. In the meantime, if you're going to have dinner I'll join you, that is, if you don't mind."

"Be my guest. You can order the biggest, costliest meal of your life, and I'll have a giant-sized Margarita for starters."

"Ditto," Maggie said.

TWENTY-NINE

Joshua, my boy, glad to find you home. Marvin gave me a report of your rather exciting evening You owe him a debt of gratitude, indeed you do. Did I tell you he raced cars professionally as a young man? Quite talented—quite talented. The red Corvette was rented. Just a minute—hold on Joshua, Marvin's on the other line—he has more information. This may take a while—I'll phone you later.

"Dear, come have a bit of breakfast before you make rounds." Maggie in her pajamas sidled up to me. "Thank you for making me feel so young and in love again. Last night was won-der-ful." She gave me a kiss with the enticing aroma of coffee on her breath.

"The pleasure was mine." I patted her derriere lovingly. Maggie's breakfast table was a veritable cornucopia. Her concept of a *bite* was orange juice, stewed prunes, coffee, bacon and eggs, toasted bagels, two types of spread plus jellies and jams. I complained gently, "Maggie, you're a nurse. You know about cholesterol, fats, sugars, and yet . . ."

"Choose your food and amounts wisely, and you'll have nothing to fear."

"Honey, you tell me that at every meal. In the meanwhile, you prepare enough for a block party."

"My Irish mother would have been proud of me, and my father wouldn't have complained at all—not at all."

"Careful, you're beginning to sound like Roscoe."

The phone rang.

*Hello, Roscoe—the Corvette was rented from an agency in
Newport Beach?—a young woman—what was her name?
No, I don't know anyone by that name. The address on her
driver's license was fake—meaning everything about her
was probably phony. Thanks Roscoe, keep me informed.*

"You heard most of the conversation. An enlargement of the copy
of the driver's license will be forwarded from the rental agency by
special courier to Roscoe's office. It should be there by this afternoon."

Maggie became uneasy. "These people are real professionals—
false I.D.'s, fast cars, altered surveillance film, breaking into and
robbing offices and houses . . ."

"Don't forget the killings: Hoffman, Mei Ling, Stuckley . . ."

Maggie stood still, her eyes surveyed our kitchen, then in a
whisper she asked, "Do you think there are bugging devices around
here?" I laughed.

"What's so funny?" She asked.

"Now you ask?—after everything that has happened around
here? As a matter of fact, Marvin went through our office and our
home last week with a bugging detector."

"When did he go through our home?"

"Last week, I gave him my keys when he came by the office. You
needn't worry. He didn't find any bugs or cameras filming us in our
bedroom that could be sold to a porno shop."

"And what about our living room intercourse scenes?" Maggie
picked up on my kidding quickly. "You'd better leave before you get
me so excited, I won't let you go," she said.

"Do you think your sweet Irish mother would approve of this
talk?"

"She's probably turning in her grave and asking Jesus to forgive
her wayward daughter who learned nothing of this filth in her home."
Maggie gave me a moist kiss. "My dear Mom never would have approved
of my shameless love, but I know she would have loved you, Josh."

Maggie put her arms around me and held me tightly. "I won't let them take you from me, ever!"

Maggie was in the office before noon. When I walked in, she corralled me. "Josh, Roscoe asked if we could stop at his office to look at an enlarged photo of the driver's license from the car rental agency. If we're unable to go now, he would have Marvin run it by later in the afternoon."

"I don't want to wait. Let's go."

"My dear Joshua and Maggie, I'm so pleased you are here. Seeing you reminds me of Apollo and Aphrodite, or was it Athena? No matter, I worship and admire your beauty and charm. Can I offer you a little nectar or ambrosia from our well-stocked larder?"

"Some water would be fine," Maggie said.

"Millicent, would you kindly bring in some *agua frio* for our guests? Yes, that's right, dear, cold water." Roscoe turned off the intercom. "She's lived in Southern California over twenty years and can't understand six words of Spanish. Now where were we? Oh, yes." He pushed aside enough folders and loose papers on his desk to accommodate an envelope he took from a top drawer. Pulling out a grainy six by eight enlargement of a California driver's license, he turned it right side up for us to peruse.

We looked at it, then, simultaneously looked at each other, "That's Elise!" Maggie blurted.

"It sure as all hell is. So she rented the car and had a male companion drive it. I assume it was a male."

"You know this girl?" Roscoe asked. We nodded. "Good, good! The noose is tightening. The name on the driver's license is fictitious, but it may be useful to Korbin who will check the local hotel and motel registrations." Roscoe rubbed his chubby hands in anticipation. "Little lady your freedom days are numbered."

"How did she pay for the car?" I asked.

"Marvin was told, crisp fifty dollar bills."

"Has the car been returned?" Maggie asked.

"No, and there are a number of agencies in cities along the coast where the car can be returned. All agencies have been alerted: as soon as it rolls in, an attempt will be made to detain the driver while the police are notified. Joshua, dear boy, you appear perplexed. Is there a problem needing clarification?"

"How long can Elise be held, and on what charges?"

"More charges than you might imagine: suspicion of murder, in the case of Dr. Stuckley, reckless endangerment on the freeway, evading arrest, and many more, dear boy. Rest assured, as soon as the police nab her, the key to many mysteries will be provided."

"I hope you're right," Maggie said.

"I was saving the best news for last." From a top desk drawer he removed a letter with the official seal of the Los Angeles District Attorney. He cleared his throat, put on his Ben Franklin-type glasses and read. "Dear Mr. Farquhaar:

This is to inform you that all charges emanating from this office and involving your client, Dr. Joshua A. Harrington, in the matter of the wrongful death of Mei Ling Bolton, blah, blah, blah . . . have been dropped for lack of sufficient evidence, blah, blah, blah . . ."

He handed me the letter with a broad-beamed smile that transformed his round face like a compressed beach ball. He slapped my back. "This is an occasion for revelry, my dear friends. Yes, perhaps, a Bacchanalian orgy!"

Although I felt a sense of relief, I was not entirely without concern. "Now what about the matter of my revolver being used in the murder of Basil Stuckley?"

"Piffle, Joshua, I say piffle! Don't let that concern you one iota! There is nothing to tie you to the—I say, there is nothing to tie you to that dreadful murder."

Riding back to the office, Maggie asked, "Well, how do you like the turn of events?" Before I could answer, she continued, "I always knew there was something phony about that little tramp, that whore, that bitch. She was going to kill us! Oh, I'd like to get my hands on her! She would have made a play for you, too, if I hadn't stopped her. She knew I didn't trust her. Why was I so nice to her when she came to the house with Korbin?" Maggie looked at me. "Well, say something!"

"I will as soon as you give me an opportunity. The way I figure it, she was employed by Magna Pharmex, if not officially, then by one of its renegade officers—let's say Mueller—and her job was to spy and collect data since both Stuckley and I had been conducting clinical research on Dolorean β."

"What exactly do you think she was hired to do?"

"My guess is, get all records pertaining to those patients who had unfavorable responses to the drug."

"You mean those who died?"

"Especially those who died, but there were others who had symptoms of nausea, vomiting, dizziness, chills, fever. Even increased joint pain. She probably went after those records also."

"Was she supposed to remove those records?"

"She or someone else acting with her *did* remove our office records, remember? They broke into our file cabinets with a crowbar or some other tool."

"Of course I remember. There was also that attempt to steal our home records, the night you had your face pummeled. And you could have killed the intruder with that shot you fired. Oh, God, what a night! I hope the police lab kept that blood sample for DNA testing. Is there a national DNA data bank?"

"Not that I'm aware."

THIRTY

Towards the late afternoon, Carmenita handed me several telephone messages. A cryptic note read, "Closing in." M. Korbin. Another message read, "Good news imminent, call me." R.U.F.
Between patients, I phoned Farquhaar.

> *What's the good news? Whoa, slow down, I can't understand you—yes—parking lot—where? Thanks.*

Maggie seeing me on the phone approached and asked about the conversation. "Roscoe said Marvin called to tell him he located the red Corvette at the Springs Hotel parking lot."
"Terrific! Are the police going to pick them up?"
"I don't know what arrangements were made between the P.I. and the cops. Roscoe mentioned that Marvin has a telephoto camera zeroed in on the car."
"I hope he doesn't have to wait in this awful heat—one hundred fifteen degrees, a guy could melt."
We saw three more patients when a mother brought in an eight year old wearing a baseball uniform. His forearm deformity indicated a fracture above the wrist. Although the time was near closing, the girls willingly remained to help with this emergency. An x-ray revealed a displaced fracture of both bones of the lower forearm. Following careful preparation, I set the fracture and applied a fiberglass cast.

I thanked the girls for remaining overtime while Maggie put the cast room in order. The patient and his mother were led out the front door. The time was six-ten.

"Well, my dear, you've put in quite a day. Are you ready to leave?" I asked.

"More than you can imagine."

The phone rang, "Let it ring, Maggie, the doctor's answering service will pick it up."

A voice on the other end came through on the audio line.

Joshua, if you are still in the office pick up the phone. If not, I'll ring you at home.

It was Roscoe. I grabbed the phone.

Hello, hello, are you there? Good—Maggie will be listening on another phone. Go ahead.

Joshua, our boy Marvin finally spotted the elusive Elise getting into the red Corvette at the hotel parking lot. He followed her out to the I-10 going west. He put a call into the Highway Patrol. We should be hearing from him again when she's handed over to the Palm Desert Sheriff's office. By the way, Elise's alias at the hotel registration desk read, Mrs. Margaret Harrington. Aren't you flattered Maggie? I'll call as soon as I hear anything new.

"The nerve of her using my name. I hope she rots in prison under her *own* name. I'm willing to bet she's in the thick of all the mayhem. In spite of her denials, she's probably the one who killed Basil."

"I doubt it," I said.

"Maybe she was the cat burglar who sneaked into our home."

"Ridiculous, no gal could have hit me that hard."

"Hah, don't ever challenge me, little darlin'." Maggie punched my arm playfully.

"Let's get out of here before we have a real boxing match."

"The only good part of that would be kissing and making nice-nice afterwards." Maggie smiled.

"When did we ever need an excuse for making nice-nice?"

Maggie stood in front of me and threw her arms around me. "Never."

We walked towards the back door and shut the lights. As we passed through the door, someone shouted from the parking lot. "Wait, señor, Doctor." It was Yolanda from the maintenance crew carrying cleaning equipment. I held the door open for her and her co-worker, but the male member of the team was missing.

"Charlie hasn't returned to work?" I asked. When she didn't respond, I thought I really shouldn't have asked since she didn't understand. After a pause in which she probably mulled over my question she blurted, "*Si, si,* he back to work, *ahora.*"

"*Bueno, bueno!*" I left before the conversation became difficult. I had already depleted most of my Spanish vocabulary. As I drove off, I looked in the rear view mirror. A man carrying more cleaning supplies emerged from the same vehicle as the women. He seemed to be burdened by the weight of his supplies and hobbled into the office. "They're a hard working lot," I said.

"Yes, they are," she said perfunctorily, her mind obviously elsewhere. "Do you think the police have her in custody yet?"

"Elise?"

"Of course, Dear!" Maggie sounded impatient. "Do you think she's spilling her guts, naming names and accusing some big shots from Magna Pharmex?"

"She has a lawyer. Either she'll opt to remain quiet, or she'll be advised to cut a deal to lessen prison time, depends on what the prosecution has to work with."

"Josh, they broke into our office and took all the files on patients getting clinical trials of Dolorean β, didn't they?"

"Right, whoever *they* are. Why do you bring that up?"

"Well, I've been thinking, didn't Basil have records on patients taking Dolorean β?"

"I'm sure he did."

"Are those records still in his office?"

"Perhaps. Why?"

"Someone might try to retrieve them as they did yours."

"Basil's been dead about a month, why would they have waited?"

"Our office building has been watched by the night duty police more carefully since then."

We were in the house five minutes when the phone rang.

Joshua, they got her! Now we're going to learn a few facts.

Roscoe, who was with her the night we were attacked on the freeway?

Don't know yet, but we'll learn—yes, we will. Talk with you later.

Maggie's burgers were prepared as a visual as well as a gastronomic delight and the heady fragrance of grilled meat and onions made me salivate. I took my first bite, and closed my eyes in rapturous delight when the phone rang jarring my sensibilities.

"I'll get it, Dear." Maggie left the table and brought the cordless phone to me. "It's Marvin. He'd like to talk with you."

I motioned Maggie to listen in on another phone.

Hello Marvin—good work—all we have to do is rein in the rest of that gang. What's that?—he's back in town?—what for? Is there another drug convention here? Does Roscoe know? Mueller obviously feels secure knowing that his DNA markers didn't match those of the semen found in Mei Ling. Thanks for calling.

Maggie replaced the phone, " Isn't this an interesting turn of events? Mueller's back in town to coach Elise or to give her support."

"Or maybe threaten her."

The following morning at six-fifteen, Roscoe called.

Joshua, I'm going to the Larson Center in Indio this morning where hatchet Annie Borden alias Elise Sundstrom is being held. Dick Shelly, the chief prosecutor would like to talk to us. I'll buy you breakfast—yes certainly, bring Maggie along.

We drove to Roscoe's office and parked our car in his lot since he insisted on driving his ancient Saab. "Millicent brought us containers of coffee and muffins, so we won't find it necessary to stop for breakfast." Roscoe carried a cardboard box containing our food and balanced it with one hand while opening the car door with the other. "You don't keep your car locked?" Maggie asked.

"Good gracious, no! Why would anyone want to steal this dirty, cantankerous old relic? It's a bit tricky to drive, enough to discourage most thieves." At that moment, Millicent, Roscoe's large secretary wearing her signature muumuu came rushing towards us with a brief case. "Thank you, my loyal and trusted daughter of the Islands. You are as a lovely pearl snatched from the dark blue waters of the South Seas . . ." Millicent had already turned her broad back and sauntered off appearing unaffected by Roscoe's exaggeration and flattery. "Lovely girl but doesn't understand poetic phrases." Roscoe shook his head.

Like his grossly disorganized office, the interior of the Saab was a shambles, cluttered with briefs and papers in haphazard piles. The site and smell of dust plus non-descript musty odors repelled Maggie who insisted on having her coffee and muffin in the parking lot. I followed her. Roscoe apologized for any inconvenience and unceremoniously pushed the papers and briefs off the back and front seats onto the floor. "Why did you insist on taking *your* car?" Maggie asked.

"The boys at the court house recognize my car and give me special parking privileges."

We walked through the metal detectors and were scrutinized by uniformed marshals. An elevator took us to the third floor. Entering Dick Shelly's office, I was startled by the sight of a familiar but unfriendly face, the imperturbable Dr. Mueller sat ramrod tall reading the *Wall Street Journal*. Seeing me, he smiled, but a smile that could be construed as a sneer. He folded the paper, placed it under his arm and stood. He bowed slightly and in his clipped German accent said, "Dr. Harrington, good to see you again." I introduced him to Maggie and Roscoe. "We have a person of common interest here, Ms. Elise Sundstrom," he said.

At that moment, the receptionist announced, "Mr. Shelly just phoned to say he would be an hour late. May I suggest that you make an appointment for another time, or perhaps you'd like to visit a nearby coffee shop and return?"

Mueller turned to us. "Would you be my guests for some refreshments? Perhaps we can discuss our interests regarding Ms. Sundstrom before any misunderstandings develop." We followed Mueller out of the office. When he was several feet in front of us, Roscoe whispered, "Don't render any opinions and don't answer any questions. Let me do the talking."

In a nearby coffee house we sat at a table and gave our orders to an unsmiling gum-chewing waitress with a barbed wire chain tattoo on her mid arm and a stiff spike of red hair pointing like a saber upward. Her ring-pierced nose and eyebrows as well as an exposed midriff made me somewhat uneasy. Mueller sat across from Roscoe. Their appearances were a study in contrasts: Mueller's narrow face and serious demeanor contrasted with Roscoe's smiling, cherubic face. Mueller's tailored hand-stitched suit, white shirt with starched collar and striped tie was in contradistinction to Roscoe's ill-fitting seersucker suit, unbuttoned wilted shirt collar and soiled tie that hung limply over his bulging bay window.

When Mueller brought his arms forward on the table his jacket sleeves retracted to reveal French cuffs with gold cuff links. The initial "J" on his left cuff link caught my eye. "Forgive me for asking, Dr. Mueller, what does the "J" stand for on your cuff link?"

He smiled stiffly. "Joachim, my name is Joachim Kurt Mueller. Why do you ask?"

"I was introduced to you initially by Dr. Becker, who called you Kurt."

"Yes. To my friends I am known as Kurt."

"May I ask, have you lost or misplaced a cufflink recently?"

"I . . ." Mueller stopped and gave me a sharp look. "Have you found a cuff link of mine?"

"Perhaps. It was found in Mei Ling's room under the bed."

Mueller's expression changed to haughty dismissal. "No, no. I haven't lost any cuff links."

The waitress brought our drinks. Mueller, like the three of us, had a glass of iced coffee and sipped it through a plastic straw. After ten minutes of polite conversation, Mueller said, "Well, my dear friends, shall we discuss our person of mutual interest?"

Roscoe signaled our waitress who sauntered over and stood next to him. Her exposed midriff with a ring clipped to her navel was about four inches from his face. He stared at the ring then looked up at her. "I would like a jelly-filled doughnut, and I should tell you that I am completely enchanted by your umbilical adornment."

"Huh? What's that?" She asked.

"It is of no consequence, my dear, just bring the doughnut and be good enough to use tongs when selecting it."

THIRTY-ONE

"Dr. Mueller what interest do you or your corporation have in this young lady's problems?" Roscoe asked.

"We are concerned for her welfare. Her father was a chemist with Magna Pharmex for many years, and we prevailed upon Dr. Stuckley to give her a job, so naturally we feel a responsibility towards her."

Roscoe's brow arched as he drew his head back. "You traveled all the way from Geneva to do that?"

"Yes, of course, we feel that the girl may be unfairly accused of serious charges."

"You're quite right about the serious charges. It was her rented vehicle that almost rammed my client off the freeway."

"Really? Did anyone actually see her in the car at that time?"

Mueller was being cagey and ready for verbal jousting. Maggie was chomping at the bit but maintained her pledge of silence.

"She was with Dr. Stuckley the night he was murdered and remains a primary suspect." Roscoe slowly outlined the rim of his glass with his index finger as he watched Mueller's expression.

"Nonsense! She had nothing to do with Dr. Stuckley's murder. After all, there was the possibility they would marry soon. She had nothing to gain and everything . . ."

"Then why did she run off and fail to report to the police? She knew she was a suspect," Roscoe countered.

"The poor girl was confused and frightened. She needed time to think."

"You seem to be well-informed about her state of mind and activities," Roscoe said.

Mueller tented his fingers under his chin. "We are like a large family. We communicate frequently and are attuned to our members' needs."

"I hope you don't mind my asking, but what are you doing at the prosecuting attorney's office?"

"I'm here to give Elise advice and to see that justice is done."

"That's noble of you, sir, but Ms. Sundstrom has a capable law firm representing her . . ."

"Of course, but they cannot advise her like an old uncle would."

"I see." Roscoe withheld further comment.

"Well, folks, I enjoyed our little chat, if you will excuse me I will go back to the courthouse now. Please stay and enjoy your drinks." Mueller left half of his iced coffee. He wiped both his nose and mouth with a napkin and signaled the waitress for the bill. After he left, I reached for a clean napkin from a nearby table and placed Mueller's straw and napkin on the clean napkin as Maggie and Roscoe watched.

"Maggie, do you have a rubber band in that carry-all purse?" She reached inside blindly and pulled out a rubber band that I placed around the clean napkin. "Roscoe put this in your brief case. We'll request a DNA test on this and compare it with the DNA in the semen found in Mei Ling."

"Capital idea! How clever of you, Joshua. How absolutely clever."

We walked back slowly to the courthouse, went through the metal detectors again then took the elevator to the prosecutor's office. Mueller had already been seated in the waiting room and nodded to us. Dick Shelly, the chief prosecutor emerged from the receptionist's office, gave Roscoe a firm handshake and placed his arm around his shoulders. He introduced himself to Maggie, Mueller and me. When Mueller explained his relationship to the indicted Elise the prosecutor looked askance and inquired if the defense attorneys knew of his visit to the prosecutor. When Mueller said no, Shelly advised him to speak with his attorneys *first* and escorted him to the door. "I'd be happy to talk with you sir, but I think the defense would rather you didn't." Mueller somewhat confused, hesitated as Shelly pushed him gently out. After Mueller left, Shelly asked us to step into his office.

"Roscoe, you old reprobate, we're finally fighting on the same side. That's a real switch. Come sit and tell me all you know about this gal who's being arraigned this morning. For the next hour and a half Maggie and I with Roscoe's legal comments answered questions and talked with the prosecutor who took notes and had our conversation recorded.

"We've got a good case against this gal, but it certainly isn't air tight," Shelly admitted. "If she shot the doctor how did she get hold of your gun?" He looked to me for an explanation.

"Someone must have had a key to our house and located the revolver," Maggie said.

"Was your house key ever out of your possession?"

I thought for a moment, *"Yes, come to think of it,* my keys were found in Ms. Bolton's purse on the night or rather on the morning she was murdered. The keys were recovered by the L.A. police and turned over to me later that afternoon."

"Who handed those keys to you?"

The question rattled me. "I-I don't remember . . . Detective Mannheim . . . maybe Detective Hernandez."

"I see," Shelly said. "If any further questions cross my mind I'll get in touch. Meanwhile, don't discuss the case with anyone. We'll have another pretrial meeting, and I'll give you adequate notice."

Outside Maggie said, "Oh, I hope this case is settled before it goes to trial."

"My Dear, that is a good possibility—yes, a good possibility." Roscoe removed his seersucker jacket to reveal a shirt wet with perspiration on the backside and under his arms. "This weather is beastly." Roscoe reached for the hot door handle with his handkerchief and opened the unlocked car. "Joshua, whatever possessed you to want to examine Mueller's straw and napkin? The Swiss forensic pathologist made it quite clear that there was no way . . ."

"Roscoe, I know what he reported. I talked with him by phone also, remember? When I heard that report clearing Mueller of having had sex with Mei Ling that night I was as disbelieving as you were. In fact, I had difficulty accepting Dr. Hegel's report. Truth is, I still don't believe it. Maggie knew my bitter disappointment and went to the computer search engine to get information on the lab in Geneva where the DNA test on Mueller was performed."

"Roscoe, please turn on the air conditioning," Maggie Pleaded from her back seat.

"Sorry, there isn't any. Once we get out of local traffic there should be enough breeze to afford comfort."

Maggie murmured, "Oh, Lord, spare me."

Roscoe turned to look at me. "Joshua, don't keep me in suspense, for heaven sake, what information did you get on the Swiss lab and Dr. Hegel?"

Maggie spoke, "Dr. Alois Hegel has a reputable background and good credentials, however," she paused for emphasis, "the *Laboratoire Suisse Centrale* where he is in charge is a wholly-owned subsidiary of Magna Pharmex."

"Oh ho! The plot thickens." Roscoe cried, "I love it! I love it." He pushed the horn button, no sound. He pushed again harder. A loud "Beep!" startled us. "See? Sometimes you've got to do it twice." Roscoe was elated with his pithy example.

"Neither of you commented on Mueller's gold cuff link with the initial 'J' like the one found under Mei Ling's hotel bed," I said.

"A keen observation, my boy—a keen observation. How I should enjoy castrating that stiff-necked prick. Sorry about that Maggie. A penis is much too decent and proper an appendage to be assigned to that vile creature.

"I should have Marvin take Mueller's saliva and mucous samples to the Riverside lab for comparative DNA studies. Where do you think Mueller is staying in the valley?" Before either of us could respond, Roscoe submitted his own guess, "The Springs, of course. Maggie, you have a cell phone, call the hotel and verify my hunch, would you?" He remained quiet while Maggie contacted the hotel and asked to be connected to Dr. Mueller's room. She inquired about his room number also, but was told that information could not be given.

"You're right, Roscoe. He's registered there," Maggie said.

"Good!" Roscoe cried, "I knew that diabolical mountebank would be staying at one of the swankiest hotels."

Maggie leaned forward to speak into Farquhaar's ear. "Do you think he shared a room with Elise?

Roscoe shouted above the wind and traffic noise. "That, my dear, is well within the realm of possibility. Let's hope they did, that would make the cheese more binding, and for a couple from Switzerland, what could be more appropriate?" Roscoe enjoyed his little joke. "Now when those two homicide mavens get a search warrant for Mueller's room, they'll know where to go."

"You're expecting the DNA samples to be a match. We could all be terribly disappointed again," I said.

Roscoe turned around to speak to Maggie making me nervous while traffic on the freeway sped at seventy to eighty miles an hour.

"Didn't Elise tell us while at our home that some Swiss gentleman had been taking care of her since Stuckley's murder?" Maggie asked.

"I believe she did."

"Mueller was harboring a murder suspect, terrific! Yes sir, aiding and abetting." Roscoe pounded the steering wheel. "The Herr Doktor is not too clever. He's like many arrogant smart asses that have expertise in one field and think they are smarter than most and can break laws indiscriminately. What they fail to realize is that when it comes to crime, they are rank amateurs. An experienced cop can out-guess any stupid novice nine times out of ten, yes sir, nine times out of ten and . . ."

"Roscoe, supposing the DNA on Mueller's straw and napkin remains unmatched."

"Joshua, why must you be so cynical?" He became contemplative and in a quieter, modulated voice said, "Don't worry, the guilty party eventually will rise like dung on a stagnant pool."

We left Roscoe in his parking lot. Maggie emerged from the cramped Saab, brushed her dress, then walked rapidly to our SUV. "Josh, please hurry and put on the air conditioner so we can breathe cool air. I thought I'd die in that cramped and messy box."

THIRTY-TWO

From my office, I called my stockbroker,

> Curtis Green. *Curtis, I need information: give me the
> latest stock quotation on Magna Pharmex—has the stock
> been gaining or losing ground?—look at the latest annual
> report and tell me who the big stock owners are—actually,
> I'm interested in one person—J.K Mueller. Also, is there
> any news of a buy-out or partnership or sell-out? Call me
> back—thanks.*

"Excuse me," Carmenita said, "Dr. Harrington, Detective
Mannheim called and said he and Officer Hernandez would like to
ask you a few questions later this afternoon."

"What again? If there's a break in our schedule we'll squeeze
them in, otherwise, they can come by after office hours or tomorrow.
I'm tired of disrupting the practice for those jokers."

Maggie came into the room, "Josh, pick up line two. It's Curtis
Green.

> "Yes, Curtis—*the stock has lost further value this quarter?
> J.K. Mueller—Hold on, I'm going to repeat this so Maggie
> can hear—He owns 225,000 shares.*

Maggie whistled.

At the stock's current price that's in excess of ten million dollars—three years ago it was worth more than twice that—two big pharmaceutical firms withdrew their offers? I see. Thanks.

"Would you say that Mueller would like to put a halt to Magna Pharmex's slide into financial oblivion?" I asked.

"The question is whether he would commit murder to do it? What do you think, Josh?"

"In one word, Yes."

In the late afternoon, Mannheim, like a giant vulture, came into the office, his narrow head and neck bent forward and his shoulders drooped. I should have been more cordial, but the sight of him always evoked a kind of antipathy when I studied his beady, penetrating eyes. Even Hernandez, by association was becoming unwelcome.

"What glad tidings do my funereal friends bring me?" Mannheim was not amused and remained expressionless while Hernandez ignored the comment.

"Doc, we heard that Mueller's sputum was sent to the Riverside lab for DNA analysis."

"That's right, any objections to that?"

"For the future, we would appreciate being informed of any covert activities,"

"Covert activities? You've got to be kidding. There was no attempt to conceal anything from anyone except the suspect." Mannheim did not pursue the subject. He set his bony backside on the corner of my desk, took a deep breath as though to get enough wind to pass through his quivery vocal chords. "Doc, what was Stuckley's relationship with the Magna Pharmex Corp just before he was murdered?"

"You're aware, that he severed ties with the company some weeks before his murder."

Mannheim's eyes followed me. "Why was that?"

"I think he felt a moral obligation since he suspected that one drug had serious toxic effects on some patients."

"What do you mean serious toxic effects?" Hernandez, discarded his mantle of silence. Before I could respond, he continued, "You mean he actually prescribed a drug that killed some patients?"

"Well, yes, to put it bluntly, that was a strong possibility." My answer made me uncomfortable, but I knew of no way to make the truth sound less condemning.

"Do you think Stuckley prescribed this drug knowing it caused death?" He persisted.

"No, I can't believe that." What did Hernandez want? A dialogue in morality and ethics? I was not going to attempt the justification of malpractice or poor judgment.

Hernandez was spoiling for a verbal battle of which I wanted no part. He showed uncharacteristic truculence and seemed frustrated with my aborted argument. I turned to the brooding Mannheim, "Fellows, what is it that you want to discuss?" Hernandez stepped in front of Mannheim. "We want to know about any of Stuckley's patients who died as a result of experimental drugs or unconventional treatments." He struck a challenging posture: his chin jutted, his arms folded across his chest and his legs formed a wider base.

"I don't have that information, besides aren't there certain legalities involved here? Don't you need a court order to examine his patients' records? It seems to me you're clearly in violation of doctor-patient confidentiality, aren't you?"

"Look, we're trying to solve a murder here, Doc. So far we're not doing too well," Mannheim said.

"How does any of this activity help solve his murder?"

"Some unhappy relative or friend might have wanted revenge," Hernandez adjusted his holster.

"Tell you what I can do: I can ask Stuckley's attorney whether he thinks you can go through his patients' records."

Mannheim's shoulders slumped further, and he heaved a sigh, "Yeah, you do that, Doc." He assumed his usual lead position by stepping in front of Hernandez. As he headed towards the door he stopped, turned and said, "Doc, remember we're working towards the same goal, tell the attorney and his special investigator, no more grand-standing. We should be consulted first, right?" The time was six-fifteen p.m.

I ushered them to the rear door facing the parking lot. At that moment, the cleaning crew arrived. Mannheim stepped aside to allow the two women with their cleaning paraphernalia to enter. They nodded and thanked him. The third member of the crew, Charlie, while limping slightly pushed a grocery-type cart with cleaning supplies. Before he passed Mannheim, he pulled his cap down over his face and turned his head to the opposite side.

Mannheim walked to the parking lot but stopped suddenly causing Hernandez to bump into him. Mannheim returned to the suite. I watched him follow Charlie who was about eight feet in front of him. Mannheim pulled his pistol and directed it at Charlie's back, "Hey you! Stop! Put your hands over your head, walk back towards me, slowly. Keep your hands up—now face the wall and lean against it. Spread your legs!"

Hernandez jumped behind Charlie and frisked his, chest, back, legs, and ankles. "Clean," he said.

"What's your name?" Mannheim asked.

"Charlie."

"Charlie what?"

"Charlie Ironsmith."

Mannheim smiled sardonically. "You must think you're pretty goddamned clever, and we're awfully stupid, you son-of-a-bitch. I understand enough German to know that Ironsmith is an English translation of Eisenmacher."

Maggie who joined us was wide-eyed. Mannheim replaced his pistol in his shoulder holster. "Take off your cap and drop it, now. Put your hands high on the wall." Hernandez kept his pistol aimed on Eisenmacher. Mannheim grabbed Eisenmacher's thick, black, curly hair and yanked it off to reveal a slick bald head slathered with a yellowish holding gel. Maggie gasped. Mannheim forcibly turned Eisenmacher's head and ripped off his black false mustache. "There, I think we're finally down to the real you.

Maggie whispered, "Josh, look at his face. He's the man in the restaurant who had that listening device, isn't he?"

I studied his face, "I think you may be right, but the other one had a military-style haircut."

"He probably has more than two wigs."

Mannheim motioned with his head for Maggie to leave. "Little lady why don't you wait in the consultation room until after our interrogation?"

Maggie reluctant to leave was encouraged by Josh to do so.

Mannheim glared at Eisenmacher. "What have you got to say now, Eisenmacher?" Before he could respond, Mannheim continued, "You're the one who stole the sample medication and busted into the cabinets to steal the charts. Who were you working for?" Mannheim grabbed his neck and banged his head against the wall. Answer me!"

"Fuck you and your Mexican pansy!"

Hernandez leaped at Eisenmacher, yanked his shoulder around and slammed his beefy fist into Eisenmacher's mid section. Eisenmacher grunted and doubled over, then Hernandez kneed him in the face. Eisenmacher fell to his knees moaning, and cradled his face, his nose dripping with blood. Hernandez bent over him, "Listen, you shit head, if you want to leave here alive don't mouth-off and answer our questions. If you don't . . ."

Eisenmacher mumbled, "Fuck you, asshole!" Hernandez with hands clenched over his head came down like a power hammer on Eisenmacher's neck. He toppled over to the side.

"Easy, Bob, we've got to keep him alive," Mannheim intervened.

Eisenmacher whimpered, "What the hell do you want from me?"

"Who are you working for?" Eisenmacher hesitated until he saw Hernandez raise his hand again.

"All right! All right! The guy's name is Mueller. Dr. Mueller."

"What were you planning to do here tonight with that cart?" Mannheim asked.

Eisenmacher kept his eyes on Hernandez. "I was supposed to take charts out of Stuckley's file cabinet and bring them to a warehouse."

"Were you driving that red Corvette with Elise? Did you try to run Dr. Harrington off the freeway?" Eisenmacher hesitated too long and Hernandez with his thick open hand reached down and slapped Eisenmacher's face with such force that his head rocked and spattered blood on the wall.

"Yes, I was driving. Don't hit me again."

"Did Mueller put you up to that?" Eisenmacher nodded. Hernandez continued, "Does Elise work for Mueller too?"

"Yes, for Christ's sake, now let me alone!"

"Who killed Dr. Stuckley?" Mannheim demanded.

"I don't know."

"Who killed Mei Ling Bolton?" Mannheim continued.

"How the hell should I know?"

Hernandez made a menacing gesture, and Eisenmacher jerked his head reflexively and put his hands over his face. "I told you I don't know, that's the truth."

"Who killed Mr. Hoffman?" Mannheim continued to grill him.

"I don't even know that name."

"Stand up!" Hernandez shouted. Eisenmacher stood with legs shaking and backed away while Hernandez ordered him to place his hands behind his back then cuffed him.

Josh left to get Maggie, and they returned with damp towels. Maggie attempted to sponge Eisenmacher's face. Initially he pulled away, then reluctantly allowed her to clean him. His nose already deformed, swelled and dripped blood.

"Are you the one who broke into Dr. Harrington's office and stole patients' charts from the file cabinets?" Mannheim asked.

Eisenmacher, eyes cast down nodded.

"And did you break into Dr. Harrington's home?"

Again, Eisenmacher nodded.

"Where are the cleaning women?" I asked Maggie.

"I had them stay in the other half of the suite."

The detectives propped up the battered, bloodied and unsteady Eisenmacher and escorted him to their car.

Maggie and I started to clean the bloodstains from the wall and tiled flooring. "I thought police brutality was a thing of the past," she hesitated, "however, in this case it was probably justified," she said.

We arrived home too exhausted to eat. I kicked off my shoes and lay on the sofa. I turned on the local news. Scenes of freeway carnage, shootings among rival gangs, a drowning in a pool . . . I was asleep before the program ended and was awakened by a gentle kiss. "Come to bed, Darling," Maggie gave me her hand and guided me to the bedroom.

At six-thirty a.m. I was awakened with the smell of coffee and Maggie's delicate lips on my mouth. "Rise and shine, Darlin', there's a won-der-ful day awaitin'." I knew better than to ask the meaning of her forecast. Her cheerful answer usually consisted of platitudes and homilies, all of which I had heard before. The time was eight a.m. when Maggie straightened my tie and brushed lint off the shoulders of my suit jacket. The phone rang.

Roscoe, whoa! Slow down—I can't make out what you're saying—give me that again—the DNA studies on Mueller's sputum showed ten points of similarity with the specimen from Mel Ling—a super positive match. Hooray! I know, it's the gold standard for ID and conviction. That takes care of Mueller's claim of innocence. Ten to one says he's the one who murdered her. I've got some news for you, too— Mueller's henchman, Eisenmacher, is in police custody—he says he knows nothing about Stuckley's murder—yeah, I'm inclined to believe him. Hernandez put him through his own version of the Spanish Inquisition that should have discouraged any lying.

THIRTY-THREE

The traction on young Jerry Fleishner's fractured thigh needed adjust-
ment—not an unusual occurrence since traction was a dynamic system
of balanced forces requiring frequent monitoring. The assisting nurse,
Pat Dudley, pulled the ring on the Thomas splint towards the patient's
groin while I moved the supporting sling under his thigh. My cell
phone rang. "I'll get that call as soon as I adjust this sling," I grunted.

> *Hello! Roscoe, what's so damned urgent that you had to
> call me a second time this morning just when I'm in the
> midst—what? Are you sure? Was a positive ID made?
> You're sending the special investigator to the coroner's
> office? Good. Lunch at the Desert Willow at 12.*

"Dr. Harrington, is anything wrong?" Nurse Dudley asked.

"No, no. Please finish tightening the slings on the traction. I'll
see the next three patients alone." I wanted to hurry through rounds,
so I could verify what Roscoe had told me. The patient aware of the
flurry appeared anxious. "Don't worry Jerry, you're doing fine. I'll
see you tomorrow after your portable x-rays."

Maggie met me in the lobby of the Desert Willow clubhouse,
a magnificent structure for a publicly owned dining room and golf

course. Our table overlooked the challenging, rolling greens of the expansive eighteenth hole. Maggie reached for my hand and gazed into my eyes with all the affection of a lovelorn bride, or was it with the confidence of a practiced temptress. Either way, I figured it was good.

Rushing through the entrance like a minor storm, Roscoe U. Farquhaar, Esquire, champion for the defense, seasoned investigator and accomplished raconteur waved a folded newspaper above his head. He approached our table with a perilous disregard for the waiters and waitresses. His familiar unbuttoned seersucker jacket partially obscured his bold patterned Hawaiian shirt that in turn failed to conceal his considerable abdomen. His round pink face seemed to glow as though it had just been scrubbed and polished.

"Well, well, my lovelies, have you seen the second page of our esteemed Desert Sun?" Roscoe still standing, opened the newspaper and placed it before us on the table. I reached for it just as Roscoe snatched it back with a triumphant declaration, "This victory must be shared, but mine is the lion's share." He read with his usual bombast, 'Chief chemist of large Swiss pharmaceutical firm drowns in hotel swimming pool. Incident highly suggestive of suicide. The body of fifty-four year old, Dr. J.K. Mueller, of Geneva, Switzerland, a guest at a prestigious Palm Desert Hotel, was found fully-clothed, lying face-down in the swimming pool last night at 8:45 p.m.'

"Oh, my God!" Maggie clapped her hands to her face, "Why did he commit suicide?"

"Thank heaven for little girls with inquiring minds. Let me propose a summary of events as they occurred in the last twenty-four hours: the lab in Riverside notified Mannheim as soon as the DNA studies were confirmed on Mueller. Mannheim telephoned Mueller and advised him of the results. Mueller must have known he faced the possibility of death or a lifetime conviction. But here's the baffling part." Roscoe's eyes widened as he remained standing. He leaned across the table and looked at me then at Maggie. With his right index finger, he poked the air as though delivering the sermon on the mount when he was interrupted by a waiter.

Roscoe sat and with a complete change in mood picked up the wine list. He looked at the waiter."My good fellow, do you have an excellent domestic Chardonnay?"

"Yes, sir, we have a Napa Valley Reserve at thirty-two dollars . . ."

"Bring it on son, bring it on! Cost is no object."

Cost was no object I thought, since he had no intention of picking up the tab.

"Roscoe, a bottle for three of us at lunchtime may be a bit much," Maggie protested.

"Nonsense, Lassie, this occasion calls for a bit of toasting and imbibing." He grabbed a roll, tore it open and placed a pat of butter in it.

"Do you have the coroner's report?" I asked.

"As a special favor to me, he conducted the autopsy this morning."

"And?"

Roscoe raised a finger denoting time-out as he chewed a mouthful. The waiter brought the wine and an ice bucket, opened the bottle and poured a sample into Roscoe's goblet. With his usual flare, he sniffed, rotated the glass, held the wine high, sloshed it around his palate, smacked his lips, and pronounced, "Absolutely, dee-vine. Pour please, my good man."

Maggie sighed impatiently. I started to tap on the Table. "Roscoe, enough with the dramatic pauses, what did the coroner say?"

"Patience, dear boy, patience, you will be interested to know, Mueller did not die from drowning. That's right, he was dead before he struck the water."

"I don't understand," Maggie said. "The newspaper article hinted suicide was a strong possibility."

"Ostensibly so, yes, ostensibly so." Roscoe was holding court, his favorite role with an audience of just two. "CSI gathered what evidence they could from his hotel room . . ." Roscoe paused to take a gulp of wine. "Among those items of interest was a vial half-filled with clear yellow liquid, unmarked, set upright on the coffee table. A chemical analysis had not yet been completed, but it looked suspiciously like a highly toxic substance, probably the same one that killed Hoffman and Mei Ling."

"Why do you say that?" Maggie asked.

"Good question, Lassie. Mueller's liver showed the same gross anatomical changes as did Herr Hoffman's and coincides with the description of Mei Ling's liver given by the L.A. coroner. The microscopic sections will give us a definitive diagnosis, but there is no question that a potent hepatotoxin caused the lethal effects."

"How did he wind up in the pool fully clothed?" Maggie asked.

"That *is* puzzling, however, Dr. Thomas, the coroner attempted to recreate the final moments before death. He postulated that at some time during the afternoon, Mueller took the poison knowing that death would occur between one and four hours. He composed a five page letter, a sort of apologia, explaining his nefarious acts, Herr Hoffman's murder was necessary because Hoffman planned to see Dr. Harrington to tell him about Mrs. Hoffman's death due to Dolorean β. When he arrived in Palm Springs, Mueller who knew of Hoffman's visit invited him for a cocktail. A cocktail which he spiked with the poison. By the time Hoffman got to your office, he was almost dead, and then, of course, he died."

Roscoe turned to me, "His letter went on to say, some time after you left Mei Ling in the L.A. hotel, Mueller went into her room through the connecting door and during the course of the evening he poured poison into her Champagne flute. He also admitted having intercourse with her."

"Did he say why he killed her?"

"He did. Mei Ling had become concerned about reports linking deaths and illnesses to patients undergoing clinical trials of Dolorean β. She wanted an immediate recall of the drug. You also knew Mueller stood to lose the rest of his tidy fortune in stock holdings if that were to happen. Magna Pharmex had put all its eggs in that basket and failure would have spelled bankruptcy. Furthermore, it was rumored that Mei Ling was about to replace him as head of the new products division, and that in itself probably would have pushed him over the edge. He asked forgiveness from his wife and children and had the audacity to say merely that he was sorry for the pain he caused Mel Ling's parents."

"What about those freeway attempts to kill us?" Maggie asked.

"He regarded Dr. Harrington as one of his principal sources of displeasure and wanted his negative reports on Dolorean β destroyed. When that was accomplished he wanted the doctor himself destroyed."

"Did he say how he planned to do that?" I asked.

"Yes. He and Eisenmacher plotted the office and home break-ins to remove the incriminating reports on Dolorean β. When they were convinced they accomplished that, they planned the freeway accidents."

"What an evil, despicable animal," Maggie said.

"Getting back to the suicide, "How did he wind up in the pool?"

"Ah, yes, the pool." Roscoe signaled the waiter, "Young man, would you take our orders?" Maggie and I ordered burgers. Roscoe ordered a filet mignon from the dinner menu.

"Roscoe, you were saying?" Maggie prodded him. "

The coroner hypothesized that Mueller after taking the poison went to his balcony overlooking the pool and had perched himself precariously near or against the rail. At the time of death or shortly after, he pitched forward, struck his head on the poolside—there was a crack in his skull, and fell into the water. His lungs, were not filled with water as they would have been had he drowned. There was no lividity or bruising, no discoloration around his skull which indicated that circulation had stopped before the fall."

When the food arrived, Roscoe swabbed his lips with his tongue and held his knife and fork upright in anticipation. He hummed softly and his eyes danced over his plate. Maggie poked me to stop staring and to begin eating my own mundane fare.

"Mueller said nothing about Stuckley's death?" I asked. Roscoe was in deep-eating concentration when suddenly he realized I had asked him a question. "Oh, yes, yes, sorry Joshua. As a matter of fact, he did say he regretted learning of Dr. Stuckley's murder, but he emphasized that he was in no way responsible for it. He stated further that he was indeed fond of Basil whose reports on test trials of Dolorean β were only helpful to the company's future sales and his personal wealth."

Farquhaar was well into his steak when I interrupted. "What about his relationship with Elise? We got his avuncular account of how he came here from Geneva to see that she got fair treatment in a pending trial."

"My dear boy, only the most naïve extraterrestrial could believe that unmitigated bullshit." He glanced at Maggie and said, "Please excuse my exuberance, my dear. Mueller was fearful Elise would sing her siren songs to enchant and mesmerize the authorities who in turn would provide her with freedom and wish her Godspeed. Of course, Mueller provided her with shelter—his shelter, after Stuckley's murder and bought her clothes and trinkets hoping to keep her from talking to the cops. He carefully had her rehearse her responses. In addition he wanted her to assist Eisenmacher in getting rid of you. You asked if he slept with her? But of course, dear boy, but of course."

"How do you know all this?" Maggie asked.

"My dear, to be a successful attorney one must be a student of human behavior, a kind of psychologist, a sociologist who understands and can accurately predict interpersonal relationships . . ."

"So you're just guessing," Maggie said.

"That which I presume to know is based on years of experience and observation. My ability to fill in the dots, so to speak, is no less than uncanny." Roscoe turned his head, put his napkin to his mouth and produced a volcanic belch without apology.

"Roscoe, now that Mueller's gone we're left with few suspects in Stuckley's murder. Where do we go from here?" I asked.

Despite having had three glasses of wine, Roscoe seemed amazingly focused. "How many suspects can we dredge up?" He pulled out a small dog-eared spiral note pad from an inner pocket of his suit jacket, licked his thumb and index finger, and turned to a blank page."Let's list some suspects. Number one: Elise, although quite frankly I have serious doubts about her. If either of you think differently let me know. Number two: Eisenmacher, although there is no logical sequence of events suggesting him as Stuckley's murderer. Who else is there?"

"We haven't excluded Mimi, Basil's wife, or his two sons," Maggie suggested.

"I don't believe Mimi is a likely candidate, she inherits nothing from Basil, no insurance, a house encumbered by a hefty mortgage. With him alive, at least she collected an occasional check for child support. As for the boys, well, from a logistics point it doesn't make much sense. They, one or both, would have to drive from Beverly

Hills, a distance of over a hundred miles, then they needed to gain access to the office, but more than that what would be their motive?"

"What about a disgruntled patient or a dead patient's family?" I asked.

"Your suggestion has merit, Joshua, and I do not wish to debunk it, but is it not possible that someone in Basil's office would be aware of such a vindictive person? For instance, would not Elise have known?" Then to answer his own question, "I think she would have said something about that. If for no reason other than to deflect suspicion away from her."

"Basil was a well-organized guy," I said. "If he had any system at all in keeping patient responses to Dolorean β, there should have been files for categories indicating good, fair, and bad results. Maggie and I can go through those files and look for those patients who had bad results."

"I should like to be there when you do. Do you mind?" Roscoe asked.

"Not at all." I looked at my watch, "let's plan to be at the office this evening after dinner, say, eight o'clock."

Darkness approached earlier during the last days of summer giving rise to cooler evenings. Maggie snuggled next to me in the car as we headed from home back to the office. "I like your body warmth, Josh. You don't mind my closeness, do you?"

"I love having you close, so close I want to be *in* you!"

Maggie nudged me, "Oh, Josh, you're terrible, but I love it," she said moving closer still.

"Speaking of terrible, did you see that article in U.S.A. Today where Dr. David Graham lambasted Merck's new product, Arcoxia, an anti-arthritic cox-2 inhibitor? He said it might be as toxic to the cardiovascular system as Vioxx."

Maggie looked at me and with a note of disdain said, "He might just as well have said the same of Dolorean β. What do you think is going to happen to the drug? Will it be recalled?"

"If there is enough unfavorable publicity and the lawyers initiate individual suits or a class action suit, it'll be withdrawn."

THIRTY-FOUR

In our parking lot under a tall halogen light, we saw the funny-shaped old Saab and knew that Roscoe had been waiting. He moved his bulky frame with difficulty. "Good evening, children, shall we start our clandestine operation of perusing files that might reveal a killer?"

"Or reveal nothing," Maggie said.

I unlocked the back door and turned off the alarm system. The maintenance crew had already gone. I turned on the lights in our suite, and we walked quietly single-file through the halls towards Stuckley's suite. The profound stillness was almost eerie. Only Roscoe's labored breathing could be heard. I felt a sudden loneliness and sadness as I passed the empty rooms where just a short time ago the movements and sounds of a busy practice had created a lively vibrancy.

Despite our medical and political arguments and our differences in life style, I missed Basil. He had a flair, a color, a point of view that I did not fully comprehend or appreciate, but I knew that life without him was flatter, less meaningful, less controversial and less exciting. In his records room there remained a stern emptiness, a foreboding against the violation of personal information crammed within the cold gray-green steel file cabinets.

An end row cabinet marked Dolorean β suggested what we were seeking. A plain wooden desk with four chairs occupied the center of the room. Roscoe with characteristic temerity pulled open the top drawer of the cabinet and began taking charts out to place on the table.

A. J. HARRIS, M.D.

"Just a minute, Roscoe, don't pull things out willy-nilly and piling them up. You'll have this place looking like your office, God forbid."

Roscoe took umbrage, "I know the precise location of every case folder on my desk, yes sir, every folder."

"That's fine, but here I insist on a modicum of organization." Basil had approximately five hundred patients taking Dolorean β, and I had hoped he would have a summary sheet somewhere depicting results. "If we don't find a summary sheet we're faced with the unholy prospect of going through all of his cases. Maggie, why don't you scout around his front office and consultation room to see what you can find?"

Roscoe impatient to uncover any information on those receiving the drug, started in on the A's. "Here's the first, Martha Adams age eighty, history of maturity-onset diabetes, controlled cardiac insufficiency, osteo-arthritis involving hips, knees and cervical spine, died after two months on a regimen of Dolorean β." Roscoe put the chart down and looked at me. "Joshua, this is hardly an indictment of the drug, given the patient's age and preexisting illnesses. No one can say the drug or the doctor is at fault here, no sir, no one."

"You're Basil's loyal friend and an excellent attorney, but don't assume the role of a medical expert. You don't know but that the patient might have lived another four to ten years or more if she hadn't taken Dolorean β."

"Humph," Roscoe closed the file and picked up a second one. He read in silence turning the pages slowly then putting the file down. He pulled out a chair, removed his jacket and placed it on the back of the chair. Suddenly he looked drained, exhausted. He leaned on the table and put a hand to his head.

"Are you all right, Roscoe?"

"Eh? Oh, yes, it's just *this* case." He spoke deliberately but softly, "This one is hardly defensible, I'm afraid." He rose, "I'm going to get a drink from the cooler."

I took the chart Roscoe left on the table and read, "Barbara Arnold, thirty-eight, mother of two, history of rheumatoid arthritis six months duration with primary involvement of hands and feet.

On regimen of Dolorean β two months. Died of cardiac and kidney failure. Family refused autopsy."

To one in the profession this was a case difficult to comprehend, but to a lay person it was not only heart-breaking, it was scandalous and suggested malpractice. Roscoe walked back into the room, sober and perhaps melancholy. He picked up a third file almost reluctantly and started to thumb through it when Maggie came hurriedly into the room with what appeared to be a large chart on approximately three feet of white butcher wrap which she had unrolled.

"I found this in the corner of Basil's consultation room." We spread it on the table and studied the neatly listed rows of names, ages, sexes, diagnoses, durations of symptoms, responses to drugs, etc. On the far right appeared the column 'deaths.'

A quick count revealed thirty-eight deaths. "My God, what was Basil doing with this drug?" Maggie asked.

"Don't rush to judgment, Lassie, all the facts are not in." There seemed to be less assurance in Roscoe's voice as we scanned the sheet. He became uncharacteristically quiet, then muttered, "This is appalling, just appalling." A quietness settled in the room when a distant *click click* was heard. The three of us looked up then at each other. I felt a sudden chill. Maggie's brows were knitted and Roscoe's mouth dropped open. "Shush," Maggie said. There was another *click, click.*

I whispered, "Sounds like a coin or a key striking the glass on the front door." The three of us tiptoed to the reception room and the entryway. In the moonlight as a backdrop, there appeared a tall, dark figure.

"Saints preserve us," Maggie whispered, "It looks like the Prince of Darkness himself." Maggie reverted to her Boston Irish brogue in moments of stress.

I turned on the outdoor light, but had only slightly better definition through the frosted glass of the door. "Open up! Open up!" The devil sounded quite human and had a familiar voice. Standing in the doorway was the macabre figure of Detective Sergeant Mannheim.

"I saw light in here while I rode down Monterey and decided to check things out."

"Well, well," a relieved Roscoe said, "if it isn't the Alpha Wolf. Where is your side kick?"

"Hernandez? He's on administrative leave."

"Why?" Maggie asked.

"For attempting to re-arrange the features on a bastard's mug without a medical license."

"You mean Eisenmacher's face?" I asked.

"Yeah, Eisenmacher's lawyers got upset and were ready to sue the city for more money than the city collects in taxes. Only now, he and that sweet patootie friend of his, Elise, no longer have a high-powered law firm representing them. Mueller's not around to pay the shysters' fees."

Mannheim followed us into the records room. We explained what we were looking for, and he agreed that finding a letter from an irate family or friend could be helpful. "You'll let me know if you come across anything. Don't go after any suspects without telling us." Mannheim turned to leave when Maggie came into the room.

"I've found a locked box in Basil's lower desk drawer marked *personal*"

"Oh?" Mannheim turned and looked at the walnut box that measured approximately four by twelve inches. "Do you need help opening that?" He reached into his jacket, removed a ring of keys, and selected a small key that did not fit. He tried another and then another until he found one that opened the lock.

"That set of keys is certainly handy," Roscoe said.

"A gift from Hernandez who is an amateur lock smith." The box was an old, well-made English piece with mitered corners and a green velvety liner. More than two dozen letters appeared in a vertical deck of cards arrangement. The oldest letters were yellowed with age. I was about to pick one up when Mannheim put a firm hold on my wrist. "Just a minute, don't touch that. I don't know what we have here, but we don't want anyone else's prints on these."

I backed off, "Sorry, you're right."

Mannheim reached in his jacket pocket and slipped on a pair of latex gloves. He read the postmark on the first and oldest envelope, "Cambridge, Mass. Aug 12, 1978." The side of the envelope had been slit open. He reached in and opened a single page letter. A solitary hand-written message read, "It is one year since Frankie died. We will never forget." There was no signature. Mannheim replaced the letter in the envelope and put it in the original order. He picked up the next envelope and examined the postmark. The origin was the same but the date was one year later. He removed the letter, the same cryptic message appeared, "It is two years since Frankie died. We will never forget."

Mannheim replaced that letter and envelope, then commented, "There seems to be a distinct pattern here. Let's see what this latest letter shows." He reached for the letter closest to the front of the box and held it at eye level. "Oh, ho, the postmark is different. This one reads, 'Indio, CA. Aug. 12, 2009.' The handwriting had changed slightly, but the message was the same. 'It is twenty-one years since Frankie died. We will never forget." Mannheim with his inscrutable stare poured over the letter, turned it over, held it to the light and smelled it. He looked at Roscoe, "If you don't mind, I'll take all of this with me."

"Hold on, there Hawkshaw, this property belonged to my dear departed friend who was also my client."

"And what are you going to do with it, Counselor, put your hand-kerchiefs and opera ticket stubs in it? There may be an answer in this box of letters. I'll give it to the crime lab. When they're through with it, you can have your precious keepsake. Would you like a receipt for it?"

Roscoe was clearly miffed and turned his back to Mannheim. "That will not be necessary. Frankly, I don't know what those super sleuths are going to determined from those letters. I knew of their existence from what Basil had told me, but I never saw them."

Mannheim with the box tucked under his arm walked towards the door. "Lock the door after I leave."

"Let's complete our assignment," I said, "and go through the charts of the deceased." Maggie and Roscoe had three to four charts apiece and were taking notes.

"Josh, here's an odd case." Maggie pushed a chart of a fifty-four year old woman towards me. "She suffered from rheumatoid arthritis and mitral valve insufficiency. Look at Basil's final notes."

I read aloud, "Patient took first dose of Dolorean β, two tabs at home in presence of husband. Ten minutes later complained of severe chest pain and fell out of wheel chair. E.M.T.'s summoned but failed to resuscitate. Autopsy refused."

"What do you make of that?" Maggie asked.

"Sounds possibly like an irreversible anaphylactic shock caused by the medication."

Roscoe was reading his last chart when he said, "There's an awful lot of medical terminology that I don't understand. For instance, Basil wrote that the patient complained of S.O.B., displayed a tabetic-like gait and dysuria before expiring. What in the name of all that is sacred does that gibberish mean?"

"Roscoe your legal lingo is just as difficult for me to understand S.O.B. means shortness of breath, a tabetic gait is a broad-based walking pattern and dysuria is pain on urination. That's a broad spectrum of lousy symptoms to be attributed to any drug." Maggie had completed her review of the charts and found no letters threatening Basil. In fact, not one of us had discovered letters of hostility directed at him by the various deceased patients' relatives or friends.

Roscoe fatigued and weary leaned back in his chair, closed his eyes and emoted, "Well, my lovelies, had we expended our labors but for naught?" Then as in a reverie he continued, "Basil, dear boy, I have determined that your judgment in treating the unfortunate and ailing had been flawed by innocence or by guile, I know not which, but flawed nonetheless."

Maggie gathered the charts and returned them to the file cabinets. "We're no farther along in our search for Stuckley's killer. Is it possible we'll never know?"

THIRTY-FIVE

Six-thirty A.M., the phone rang. Maggie disengaged her arms from around me as we both awakened. She reached across for the phone on my bedside stand, "All right, hold your horses, I'm coming."

Hello—yes it is—just a moment please.

Covering the mouthpiece and handing the phone to me, she said, "It's Detective Sour Puss."

Yes, Detective Mannheim, what can I—well, let me suggest that we meet for dinner at Shame On The Moon, six-thirty—don 'it worry about the bill, I married a wealthy woman. Maggie poked me. *Will Officer Hernandez be joining us?—I see.*

"What was that all about?"

"He has some preliminary work to do, but Mannheim feels that he has a handle on the case, wants to meet tonight."

Maggie jumped and gave me a squeeze, "Josh, that's absolutely marvelous. Am I invited?"

"Are you my bed partner?"

"Not unless you invite me to dinner." She slapped my behind then hid under the blanket inviting horseplay.

I wrested the blanket from her and started tickling her in places causing her to scream uncontrollably and begging me to stop.

"Now are you going to behave?" I asked.

"Yes, yes, I'll do anything you want me to do," she continued laughing and pulled the cover over her again.

"Okay, I'll give you an assignment—call Roscoe and ask him to join us tonight."

"Oh, pooh, I thought you were going to ask me to do something wonderful," she feigned anger.

"We've no time this morning, my Love."

Ginger, the hostess, greeted us with her usual warmth, kissing Maggie and hugging me then escorting us to the relative seclusion of the Garden Room and a round table set for four.

"I'm terribly eager to hear what Mannheim has to tell us. Do you think the killer is anyone we know?" She searched my eyes, but I hadn't a clue and shrugged. Just as we sat, a tall, well-dressed man approached out table. Maggie and I did a double-take. The stranger was none other than Mannheim. He looked twenty years younger with a recent hair cut and trimmed eyebrows. He wore a sport jacket, open collar polo and beige trousers, which created an appearance quite different from his usual dismal on-duty attire.

His gate and mannerisms seemed more relaxed, and his visage not at all cadaverous. There was a hint of a smile on his lips, but that might have been more illusion than real. "Thank you for inviting me, it wasn't necessary but appreciated." We shook hands and sat.

Coming into the Garden Room which was one step below the main dining room, Roscoe flew towards us having missed the step but regaining his balance as he was about to careen into our table. "Forgive my dramatic entrance. Please don't stand." He opened his arms, "Ah, my favorite people appear before me like heavenly apparitions." Then he looked at Mannheim. "As well as one of my less than favorite earthlings, Homicide Harry. Detective, did you remember to bring my letter box?"

Mannheim responded by shaking his head. "Of course not."

TAKE 2 TABS THEN DIE

"I hardly expected you to," Roscoe said. He sat and rubbed his chubby hands in gleeful anticipation, "What startling news can we expect from a luminary of our magnificent homicide detail?" Without waiting for an answer, Roscoe signaled a waiter and asked for a wine list.

Midway into our first course, the Caesar salad, Mannheim announced his retirement and his leaving the Palm Desert area, his home for the last twenty-five years.

"Where will you be going?" Maggie asked.

"Bozeman, Montana, to a friend's ranch."

Maggie registered doubt. "I don't see you roping steer, branding cattle or milking cows."

"You got that right, ma'am. I'll be spending time with a little filly . . . one I've had my eye on for quite some time."

"I didn't know you were interested in horses."

"I ain't."

"Oh."

"Will Officer Hernandez take over the department?" I asked.

"No. Bob Hernandez will be going elsewhere."

Roscoe surreptitiously opened his belt and leaned back into his chair. "Ah, another Lucullean repast with such delightful company." Then he looked at Mannheim. "As much as I was enthralled to learn about your retirement, that was not quite the revelation I was hoping to hear. Do you have an announcement in the murder case?"

Mannheim toyed with the last fork-full of his cake dessert. He knew the three of us were watching him expectantly. He continued to look at his plate and in his usual monotone announced, "I know who murdered Doc Stuckley."

Maggie, wide-eyed, sat on the edge of her seat. Roscoe folded his hands over his bay window and stared at Mannheim. My pulse had quickened, and I too sat upright.

When he knew he had our attention, Mannheim said, "The first inkling I had came when I recognized the handwriting on those letters. I had seen it many times before, although I resisted the thought that I might be right, but other things came into focus—someone who lived in the Boston area and moved here relatively recently, someone who had the ability to open locked doors, that is, your home and your office. When I mentioned that DNA studies were to be made from saliva used to seal the envelopes from letters taken from Dr. Stuckley's office, he spilled his guts and seemed to be relieved."

"You're talking about . . ."

"Officer Hernandez," Mannheim said flatly.

"Officer Hernandez!" Maggie gasped, "Oh, no!"

"Yeah, he's in custody now. With a good lawyer he's probably facing twenty-five to life."

"Good grief, why?" Roscoe asked.

"According to your own recollection of Doc Stuckley's practice in the Boston area twenty-eight years ago, he treated a lad for a football injury to the leg. That youngster died while getting an experimental drug Stuckley prescribed. The kid brother, who idolized his older brother Frankie, suffered a terrible emotional shock, made worse when his mother was committed to a hospital for severe depression following his brother's death. That younger brother is Bob Hernandez who never forgot that terrible time. He blamed Stuckley for Frankie's death: That hatred smoldered and became more intense with the passing years. On Frankie's birthday, he would send that same letter every year to Stuckley. We saw thirty-one of them."

"Why did he use my weapon to kill Basil?"

"With his skill as a locksmith, he found it easy to slip into your home, locate your weapon, kill Stuckley, and replace your revolver before you knew it was gone. Using your weapon he thought he could deflect any suspicion that . . ."

"But why me? I never harmed him . . ."

"His thinking was screwed up. He saw things as totally good or totally evil. To him the bad guys had to pay a heavy price for their crimes. For instance, he would have killed Eisenmacher with his bare hands if I hadn't intervened. As for you, Doc, he wasn't quite sure you didn't kill Mei Ling Bolton. If he knew for sure that you had killed her, he might have used your own gun to kill you too. He has mental problems, that's for damned sure!"

"Why did he take so long to seek revenge on Dr. Stuckley?" Roscoe asked.

"Counselor, he waited for an opportunity to get close to Stuckley in a sort of unobtrusive way. If that sounds crazy, well, it probably is. Why don't you ask him? Just be sure there are iron bars separating the two of you." Mannheim pushed his chair back then stood looking down at us. "The crime against Doc Stuckley's been solved, but I take no great satisfaction in that. I regret a cop was involved. On the other hand, his victim might have been responsible for the deaths of thirty-eight innocent people, and he was licensed to do it. Well, thanks again, folks. If you're ever in Bozeman, look me up."

The three of us watched him as he walked away, and I could have sworn that he swaggered just a bit—like good ol' John Wayne.

ABOUT THE AUTHOR

After serving in the Pacific Theatre as a field and hospital medic in the U.S. Army, Alvin J. Harris, M.D.F.A.C.S. graduated from the University of Illinois, College of Medicine. He completed an internship and residency in Orthopedic Surgery at the Cook County Hospital in Chicago, Illinois, where he instructed medical and nursing students as well as physicians in post-graduate courses.

In Los Angeles, California, he served on the staff of the Children's Hospital, guiding residents in clinical and surgical techniques. While tending to his private practice, he served as chief of the orthopedic section at the Presbyterian Hospital in Van Nuys and the Holy Cross Hospital.

He practiced for twenty years in Washington State and founded the Sequim Orthopedic Center. In addition to private practice, he examined and treated prisoners with orthopedic problems for the State Corrections Department and learned about prison protocol. As an expert witness, he testified in litigation resulting from vehicular accidents, physical abuse, and trauma.

When he isn't writing, Al attends lectures at the university or researches information for his novels. He occasionally squeezes in a game of golf with his wife, Yetta. His other novels include *Death Dear Doctor* and *Satan Stalks Sinatra Drive*. His fourth book, *Death in the Saddle (Not a Western)* will be ready for the press in the summer of 2011.